West's knee nud and quickly mov there?"

"No." Her half laugh sounded breathless because she was trying to move away from him, too. Regardless of how they shifted, they still made contact. And now she imagined that she could feel the warmth of him right through his jeans and her yoga pants. "Tables are really small."

"There are worse things." He nodded his head toward Jason and the Stephen King novel. "I blame my mother for his taste in reading." The corner of his lips lifted. "We call her the horror queen."

"Good thing I know about her penchant for vampires and zombies," Alexa managed. "Might not be flattering."

"Grandma calls herself that, too," Jason assured. "Can I have waffles with strawberries and whipped cream?"

"I think you're a bottomless pit," West said. "Considering you had two bowls of cereal and half a package of bacon already. But yeah. If you're really hungry enough." He caught the attention of their waitress, who immediately headed their way.

"I'm always hungry," Jason told Alexa, as if he were imparting some big secret. "Grandma says I'll be as tall as my dad someday."

Despite herself, she looked through her lowered lashes toward West.

Tall.

Handsome.

She grabbed her water glass, suddenly parched.

Dear Reader,

I am honored with another visit to Cape Cardinale, where the wind is stiff, the Pacific Ocean is untamed and the townspeople are usually in one of two camps—those who never want change and those who cannot wait to get away.

West D'Angelo used to be one of those who couldn't wait to get away. From the sameness of the small town, and from the heavy expectations of being the only child of one of the town's homegrown and beloved physicians. But now West is back. Older. Wiser. And stepping into those shoes of his father that he'd never intended to wear. But his determination to be a good father to his young son after the death of his wife overrides everything.

West's son, Jason, however, thinks what his dad needs *most* is a new wife, and he has the perfect person in mind—Alexa Cardinale, who works at his school. What Jason doesn't consider is the fact that Alexa has no intention of remaining in town once she's fulfilled the terms of her estranged father's will or the fact that neither West nor Alexa thinks there is any room—or interest—for romance in their lives.

Jason, though, is a pretty brilliant kid...

I'm hoping you'll feel the same!

Allison Leigh

THE ROMANCE REMEDY

ALLISON LEIGH

SPECIAL EDITION

Harlequin®
SPECIAL EDITION™

Recycling programs for this product may not exist in your area.

ISBN-13: 978-1-335-40229-5

The Romance Remedy

Copyright © 2025 by Allison Lee Johnson

Harlequin Enterprises ULC
22 Adelaide St. West, 41st Floor
Toronto, Ontario M5H 4E3, Canada
www.Harlequin.com

Printed in Lithuania

MIX
Paper | Supporting responsible forestry
FSC® C021394

Though her name is frequently on bestseller lists, **Allison Leigh**'s high point as a writer is hearing from readers that they laughed, cried or lost sleep while reading her books. She credits her family with great patience for the time she's parked at her computer and for blessing her with the kind of love she wants her readers to share with the characters living in the pages of her books. Contact her at allisonleigh.com.

For Casey and Jen and a beautiful future.

Prologue

"*No*, Mom."

Alexa Cardinale closed her eyes and tightened her hand around her cell phone. Keeping her tone calm was an effort, particularly when she had to raise her voice just to be heard over the rain drumming on the roof of her car. "I told you before that I wouldn't make it home for your birthday this year."

"But you haven't been home once since you moved to Cape Cardinale. It's been months," Nadine Cardinale complained.

"I've been busy with my new job, remember?"

"But you're not even a real teacher there!"

Alexa sighed. Her position at a local elementary school was nothing to brag about—an instructional aide—but it afforded her the ability to still pay her bills. "Thanks for the reminder."

Her mother wasn't the least sidetracked. "Talk to that lawyer and explained our situation—"

"*Your* situation," Alexa clarified. "And it doesn't change anything, Mom." Fitzgerald Lane was the lawyer handling her father's estate. Alexa liked him well enough, though she doubted he'd be swayed by her mother's latest dramatics.

"I'm sure Carl plans to propose to me!" Nadine's voice rose even more. "You should be here for that!"

Her hopelessly romantic mother had been certain of that very thing with Mark and Brian and Neil, too. But none of them had been of the sticking variety.

The only one who'd ever married Nadine had been Alexa's father, Pietro Cardinale. He hadn't been of a sticking variety, either. Not with Nadine, nor with any of his other wives.

Nadine's problem was that she'd always had miserable taste in men.

Like mother like daughter.

But Pietro hadn't cleaned out everything Nadine possessed on his way out the door.

Alexa couldn't say the same about *her* ex-husband.

She stared through the rain sheeting down the windshield of the seriously used car that she'd bought when she'd moved from San Francisco. She'd christened the little Volkswagen with the name of Betty, but the only positive thing she could say about her was that she was—mostly—a cheerful yellow color. Other than that, Betty was twenty years old with an engine that stalled out if she went through too deep a puddle.

And in Cape Cardinale, Oregon, there always seemed to be a lot of puddles.

But the price had been right, and Alexa only needed the car to get her through to next summer when this ridiculous sentence would be complete. One year of living with her two half brothers and her half sister in a broken-down shack of a beach house. A beach house that might—or might not—fetch a whole lot of money once the terms of the inheritance were met.

That's the only thing their supposedly bazillionaire father had left to them in his will. A beach house with strings.

So far, they were only a few months into the arrangement and it was a wonder that no blood had been spilled. It wasn't easy living 24/7 with people you barely knew.

Alexa stared balefully down at the beach. The house was barely visible from where she was parked at the top of the hairpin-laden road that scared her every time she drove on it.

Her mother was still on her tirade. "I'll talk to Fitz about Thanksgiving." She spoke over her, hoping to bring an end to it. The holiday was two months off and Nadine would either still be obsessed about Carl or distracted by her next shiny object.

Unlike Nadine, Alexa didn't get distracted. There was a pot their father had left them at the end of the black rainbow. Namely, selling the property. Which would get Alexa back to California where she would *not* have to live with her mother again, or anyone else for that matter, because she would finally have enough money to buy something of her own. Even if it was an apartment the size of a shoebox, it would still be *hers*.

And nobody could take it away.

She realized the rain was starting to ease up. "I'll see if I can come up for just the day." Despite the fact that Fitz's daughter, Sophie, was getting married the weekend following the Thanksgiving holiday to Meyer Cartell—Alexa's older half brother no less—she doubted Fitz would give them any leeway. He took his responsibility very seriously. Even where Meyer was concerned, since he, too, was sentenced to live in the beach house.

"Really?" Nadine's voice went up half an octave in her excitement and Alexa very nearly crossed her fingers.

The easier solution would have just been to invite her mother and Carl to visit her in Cape Cardinale for Thanksgiving, except the last time Nadine had been there was for Pietro's funeral. And *that* had been an unmitigated disaster.

All four of Pietro's ex-wives had been inexplicably drawn together in support of his present wife, Lotus, for the funeral. As if the years…decades…of acrimony that went be-

fore had never occurred. Toss in the fact that Pietro was
a pretty famous figure in the art world whose death had
sparked as much media attention as his lavish lifestyle had,
and the event had been more circus than solemnity.

It was only after all the falderal had died down and the
will had been read that they'd learned their father hadn't
had anything left of his once-massive estate except for the
tiny Oregon house where he'd been born.

The lavish homes all over the world?

Gone.

The investments and priceless artwork?

Gone.

Alexa had never expected to get anything from her father
in his death. Not when she'd never gotten anything from
him during his life. But learning that everything he'd ever
amassed in his life was gone had been a shock to all of them.

Including Nadine, whose righteous indignation over the
entire situation still flared up way too easily. Her alimony—
which could have kept her in comfort for life if she'd ever
thought to supplement it with some earnings of her own—
had ended the day Pietro had died.

"Alexa? Are you still there? I can really count on you for
Thanksgiving?"

She sighed. Flexed her fingers around the phone again.
"Yes, really," she said belatedly. She knew better than to
say she "promised."

It was a word that she and her mother both avoided.

Promises.

They were far too easily made and far too easily broken.

Chapter One

"He promised he would pick me up on time."

Sitting next to Alexa on a bench in front of Howell Elementary School, Jason D'Angelo's young voice was almost inaudible.

"Doctors sometimes have unpredictable schedules. Things happen." Her tone was calm, but inside she was seething. This was the third time West D'Angelo had been late picking up his son in the four short weeks since Jason had enrolled at Howell. "Your dad will be here." Sooner or later.

The assurance didn't help Jason any. He continued swinging his leg, thumping the toe of his tennis shoe against the bulging backpack sitting on the ground in front of him.

"Congratulations on the test today, by the way."

"Math's easy."

Everything for Jason was easy. Except fitting in. "I liked the picture, too," she added.

Jason's lips twisted. He was too young to look so forlorn. "Mrs. Tone didn't."

In Alexa's opinion, there wasn't much that Ernestine Tone *did* like.

The woman had been teaching for nearly fifty years.

Alexa for eleven. Didn't matter that she had two master's degrees under her belt while Ernestine had only a girdle under hers. Alexa was an unwanted instructional aide in her classroom and from day one had treated her more like a half-witted servant than an educational collaborator.

But the job was the best that Alexa could get in a town that had only a few schools to begin with, none of which had had even a part-time teaching position open.

Fitzgerald Lane's claim that it would be easy for her to find a teaching job during the year she'd be spending in Cape Cardinale had been hogwash. Alexa's only comfort was that when she did go back to California next year, the same job she'd left behind would still be waiting for her.

One hundred and fifty-five days down. Two hundred and ten to go.

"Next time, draw Mrs. Tone a bouquet of flowers," she suggested, "instead of a bunch of zombies running her down." Jason had captured every detail about the teacher from her tight helmet of gray hair to the design on the pendant watch that hung around her neck from a thick chain. The gruesome zombies had been equally vivid.

"They weren't after *her*," Jason said. "They were after the turkey."

"There was a turkey?"

He dove into the backpack and pulled out the crumpled test. On the front of it was a red "A." On the back of it, a red "F" scrawled atop the pencil sketch. He tapped the sketch and she realized that there was, indeed, a turkey. Complete with dragon-like talons looking prepared to strike. Whether at the zombies or at the teacher who was in the way was subject to interpretation.

"I didn't notice the turkey before," Alexa admitted. "But the F doesn't mean anything. The grade on the test does."

Jason shoved the page into the depths once more and

yanked the zipper closed. "Mr. Mirizio in Chicago was way cooler than her. He never minded zombies."

"My class in California was cool, too." She'd taught a second- and third-grade combo class. And, unlike Mrs. Tone, she'd actually *appreciated* the work that her classroom assistants provided.

"If my mom was still alive, we could've stayed in Chicago." The message was plain. Jason didn't want to be in Oregon.

She felt for him. She didn't want to be in Oregon, either.

"I'm sorry about your mom." She knew from his file that his mother had died a few years earlier. She also knew he'd skipped straight from second to fourth grade when he'd come to Howell. He was tall for his age but that didn't mean he fit in with his older classmates.

"It'll get easier here," she said. "It just takes some time." The school year had already been in session for a month by the time he'd enrolled, and he was still on the social fringe of his class.

It was hard to break into the social cliques that formed in classrooms. Particularly when you were a year younger yet noticeably more advanced in nearly every subject.

He scrubbed his fingers in his unruly brown hair. "I don't care if I got friends." Though clearly, he did.

"Hey." She nudged his shoulder and winked. "You've got me."

His face brightened. "I'm glad Mrs. Tone made you be the one who had t' wait with me. I wouldn't have turkeys *or* zombies chase you."

She chuckled. Zombies were featured in nearly everything Jason drew. And he drew a lot. On the corners of his test papers. In his workbooks. On his gangly arms. "That's very nice of you. You seem to be pretty interested in them. Zombies, that is."

His shoulder jerked again. "My grandma watches *The Walking Dead* reruns when she thinks I'm reading. Well, that and her lovey shows."

"*Lovey* shows?"

"You know. The stuff on daytime." He pressed his lips together in a big fishy kiss. Then he kicked his backpack again. "She's going to make turkey for Thanksgiving," he added, sounding suddenly glum.

"Don't like turkey, huh?"

"I don't like hers," he said fervently. "It's like chewing—" He broke off as if he couldn't think of anything to adequately describe the horror.

"My mother's turkey is always dry, too," she confided.

"This dry?" He stuck out his tongue, pretending to choke.

"Well, I'm not sure about *that* dry," she said wryly. "But I've always survived it. I imagine you will, too. Will you be at your grandmother's house for Thanksgiving dinner then?"

"Probably. She always visited us in Chicago before, but my dad always had to work."

How many times had Dom gotten out of a family commitment because he'd "had" to work? She'd only learned after the fact that a good deal of her ex-husband's so-called work had been a nurse named Tiffany.

Jason looked up at her. His eyes had lost some dispiritedness. "Do you gotta go somewhere for Thanksgiving dinner?"

"Not this year." Alexa didn't have to worry about meeting Carl for the simple reason that he hadn't proposed at Nadine's birthday party as expected.

Big surprise.

In the same manner as his predecessors, the man had vacated Nadine's life nearly as quickly as he'd entered it. It had only been two months since then, yet Nadine had already made plans to go skiing in Canada over the holiday with Sergio Something-or-other.

"Maybe you could come have dinner with us."

She smiled gently. "Maybe you should check with your grandma before you start inviting the masses." A movement on the far end of the parking lot caught Alexa's attention and she pointed. "Looks like your dad is here." Finally. She brushed her hands down the front of her ruffly purple skirt as she stood.

Jason, on the other hand, waited until the tires of the dark sedan rolled to a stop in the water-clogged gutter before sliding off the bench and picking up the backpack. The webbed straps strained as he hefted it over one shoulder, and she automatically reached out to lift a little of the weight off him even as she opened the rear passenger door for him.

She barely glanced at the man in the driver's seat who was watching Jason leap from the curb into the car to avoid the gutter water.

She knew what the boy's father looked like. Which is why she was certain Jason would grow into his looks *just* fine.

West D'Angelo was numbingly handsome with thick, dark hair, intensely blue eyes and an honest-to-goodness cleft in his perfectly sculpted chin.

He didn't even acknowledge her, though. "Sorry, Jase. I thought your grandma was picking you up today."

His voice was the kind of deep that inspired shivers.

If a person was inclined to that sort of thing.

Which she wasn't.

Jason dumped the backpack on the floor next to his feet and began fastening his seat belt. "'S okay," he mumbled.

Alexa's heart ached a little. She wanted to tumble the boy's hair where it lay across his forehead. She wanted to give his father what-for for being late again, regardless of the reason.

She really wanted to blame the frisson running down her spine on the barometric pressure.

She straightened away from the car. "See you tomorrow, Jason." She gave Jason's father as much acknowledgment as he'd given her.

Which was to say, none.

She'd barely backed away when the car started moving again, sending a small wave of rainwater up and over the curb, right over her gold-canvas tennis shoes.

Jerk.

She went back to the bench, retrieved the messenger bag that held her own things and squished her way around the main building to the back parking lot where the staff had assigned spots right near the school building's rear entrance. She bared her teeth as she passed the slot reserved for E. Tone, but by the time she finally reached her yellow car at the far end of the lot, she'd given up on her annoyance.

It took too much energy.

She dumped her bag on the passenger seat and peeled off the wet shoes. "All right, Betty," she said as she inserted the key. "Let's cooperate today, shall we?"

It took a little coaxing, but Betty's engine came to life and they drove through the town of Cape Cardinale.

She shared her name with the place, but until her father died, she'd never been there. The small town had its charms, to be sure. But it wasn't home to her. She had no more interest in making it so than Pietro'd had. He'd brushed the sand off his Italian loafers when he'd been a young man and never looked back. He'd been more interested in the rest of the world.

Small town or not, though, it took a surprising amount of time to drive through it. By the time she'd passed Ocean-view Church—where her famous father's circus of a funeral had been held—the sun was almost set.

"Seven months to go," she told herself.

Then she could go back home to California where she belonged.

She. Could. Not. Wait.

"Do you have any homework today?" West plucked his son's backpack from the back of the car before pushing the door closed.

His question went unanswered. Jason had already gone inside the house, leaving the interior door open that led from the garage into the laundry room.

West retrieved his briefcase from the trunk, absently noticing that his son's backpack was the heavier of the two, and wearily went inside.

Dirty clothes were piled atop the counter next to the washing machine, and he sent a small avalanche sliding onto the floor when he tried nudging his briefcase onto the counter as well. For a moment, he looked at the pile of jeans and mismatched socks littering the floor.

The effort to reach down and pick it all up was just beyond him and he left the mess alone. The washer and dryer in the rental house might be ultramodern, but they didn't jump up and do the laundry on their own.

His mother had been unsubtly hinting about him hiring someone to help with the housework, but so far, West had been ignoring her, too. He could only focus on so many things at one time and the chore was at the bottom of the list here just as permanently as it had been in Chicago.

He'd thought things would be easier once he was back in Cape Cardinale. But he'd been wrong.

There were still memories of Janine at every turn.

A squawk greeted him when he entered the kitchen.

"Hey, Max." He barely glanced at the oversized birdcage positioned near the windows of the breakfast nook. Maxwill Sing was the canary's official name. Janine hadn't lived long enough after naming her impetuously purchased bird to learn how ironic the name was. Because Max definitely did *not* sing, despite supposedly being a songbird.

The bird expert that West consulted had assured them that Max was a healthy, normal canary. And healthy, normal canaries—particularly males—tended to sing. Sooner or later.

It was later. Yet the most Max ever did was ruffle his feathers and squawk.

Not that it made any difference, but West stopped in front of the refrigerator to study the calendar affixed there. Nearly every one of the squares had something written on it—including who'd been assigned that day's duty of retrieving Jason from school. "G-ma" was clearly written on today's square in Jason's handwriting.

The erasure of "Dad" beneath it was evident but only because West was looking for it.

Until he'd gotten home from the clinic to find the house empty, it hadn't occurred to him that his son might have changed the original schedule at which West had given a passing glance on their rush out the door that morning.

Panic had ridden alongside him in the car all the way back to the school that afternoon, particularly when his call to the office had gone unanswered.

Relief had only set in once he'd seen Jason sitting on the bench alongside the teacher's aide from his classroom.

On the heels of relief, though, was a sea of regret.

The first time he'd been late a few weeks ago had been unavoidable. His mother had driven over to Portland and there'd been an emergency at the clinic. West had called the school that day, though, to warn them he'd be late.

He'd been tempted to send one of the interns, but the

imagined censorious judgment from his late father had stopped him.

The second time had been purely West's fault. No emergency. Just a conference call from Chicago with his business partner, Sean Robinson, that had gone on too long. So, yeah, he'd deserved the thinly veiled look of disgust on the teacher's aide's face when he'd arrived.

Today, he hadn't been in the mood for any of it.

No matter how pretty she was.

And now he owed an apology to his mother on top of it for the terse message he'd left her as he'd broken speed limits crossing town to the school.

He yanked open the fridge hard enough to dislodge the calendar from one of its two hooks and extracted a bottle of imported sparkling mineral water.

His mother kept ordering the stuff for him. She thought she was doing him a favor, because Janine had always kept the imported water on hand. He really did need to have a conversation with his mother. Not about the cost of the water. That was insignificant.

But about everything else. Namely her assumption that he wanted to replicate their Chicago life here in Cape Cardinale.

Later. He'd do it later.

Now, he twisted off the cap, tossed it on the counter and went in search of Jason.

The house was enormous. His mother's idea of a suitable home for her only son and grandchild. "It's on Seaview Drive," she'd gushed when she'd told him about the place. "The neighborhood has the best ocean views in all of Cape Cardinale. I've always wanted to live up there."

Admittedly, the neighborhood did have spectacular views. But that didn't mean the house suited them.

Enormous didn't make up for functional.

A day didn't go by without some new challenge hitting him smack in the face.

Water-heater failing.

Toilets backing up.

Dishwasher flooding the kitchen floor.

Mercifully, the roof was—so far—remaining sound.

He knew he'd have to find something more permanent sooner or later, but that involved yet one more decision. To date, his track record where personal decisions were concerned wasn't wildly impressive.

For now, he had the rental management company a text message away.

He finally found Jason sitting on the floor next to the monolithic dining room table that had once sat in West's grandmother's house. When she'd died, his parents had taken it in.

Now that he was back in Cape Cardinale, it was evidently his turn to suffer the monstrosity as well as its accompanying twelve chairs. Maybe his mother had found this particular rental for him just to house her mother's ugly dining room furniture so she could finally sell his childhood home and move into the retirement community she'd been talking about for years now.

Stranger things had been known to happen.

Look at him. Returning to Cape Cardinale after swearing twenty years ago that he never would.

He focused on his son's head.

When it came to Jason's well-being, anything and everything was back on the table.

He decided that challenging him now about changing the pickup calendar could wait. Jason came first. If this was one of his son's way of testing the theory, West couldn't blame him.

"What're you doing there, bud?"

Jason didn't look up. "The signal's better here than any-where else in the house."

The chandelier hanging over the table was dark. Jason hadn't needed to turn it on. Not when there were sixteen vintage-style post lanterns outside the window with the wattage power of runway lights. They lined the brick path from the curb to the front door and came on whenever the sky got cloudy—which was most of the time.

He crouched next to his son, wincing a little at the stiffness in his left knee. He was thirty-eight for God's sake. But for months now, his knee had been cracking like he was twice that. "Signal for what?"

Jason tilted the tablet in his hands, revealing the video chat on the screen. *Internet, Dad. Duh.* Jason didn't have to say a word for West to hear his son's thoughts.

"Hi, Doctor D," Luc Mai greeted from the other end of the video chat.

The Mais had been their neighbors in Chicago. Luc was a year older than Jason, but that had never mattered. The two boys had bonded as friends when they'd been toddlers, and nothing had come between them since.

Not even the fact that West's wife had been sleeping with Luc's father.

Not that Jason or Luc knew anything about that.

West and Carla Mai had agreed on that particular fact. They'd been two people who'd barely known each other but who'd found a deep accord in the betrayal that had changed all of their lives. If Janine and Owen Mai hadn't perished together in a car crash, they'd all still be none the wiser.

Certainly, Carla would have been happier in her ignorance. She'd made that more than plain.

West, on the other hand, felt differently.

He'd believed in a fantasy. Knowing it hadn't existed after all would stop him from ever making that mistake again. He just wished he could shed the ghost of his wife that still haunted him. Usually when he was screwing up the job of D.A.D.

"Hi, Luc," he greeted the kid on the screen. "How's your mom doing?"

Luc shrugged. Nine-year-old obliviousness at its finest. "She's in the kitchen. Cleaning up from supper."

"Speaking of…" West nudged Jason's arm. "We need to start thinking about supper. You can have five more minutes of ZombieCart." It was their favorite video game. He straightened, setting off another round of snap-crackle-pop.

"Can we have pizza?" Jason's voice followed him out of the dining room.

"Yeah." It wouldn't involve anything more complicated than dialing his phone, which West did while he headed up the massive staircase to his bedroom. It was the only room in the house that actually did have an ocean view. He was on the opposite side from the front lampposts and though the moonlight wasn't very bright yet, in the distance, the Pacific still glimmered like a dark jewel.

He barely glanced at it as he gave the pizza order. When he was finished, he tossed his phone down on the bed and peeled out of the clothes he'd worn that day.

Scrubs had ruled his wardrobe in Chicago.

Here in Cape Cardinale, it was shirt-and-tie all the way. That's what happened when a physician spent as much time playing business administrator for a nonprofit clinic perpetually on the hunt for funding as he spent doing the work he'd trained for all of his life.

He flipped on the shower and didn't wait for it to get warm. Depending on the vagaries of the house's temperamental plumbing, that was a feat that could take seconds, or not at all, before stepping under the spray.

At least the water pressure was good.

The spray was so sharp it practically stung, and he turned his back to it, closing his eyes in deep appreciation.

You always did love the shower. Janine could have been standing right beside him, so clear was her voice.

But her ghost was only in his head.

A grief hallucination, said the psychologist.

A need for more prayer, said the priest Sean had sicced on him.

Too much alcohol came from the bartender at his favorite bar back in Chicago.

They were all right. And yet none of them was.

"Go away, Janine," he muttered aloud.

She faded away but left the memory of Jason's teacher's aide in her wake.

The disapproval *she'd* emitted in waves when he'd picked up Jason at the school outsized her diminutive stature. But she had pretty blue eyes. He lifted his head, slicking his hair back wetly from his face as he stared blindly at the ostentatious mauve gold-rimmed tiles surrounding him and cast about for the woman's name. Jason had been at the school for a month now. What the hell kind of father was he that he couldn't remember important details like the names of the people with whom his son spent most of his weekdays?

The blue of her eyes was more robin's egg than sapphire.

The intrusive thought nudged aside his sudden worry over his apparent mental decline.

Probably not a natural color. Contact lenses no doubt. And the blond hair was probably from a bottle. Not that she looked like she spent a lot of time on her hair. It reached the top of her shoulders and the waves always looked like she'd just rolled out of bed. Rumpled. Soft.

Sexy.

He reached for the soap and turned into the water, blocking that particular notion.

His wife's hair had been dark. Glossy and as smooth as a raven's wing. Even when she had rolled out of bed, she'd never looked rumpled.

He shoved his head under the water and turned the handle until the needle-like spray stung like a million little shards of ice.

He had an extra-large meat-lover's on its way.

That's what he would think about.

Cardinale.

The name suddenly popped into his head. The aide from Jason's class was Mrs. Cardinale. How he could have forgotten it for even a minute was beyond him. The town was Cape Cardinale, for God's sake.

He shut off the water and grabbed his towel.

The thing that was most important was the "Mrs."

Emphasis on the Missus.

And even if she weren't married, it didn't matter what sort of blue her eyes were or whether or not she was appealingly rumpled.

The last thing West wanted *or* needed in his life was another female.

End of story.

Chapter Two

Alexa curled her fingers into a fist and pounded harder on the bathroom door. So hard that the faded wood bounced in the frame. It was a wonder the ancient hinges even held. "Some of us have to go to work you know," she yelled through the door.

The only response she earned was the sound of water running.

"Problem?" Cutter was the second of her male half sibs. He was younger than her by five years and taller than her by nearly a foot. He was currently yawning and scratching his bare chest as he walked through the front door of the dinky house. Didn't matter that the early morning air rushing in alongside him was bracingly brisk. He "stayed" at the beach house per the terms of the will.

But in reality, he ordinarily stuck to the camper trailer that had just recently replaced the tent he'd initially pitched on day one of their sentence. The fact that the camper was barely a step above the tent was apparently enough to quell any possible objections that Fitz Lane might have had.

"Princess Dana," she told Cutter through her teeth, and turned to pound on the door again. "Why the *hell* does she have to hog the only bathroom we have right when she knows I need to get ready for work?"

The question was rhetorical and Cutter made no effort

to respond, instead turning into the minuscule kitchen. She heard the creak of a cupboard and knew he would be filling a mug with coffee.

Aside from the sperm donor of a father they shared, the four of them didn't have a lot in common. But not a one of them could function in the morning without coffee. So far, the electrical power that Cutter was pulling from the house to the old trailer through a complicated electrical hookup was consumed by the entirely unarchaic computers he used 24/7 to make his living managing IT systems for other companies. He'd tried to plug in a coffee maker of his own, too, and had promptly blown the electricity altogether.

It had taken the power company coming out to solve the problem.

Now, if Cutter wanted coffee, he prudently came inside the house for it.

She lifted her fist to pound on the bathroom door yet again only to fall back with a surprised step when the door suddenly swung open and a cloud of steam rolled out.

Her older sister—all five-foot-ten spoiled inches of her—stepped through the fog. She had a towel wrapped turban-style around her infuriatingly beautiful head and a thick robe wrapped around the rest of her model-perfect body. She was five years older than Alexa, but Alexa was certain that *she* had more lines around her eyes than Dana did.

"All yours," Dana said and serenely stepped around Alexa on her way to her bedroom.

Feeling ten years old, Alexa stuck her tongue out behind her sister's back before ducking into the bathroom.

It didn't pay to dawdle.

She'd made that mistake once and Cutter—ever wily— had slipped right through the door and locked it in her face. She'd pounded on the door then, too, earning only Cutter's laughter. "Snooze and lose," he'd crowed.

At that particular moment, he'd even managed to usurp Dana's number-one position on Alexa's most infuriating list.

Right then, voluntarily staying at this little house had felt like the absolute height of lunacy.

They didn't even have a guarantee that it would sell for what it was supposedly worth. The place was eighty years old and not in a good way. The only positive thing about it was the location and *perhaps* the fact that Pietro Cardinale had spent his early years living there.

Back then, he'd been just a little boy named Peter Cartell. The award-winning astral photography that brought him fame and fortune hadn't come until adulthood.

By then he'd notched one marriage off his belt, ditched his real name and adopted the name of the town as his own. Peter Cartell became Pietro Cardinale in the blink of an eye.

Using the town's name was the only thing Pietro ever did for Cape Cardinale, though. Since the funeral, that particular fact had been constantly bandied around town.

As much as Alexa considered Pietro a total failure in the fatherhood department, she didn't appreciate such comments. Just because he'd turned himself into an award-winning photographer didn't mean he owed the town of his birth one darn thing. After all, what had the town done for *him*? Apparently, nothing. Or why else would he have spent his life everywhere else but here?

She realized she was brushing her teeth with such vigor that the plastic toothbrush was on the point of breaking.

She rinsed her mouth as well as the intensely ugly pink sink then stepped into the equally ugly tub, yanked the shower curtain along the metal rod and adjusted the shower spray down from the Dana-the-Amazon realm. The fittings of the bathroom might be ancient, but Alexa was grateful to her soul for the fancy water heater that Meyer had installed before the first month of their enforced living situation had elapsed. The water heater was tankless and able to produce endless hot water for as long as there was electricity to keep it running.

Given Dana's propensity for hour-long showers, the expensive thing had probably saved a life or two.

Unlike her half sister, Alexa didn't dawdle, and her hair was still damp when she raced out of the door for her car less than thirty minutes later. She gave a wave to Meyer, who was strolling down the road from the blue bungalow a little way further up Bluff Road.

The bungalow was the only other house on their crescent-shaped beach and Sophie Lane lived there. Technically, Meyer was living at the beach house along with Cutter, Dana and Alexa, but he nevertheless spent a good part of his time up the road in the bungalow with his fiancée.

Pietro's last will and testament held an all-or-nothing stipulation that his offspring live together at the beach house for a year or what remained of the estate would go—quite literally—to the dogs. Even though Meyer was engaged to the daughter of the man enforcing that stipulation, he didn't want to jeopardize their inheritance any more than the rest of them. So, when it came to bed count, all four of them were sleeping at the beach house. Or, in Cutter's case, an extension of the beach house.

Alexa knew they all were making the best they could out of a truly strange situation. She wasn't the only one keeping her eye on the end goal.

The only one who didn't actually need the money once the property was sold was Dana, and that would have been true even *if* she weren't married to a moneybag named Tyler Mercer. Dana's mother had come from money. And even after Pietro had dumped her for Alexa's mother, she'd remarried once more. Into even more money.

As for Ty, he was a self-made real-estate developer with

projects up and down the coast. According to Dana, he saw a lot more value in their father's beach house than was apparent despite the fact that it had lain abandoned for decades until they'd moved in last June.

Alexa and Dana didn't share one of the three bedrooms the house possessed. But they did share a thin wall. Even though Tyler hadn't visited Cape Cardinale, Dana traveled almost weekly to the house they owned in Corvallis. She was always back before the day ended, though. Dana and Ty might not be physically spending their nights together, but they still spent hours on the phone, talking.

All.

The.

Time.

Alexa could hear the murmuring through the wall at all hours of the night. Her sister and Ty had been married for ages. What on earth did they still find to talk about so much?

She and Dom had run out of things to talk about after five years. On the other hand, after he'd cleaned out everything they'd possessed and left, she'd had lots to say.

Too bad the courts hadn't seen fit to listen. After all. He was Dr. Dominic Falco. And goodness knew doctors were above that sort of thing.

She should have paid more attention to the dotting of i's and crossing of t's when it came to their assets. If she had, Dom wouldn't have been able to get away with robbing her blind. But he'd been her husband. She'd trusted him.

Never again.

If she didn't want to listen to the lovebirds on the other side of her bedroom wall, she could take a leaf from Cutter's book and pitch his tent outside the house. He wasn't using it now that he'd replaced it with that old trailer.

But she had as much desire to sleep in a tent on a camp cot as she had to have a hole drilled in her head. So, mostly, she buried said head in her pillows and turned up the music on her earbuds to block out everything else.

Besides. Whether she wanted to admit it or not, the bed set that Dana had arranged—along with the rest of the furnishings for the little house—was ridiculously comfortable. Alexa had sacrificed everything else to come to Cape Cardinale. She wasn't sacrificing that one bit of unexpected comfort.

Her coffee mug was empty by the time she parked Betty in the school parking lot. She stopped in the teachers' lounge on her way to the classroom to refill it when the principal hailed her.

Alexa kept her smile in place with an effort. If Regina Bowler was going to pass on more of Ernestine Tone's criticisms, Alexa didn't know if she'd be able to take it.

Her job wasn't ideal but she couldn't just quit. She had to earn some sort of living.

Maybe she could work out at the airport.

Meyer ran things out there. But her only qualification would be from being the boss's half sister.

Cutter was a one-man shop. He didn't have any employees at all.

And Dana was…well, Dana. She didn't *do* work.

Alexa took a bracing sip of the too hot, slightly bitter coffee and squared her shoulders toward Principal Bowler. "Good morning."

The principal was seventy if she was a day. But she was spry and feisty as hell when she chose to be. Today, fortunately, didn't appear to be that day, and the woman just smiled benignly. "I was hoping I'd see you before the bell," the principal told her. "I'll walk with you."

Alexa tucked her singed tongue in her cheek to stifle the *What for?* that immediately popped into her mind. "Sure," she managed to mumble mildly, well aware of the curious looks they earned as they left the lounge together.

Nothing like a teachers' lounge.

It was always a hotbed of gossip.

The principal was shorter than Alexa's own five-and-a-half-feet, but she walked at twice the speed of everyone around her. Which left Alexa hurrying to keep up with her.

They'd reach her classroom in no time. Joy, joy.

She took a bracing sip of coffee. Not the delicious coffee that Dana kept them supplied in at the beach house, but it did the job.

"You know we've been raising money for the playground improvement fund," Regina said. "The parents' association along with the faculty."

Alexa hadn't known about it, but she nodded anyway. She had a sudden vaguely horrified thought. Everyone in town knew of Pietro Cardinale. Not everyone knew that his estate wasn't worth a fortune after all. "If this is about a donation—"

The principal started shaking her head before Alexa could even finish the thought.

Thank goodness. Alexa's currently meager paycheck barely covered the basics, even living rent-free.

"The parent chairing the fundraising committee has had to step down," Regina told her. "She hasn't been able to find anyone willing to take her place and I was hoping that you would."

Surprise made Alexa's jaw feel loose. She belatedly closed her gaping mouth. "What does it entail exactly?"

"Just a couple of meetings," Regina said swiftly. "We have to finish the fundraiser in December to ensure the equipment is ordered and installed by the end of the school year. Otherwise, the district funds budgeted to us run out and the improvements will have to be made based only on what we've managed to raise."

"No pressure there at all," Alexa said. "Exactly how much are we supposed to raise?"

Regina looked a little harried. "As close to a hundred thousand as possible."

Alexa nearly choked. "Please tell me you're already half-way there."

The principal tucked her arm through Alexa's. "Just keep the group on schedule and you'll be fine."

Since Alexa didn't know diddly about fundraising, she wasn't so sure. Particularly since Regina had neatly avoided answering. "I *guess* I can help." She couldn't keep the doubt-fulness out of her voice, but it didn't seem to bother Regina at all.

"I knew you would." Regina patted her hand as they turned into the doorway of Alexa's classroom.

Ernestine was standing in front of the blackboard just a few paces away and she focused on the principal's arm that was still linked through Alexa's with the attentiveness of a mongoose.

She gave the principal a neutral, "Good morning."

Alexa, typically, received a glacial stare.

"Good morning, Ernestine," Regina said with what Alexa could only describe as deliberate cheer before focusing her attention again on Alexa. "I'll get you the list of committee members and a report of the progress. My secretary is making up flyers for the next meeting. It's tomorrow."

"Tomorrow!"

"She'll bring them by as well before the end of the day." Regina smiled benignly as she bustled out the door.

Alexa sighed and looked at Ernestine over the top of her coffee mug. As was typical, the teacher was dressed entirely in unflattering dark gray. Add in the pendant watch hanging by a thick chain over her concave chest and, Alexa imagined, Ernestine would fit right in as a dour prison matron.

She took a bracing sip of the hot brew and pinned on a smile. "Good morning, Mrs. Tone. I hope you had a nice evening last night."

The look she got in return was even more baleful than usual. "Why?"

Alexa sighed slightly. "No reason," she said with the same forced cheer that their principal had shown. She was suddenly desperate for the week to be done because then she'd have two days of respite from the woman.

She went to her desk at the back of the classroom and dumped her purse in the bottom drawer before picking up the laminated calendar the teacher had given her at the beginning of the school year. The woman loved the laminator. "State testing is only a month away," she observed. "Is there anything you'd like me to work on with the students in preparation?"

"Work on getting the stains off the dry-erase board," the woman said dismissively.

"Okay." She kept her temper much more easily at work than she did back at the beach house though the stiff calendar nearly slid off her desk when she tossed it down. "And when that ten minutes is done, what—"

"I don't appreciate your smart-aleck tone."

Her nerves tightened. "Mrs. Tone," she said carefully, "I'm here to *help* you. You have a classroom of thirty children. That's more than—"

Ernestine cut her off with a withering look. "I may be *required* to have an aide because of this class size. But I'll thank you to remember that *I* am their teacher."

The last few words were nearly drowned out by the shrill ring of the first bell, followed a second later by the pounding of feet as students streamed through the doorway.

They pushed and shoved with typical good-natured enthusiasm, jockeying for position as they deposited backpacks in cubbies and generally worked out their wiggles in preparation for the day.

And Alexa absorbed their energy like a soothing balm.

For as long as she could remember, she'd wanted to be a teacher. The only other prospective career she'd entertained had been Tinkerbell, but that position had been already filled.

Her gaze caught on Jason D'Angelo and he smiled shyly back at her before he worked his way through the slightly crowded desks. His desk was at the back of the room, too, but on the other side of the classroom.

"Homework." Evangeline greeted her students with all the warmth of a drill sergeant. "Have it out and on your desks. Mrs. Cardinale will pick it up.

Another task that Alexa didn't object to. Just because Mrs. Tone detested her presence, it didn't have to follow that the students did.

She found a smile by focusing strictly on the students and the homework that she began collecting. When she reached Jason, she grinned even more at the drawing in the lower corner of his paper. It was a bouquet of roses.

He rolled his eyes and shrugged slightly, though his cheeks looked pink.

"Nice touch," she told him under her breath before she moved to the next row.

And so it went for the rest of the morning.

When the lunch bell rang, Alexa remained in the classroom with a fresh coffee and a cup of ramen from the vending machine in the teacher's lounge while she went through the fundraising materials that Gerta had dropped off for her midway through the morning.

She was frowning over the dismal sum of contributions

when the classroom door opened. She looked up to see Jason standing there, a brown paper sack in hand.

"Can I eat in here?" he asked.

She glanced out the windows. The wing for the upper grades was fashioned into a U that overlooked their own playground. A similar wing for the younger classes was on the opposite side of the school. It was the older kids' playground that would be receiving the new equipment; but even with only its currently ancient swing set, there was plenty of space for the kids to enjoy. "It's beautiful outside today. Wouldn't you rather be out there?"

"You're not," he said reasonably.

She couldn't help but smile. Given the choice, she'd take a sunny blue sky over fluorescent lighting. But facts were facts.

"I am inside, indeed." She bounced her pencil eraser against her papers. "And yes, you may eat in here." They'd be safe from Ernestine who'd gone off campus for lunch.

He immediately went to his desk in the far corner. He dunked his hand into his bag and came out with a sandwich. With his other hand, he began flipping through a paperback book that he pulled from his backpack.

She couldn't see the cover, but it was thicker than normal for a kid his age. It also looked quite well worn. "What're you reading?"

"*Salem's Lot.*"

She winced slightly. Stephen King was an amazing author. A personal favorite, in fact. She just wouldn't have said the book was an appropriate choice for an eight-year-old. Even one as precocious as Jason D'Angelo. "How far along have you read?"

"I just started it." He flipped the cover closed again and took a wolfing bite of his sandwich, which looked like PB&J from where she was sitting.

Her stomach rumbled slightly. A cup of instant noodles was not as satisfying as anything that had peanut butter in it, but the vending machine didn't offer actual sandwiches.

She nudged aside the folder of fundraiser notes and leaned back in her chair. It squeaked raucously, but she was so used to it, she barely noticed. "Do you know what the book is about?"

He nodded. "Vampires." His voice was thick with the second huge bite of his sandwich. At the rate he was going, he'd consume the thing in just four bites.

"It's okay with your dad that you're reading it?"

He lifted his shoulder. "'S his book." He nabbed a spot of jelly from the corner of his mouth with his tongue. "He's got lots of books. He lets me read 'em all."

Evidently, a liking for horror ran through more than one generation of the D'Angelo family. While she appreciated the carte blanche approach when it came to reading material, there was still something to be said for keeping it age-appropriate.

But she wasn't Jason's parent.

She glanced back at the papers in front of her. She was thirty-three years old with no prospects of being anyone's parent unless another immaculate conception turned out to be in the works.

She'd been twenty-four when she'd married Dom. They'd both wanted kids. A passel of them.

That fairy-tale notion died a quick and painful death. Just one more fatality among a host of them.

She'd had only a handful of dates since their acrimonious divorce three years ago. She'd endured them more than enjoyed them. Now she'd rather not even be bothered. Too much work. Too little reward.

"What're *you* doing?"

She realized Jason had polished off his sandwich while

she'd been dragging her butt through a past she usually preferred not to even think about. It was only since she'd come to Cape Cardinale that all that old stuff kept slipping in.

She tapped her eraser against the file folder again. "I'm working on some fundraising stuff."

He leaned against the corner of her desk. "For what?"

"Playground equipment." She gestured out the window. "For right out there."

"What d'you gotta do for it?"

She couldn't imagine what he would find interesting about it, but she told him anyway. "Once I have a meeting with the committee, we'll figure out how to raise more money so we can afford to buy some really cool stuff."

"Like what?"

She flipped open the thin catalog to show him the photographs of the play systems.

"We had one like that in Chicago." He stabbed his finger against one of the more elaborate—and commensurately more expensive—setups. It was a sprawling contraption with multiple towers, slides and tunnels. "When's the meeting?"

"Tomorrow after school." She pulled one of the flyers from the stack and handed him one. "You can give that to your dad, in fact." West D'Angelo hadn't been listed among the volunteers or donors. Whether because of disinterest or because he didn't know anything about the playground improvement fund remained to be seen.

Jason hadn't finished reading through it when the bell rang. She hadn't realized how much time had passed.

"You didn't get very far with your book," she told him.

"I can read after school."

Particularly if his dad is late again, she thought.

She corralled her papers and placed the bulging folder in one of her desk drawers while the kids began returning. The rest of the day passed in relative blahdom, since Ernestine gave Alexa a death glare whenever she made some attempt to be more useful than a monkey trained to fetch and carry on command.

The sky was still clear when she left the school and, since she was in no particular hurry to get back to the beach house, she stopped at the local grocery store. She'd already memorized everything the place carried, but she still managed to fritter away several minutes wandering the aisles where Halloween candy was marked down to nearly give-away and the Thanksgiving décor barely had pride of place-ment since Christmas-everything was already edging it out.

She bought a bag of miniature peanut butter cups that begged for purchase and a paperback. Not written by Stephen King, but a new author who looked promising. She also added a bottle of red wine.

Why not? Tuesday was as good a day as any for wine.

And maybe the label wasn't what Princess Dana would have chosen, but it was the best that Alexa could afford.

With her purchases made, she drove the rest of the way back to the beach house.

The place was empty when she got there. Cutter wasn't even in his trailer when she checked.

"Privacy at last," Alexa muttered and promptly opened the bottle of wine. "It's five o'clock somewhere."

She changed into jeans and a chunky sweater, popped a miniature PB cup in her mouth before securing the rest in a glass jar against the ants they could never seem to eradicate. Then she carried her wine out onto the deck that Meyer and Cutter had been reconstructing ever since they'd torn down the original rotting one. The replacement was considerably larger and would be built soundly enough to last decades, but they still had gotten only half of the deck boards in place.

They'd allowed for enough space for a few folding lawn chairs and a small table, though.

She took one of the chairs for herself and positioned the other to prop up her stocking-clad feet. Then she opened the new paperback. But she spent more time gazing beyond the beach where a couple brave souls in wetsuits braved the waves than she did at the words printed on the page.

When her sister suddenly appeared, she was so startled, she nearly knocked the untouched glass of wine over on the glass-topped patio table and the chair beneath her feet tipped on its side.

"Were you sleeping?" Dana had the strap of a bulging canvas bag over her shoulder.

"No." Alexa righted the tumbled chair and Dana sank down onto it with an audible sigh. Her hair was pulled back in a twist, but it was an unusually haphazard one.

For a woman who rarely had a hair out of place, the way-ward blond strands that had escaped were surprising.

In the last several months, Alexa had worked very hard to conquer her childish compulsion to bait Dana at every opportunity. She was usually successful, except for occa-sions like that morning when it felt like Dana was the same privileged princess that she'd always been.

Right now, she looked more like the princess of exhaus-tion.

Alexa picked up the bottle of wine. "Want a glass?"

Dana hesitated as she studied the bottle.

"Not a good enough vintage?"

Her sister's lips thinned. She dumped her canvas bag on the deck between their chairs. "It's a little early in the day for *me*."

Touché.

They were both quiet for several minutes. Dana stared out at the ocean. For the most part, a tall stone seawall kept the tide from getting too near the house. Right now, the tide was out and the rolling waves were calm. Alexa, on the other hand, studied Dana's profile.

They were only five years apart in age. If not for Dana's efforts of staying in regular contact with all of them, there would have been years and years to pass without ever seeing one another.

They had shared a few miserable holidays when Pietro had felt in the mood to remember his offspring. They even had a group text that stayed mostly silent unless it was someone's birthday.

Yet they were still virtual strangers.

"How long have you and Ty been married now?"

Dana's attention came back around. She looked vaguely startled. "Eighteen years." Her eyes narrowed suspiciously. "Why?"

Alexa lifted her wineglass. "Trying to make conversation here."

Dana's lips twisted slightly but she subsided in her chair again. "Eighteen years," she repeated again. Almost under her breath.

"Time flies when you're having fun," Alexa said.

Dana huffed out a sound that might have been a laugh. Or not.

They were silent for a while again. Not that the rolling ocean or continual breeze ever allowed for real silence.

Finally, Alexa nudged the canvas bag with her toe. "You go shopping in Corvallis or something?"

Dana glanced down at the bulging bag sitting between them almost as if she'd forgotten it was there. "Or something." She pulled a butcher-wrapped package from the bag and set it on the table. "Been craving a good steak. I bought enough for all of us." She nodded toward the gleaming gas grill positioned next to Cutter's camper. Amusement suddenly lit her face. "Seems like now's as good a time as any to find out if that thing will actually work."

Alexa smiled, too.

Dana had bought the grill, unassembled, when they'd first moved into the beach house, with the idea that they could all "celebrate" the occasion together with grilled steaks.

Only it had taken Cutter and Meyer months to actually finish putting the thing together.

"Should we warn Sophie?"

They'd prevailed upon their neighbor to use her grill that first time, and every time since.

Dana chuckled and this time there was no question that it was, indeed, a chuckle. "Maybe. The grill *looks* operational, but who knows?"

Alexa toyed with the stem of her wineglass. "Do you and Ty ever donate to stuff?"

Dana's brow furrowed. "What do you mean?"

"The school is having a fundraiser to improve one of its playgrounds."

Comprehension dawned. Dana lifted one shoulder. "Ty's business manager handles that sort of stuff for the company. But they usually support causes in the communities where they're actually involved."

"And personally?"

Dana's lips twitched. "Might be easier if you tell me how much you're asking for."

Her cheeks went hot. "I'm not asking for anything! I'm just curious."

"About a number of things, apparently."

"The committee chairperson running the fundraiser had to step down and I've been asked to replace her."

"Do you have a lot of experience with fundraisers?"

"I have a lot of experience being drafted into volunteering," she corrected. "But this would be the first fundraiser.

It's been going on since last school year, and they've collected a whopping five thousand dollars. Even with the school district funds, that's only going to get a few climbing bars and maybe a shade sail or two. Wouldn't you have thought they could get a parent to step up and take on the committee? I'm not even a permanent staff member."

"Gives them someone easy to blame after the fact."

Alexa frowned. "Well, thanks. *That* hadn't occurred to me." She lifted her wineglass and took a hefty drink.

Dana's smile widened slightly. "Then turn the thing around and make a success of it."

"Easy for you to say. It'll take ten times what we've got to make a dent."

"This is the time of year when everyone starts to feel a little extra generosity. Have a holiday-themed event or something."

"With what?" She waved her glass in the air. "We don't have a budget to be spending money to get donations."

Dana cocked her head. "Do you really want my advice?"

From pure habit, Alexa's jaw tightened reflexively. But she nodded. "Yes."

"Bet that hurt," Dana murmured. Then she turned slightly in her chair, squaring herself up to both the table and Alexa. "Find sponsors from the local businesses so you can throw a great party. Get some kickass prizes to raffle off. Or have a silent auction even. Talk about the worthiness of the cause. These are schoolchildren from their community who need something. People will give if they're asked in the right—" She broke off, frowning. "What's that look for?"

Alexa lifted her hands. "Just sitting here wondering if that's the first time the word *ass* has ever passed your lips."

"You are so annoying," Dana said, but without much heat.

"I have a file detailing everything they've done so far."

"Let me guess. A mass email to all the parents. Maybe a few flyers they've sent home with the kids."

"Pretty much."

"Do you know what the median income is here in Cape Cardinale?"

Alexa snorted. "Sure. I always take note of that sort of thing."

Dana smirked and named a figure that had Alexa's jaw dropping slightly.

"I am *not* earning enough." She took another swallow from her wineglass, emptying it. Ordinarily, she rarely drank more than a glass. But she reached for the bottle for a refill.

"The point is that there *is* money around here." Dana gestured vaguely. "Those houses up on the top of the cliff? Along Seaview Drive. Every one of them is worth a fortune."

"Is that why you're so sure we won't have trouble selling this dump?"

"This house isn't a dump. It's just old."

"The bathroom toilet is powder pink."

"And it still works. Haven't you ever wondered about that fact?" Dana circled the wine bottle with her long fingers for a moment before leaving it alone and folding her arms together atop the patio table. "Aside from the deck that was collapsing and the chimney that's not safe, everything about this place was maintained. The roof. The plumbing. Even though our father hadn't lived here for nearly forty years, he still had the place taken care of. Obviously, he cared about it."

"More than he cared about us."

"It was the only thing he didn't give up in exchange for—" Dana shook her head and lifted her fingers, as if to explain the inexplicable nature of their father "—the way he chose to live. And he left it to us."

"Or he just forgot about it, and his business manager or whoever just kept paying the occasional repair bill and here we are." Alexa pointed her finger. "You're romanticizing."

"And you're minimizing," Dana countered. "But—" she lifted her palm "—the bottom line is that, house or no house, this is a premium piece of property." She swept her hand in the air. "That's our front yard," she said. "Unobstructed, undeveloped oceanfront, situated in a beautifully protected cove. Someone *will* pay major money for it. And our father left it to us. Not to Lotus. Not to any one of our mothers. Just you and me and the boys. *That* act was deliberate. Just because he was an uninvolved father didn't mean he didn't care at all."

"I think he just forgot about all of it. Like he always forgot about us."

"Explain the reason behind the will then," Dana challenged. "The whole year-living-together thing. You can't, can you."

It was irritating when Dana was right. Because Alexa *couldn't* explain away that point.

She took another sip of wine. Worked her jaw from side to side. "How do I go about finding local sponsors?"

Dana stood and gathered her bag and the large paper-wrapped bundle. "After steaks," she said, "we'll come up with a plan. Okay?"

Alexa nodded. She watched Dana pull open the front door.

"Thanks," she finally added, though it was too late.

Dana had already disappeared inside.

Chapter Three

"*Please?*"

West looked at Jason. His son was practically straining out of his seat belt, so impassioned was his plea.

"I told you already. I don't have time to be on a committee," he told Jason. Even if he wanted to—which he didn't. He set aside the flyer that his son had been waving at him from the back seat. The same flyer that he'd been sticking in front of him since yesterday. They were crawling along the traffic lined up outside the school for morning drop-offs.

"I can make a donation," he said, also for about the hundredth time.

Jason grunted, obviously discontented with the answer.

Batting a thousand, West.

He scrubbed his fingers through his hair and crept a little closer to the designated zone marked by precisely placed orange traffic cones. One more car to go and it'd be their turn. "What if I ask your grandma? Maybe she can help with the committee."

"That's not gonna help," Jason groused.

"Help what?"

Jason didn't answer.

West exhaled. He watched a familiar blonde wearing a bright purple windbreaker with a whistle hanging around her neck approach the SUV in front of them. Two kids hopped out and scurried with her to the sidewalk and then toward the entrance to the building. When another windbreaker further ahead beckoned, the SUV went ahead past the cones.

Everything about drop-off and pickup at Howell Elementary School ran like a fine-tuned clock.

West coasted to a stop between the traffic cones and Jason's classroom aid approached, opening the back door. "Morning, Jason," she greeted brightly. "Ready for a great day?"

Her cheerfulness was as grating as the fact that she didn't even spare West a glance. It was always that way. While his attention, annoyingly, was just metal shavings to a magnet.

"I am!" Jason's glumness vanished as if it had never been. He jumped out of the car and slammed the door behind him. Not even a "g'bye, Dad."

West jabbed the button to roll down his window. "Jase."

His son paused and looked back at him.

West lifted the flyer. "I'll be there."

Jason's eyes widened. He was surprised enough that he didn't even notice when his favorite aid turned her attention to the next car. "Really?"

The meeting was to be held right after school let out for the day. There'd be hell to pay over the adjustments he'd need to make to his calendar to attend the meeting, but West still nodded. He realized he was following the purple-coated blonde in his rear-view mirror and trained his gaze on his son. "Your grandma is still picking you up as usual, though," he warned. He'd double-checked that fact with his mother, just to be sure.

Jason was all smiles. "Thanks, Dad." He hefted his backpack a little higher and turned to jog into the school.

The guy in front of the cones was gesturing for West to get moving.

He rolled up the window and with one last glance in his

mirror, followed the path of the SUV, and wound his way out of the parking lot.

Ten minutes later, he reached Beach Medical Plaza— a glorified name for the aging two-story medical building his mother owned that also housed the Cardinale Community Clinic.

He parked well away from the gigantic dumpster currently occupying the parking spaces near the entrance and went inside. The clinic occupied only one side of the building. The other held an assortment of individual medical offices they rented for a song. On the second floor, a new home health company called Cardinale Cares was remodeling every single suite—and they were willing to pay a lot more than a song.

West's father was probably rolling over in his grave that they were actually doing something for profit, but his mom had already lost one longstanding tenant to a new complex out by the airport where building was booming. Stu Hayes's medical practice had been located in their building for decades, and he'd admitted to West that it was only his longstanding friendship with Marjorie that had kept him from leaving sooner.

West didn't want his mother to lose more tenants because they couldn't afford to make long overdue improvements. Which was why he'd talked her into signing the deal with Cardinale Cares. The reno had already been well under way when he'd moved back to town. But he had expected the construction to be winding down considering it was supposed to all be finished before Christmas.

He bypassed the clinic's waiting room—already occupied with patients—and entered through the staff entrance at the end of the corridor. Ruthie Charles greeted him as usual, looking at him over the tops of her black-framed reading glasses. "Running late again." She plunked an insulated metal mug on the raised counter between them.

She'd been the office manager since he was a kid and her only concession to age was the ergonomic chair that had replaced the backless stool she'd once used. The rest of her—from big-coiffed unnaturally dark brown hair to the high-heeled pumps that matched her red lips color for color—remained almost exactly the same.

"Good morning to you, too."

She scowled and set a printout of the day's schedule next to the travel mug. The phone rang and she reached out to answer it.

He took the Yeti and the schedule and went around the corner into his office. The coffee in the cup would remain blistering hot throughout the morning, which was why he liked the mug. He'd made a lot of changes coming back home. Suffering through lukewarm coffee didn't have to be one of them.

He took a cautious sip as he quickly scanned the jam-packed schedule. From somewhere overhead, he could hear the muffled whine of a power saw.

Sandwiched between patients, he had video meetings with a variety of philanthropic organizations plus an evening presentation with a third. He was glad that his mother had suggested she give Jason dinner. Because he wasn't sure how he would have fitted that in as well.

He exchanged his jacket for the lab coat hanging on the back of his door and went around the corner, stopping in front of Ruthie's tall counter again. The last time the clinic had been remodeled was twenty years ago, and until then, her desk had been the receptionist's area. She'd never seen a need to change it, even though she'd long ago moved up in responsibility.

One thing he could say about Ruthie. When it came to

stretching a dime, she was an expert. If it wasn't for her, West doubted the clinic would have continued functioning after his father died. She was the glue that had held it together through the revolving door of doctors who'd come and gone in the ten years since.

West was the latest. The door needed to stop revolving. Not just for West's sake, but the clinic's, too.

"What happened to Otto Nash?" he asked Ruthie. Otto was supposed to have been the first appointment of the morning. Instead, Tater Jones's name occupied the slot.

"Ask him," Ruthie said blandly. "He canceled. Message came in last night."

Otto was West's neighbor. In his mid-seventies, he lived alone in a house twice the size of West's rental. He was mostly reclusive, looked like a cross between Einstein and Keith Richards, and upon first meeting him, West hadn't been entirely certain he was competent.

He'd been driving home from work shortly after they'd moved to Cape Cardinale and he'd seen Otto sitting on the curb. Clearly injured. No evidence around to suggest the cause.

West had stopped to help, but the man had flatly refused an ambulance, which would have taken him to the hospital in Corvallis. Instead, West had taken him back with him to the clinic and learned, along the way, that Otto had been hoverboarding—despite having already endured a broken leg earlier that year.

West had treated the dislocated shoulder and fractured wrist and, despite Otto's protest, ordered an evaluation from the neurologist who occupied one of the building's office suites.

But there'd been no concussion. No evidence of impaired cognition.

What West considered questionable judgment was, to

Otto, a way of life. The old guy was hell-bent on living however he wanted. Regardless of the personal consequence.

Canceling his appointment could mean anything.

"I'll check on him this evening," West told Ruthie. "Either before or after the Dunterwood meeting. Meanwhile, though, I need you to reschedule everything this afternoon after four. I have to leave early."

She raised her thinly penciled eyebrows. "Please tell me it's because you made an appointment with Roger Fox to look at your knee. He's the best orthopedist in town." She blinked facetiously. "What? You think we don't all see the way you keep favoring it?

"My knee is fine."

"Then why do you need to leave early? You never leave early."

"I am today." He plucked two plastic-wrapped suckers out of the big bin she kept on the corner of her desk and stuck them in his pocket. Rooms two and three were kids in for well-checks and vaccinations. A sugar-free sucker always helped when there was an injection waiting in the wings. "Can't be helped, Ruthie."

He left her grumbling under her breath and went down the hall to the first exam room, making sure he wasn't favoring his left leg. He pulled the chart out of the plastic bin, knocked briefly on the door, and went inside. "Morning, Tater. Been a long time."

Tater Jones wasn't as old as Otto, but West had known him forever, having been classmates with his daughter, Tanya.

Tater was just as skinny as he'd always been, and his balding head was still hidden beneath a grease-stained ball cap. "Long time," he agreed. He ducked his head, coughing into his shoulder. "Didn't figure you'd come back this way," he said when the spasm had passed.

West had moved to the small sink in the corner to wash his hands. "Didn't figure I'd come back this way, either." He yanked a paper towel from the dispenser, dried his hands and pulled on a pair of disposable gloves. "Mom is a lot of help with Jason, though." He'd known she would be. What he hadn't known was that the ghost he'd hoped to escape would trot right along with them.

"How old's your boy now?"

"Eight."

"Probably misses his mama. I know Tanya sure did at that age when we lost my Elizabeth."

"Mmm." There was no point pretending to be surprised by how much Tater knew about West's life. That's the way it was in Cape Cardinale.

He pulled his stethoscope from his pocket. "How *is* Tanya?" She'd been a go-getter even in school.

"Doing fine." Tater broke off to cough again. "Her restaurant's popular as blazes," he managed roughly.

"Rightfully so, from what I've tasted. I haven't made it over there yet, but Ruthie orders in routinely. Deep breath in."

Tater inhaled on a wheeze. Coughed it out again.

But West had already heard enough. He quickly went through the rest of his exam then stepped back until Tater met his gaze. "I'm going to have the nurse come in. We'll run a few tests to confirm, but I'm betting on pneumonia. You're going to need to give yourself some time to recuperate."

"Nah. I—" Tater coughed again.

"Then next time, I'll be seeing you at the hospital," West told him implacably, which he knew Tater wouldn't appreciate. Not because it was a hospital per se, but because it would be out of town.

The man was born-and-bred Cape Cardinale.

Those who were and who stayed were just like Tater. Proud to live and die all within a finite few square miles.

Those who didn't stay tended not to return except for visits. Namely because of deaths and births of more generations who'd repeat the same cycle.

"Fine," Tater groused. "I got no interest in leaving town just so's some nurse can see my butt showing out the back of a hospital gown."

"Figured." West disposed of his gloves. "Shannon will be right in. She's a nurse. Be nice to *her*," he warned as he washed his hands.

"I'm always nice," Tater protested.

"Sure you are." He left the room, still drying his hands.

Standing at Ruthie's counter once more, he made his notes in Tater's chart and crossed paths with Shannon after he was done. He waited long enough to see her enter Tater's room before he went inside Exam 2.

The routine was comfortably familiar and before West knew it, the day had passed.

Ruthie was the one to remind him that he'd said he'd needed to leave early. "Here are your phone messages from this afternoon. I was able to push back the zoom meeting at five a half-hour and I put the stuff for the dunderheads this evening in your briefcase."

"Dunterwood," he corrected, even though he was beginning to think her descriptor was pretty accurate. For every patient the clinic served with an ability to pay for services whether through insurance or otherwise, they served three more patients who did not. Nothing about that had changed since West's father's day. Yet Dunterwood, which had supported the clinic for nearly two decades, had suddenly announced that it was pulling its funding.

West had been trying to convince them to reconsider ever since.

"Who's the zoom with again?"

She gave him an exasperated look. "CEO with Cardinale Cares? It's either a video meeting today or not until next month."

"Right." He exchanged his lab coat once more for his leather jacket, flipping quickly through the pink message slips. None was patient-related or urgent. They used a service for after-hour calls and employed two individuals who handled things during office hours. He shoved the slips back in his pocket. Then, with refilled Yeti in hand, he drove swiftly over to the school.

He was still ten minutes late by the time he found his way to the library where the fundraising committee was supposed to be meeting.

For some reason, he'd expected Jason's teacher—the unsmiling Mrs. Tone. But the first set of eyes to greet him were robin's-egg blue and decidedly unwelcoming.

Mrs. Cardinale. The aide.

"What're you doing here?" she demanded.

His neck went a little hot. She was perched on the edge of a library table in front of six other people who were occupying folding chairs. Dressed in pink-and-purple-plaid leggings with a green-and-blue-striped sweater, she was a dizzying clash of color and pattern.

But from the very first, she'd still made something nearly dead inside him sit up and take notice.

For the most part, he'd managed to ignore that reaction. Easy enough to do when their only encounters had involved him being behind the wheel of his Mercedes.

Up close and personal, though?

He welcomed the idea even less.

Nevertheless, he'd made time for Jason's sake. So he pulled the crumpled flyer out of his pocket and brandished it between two fingers. "My son told me you needed volunteers."

She pointed. Her fingernails were short. Unvarnished.

"There are chairs in that rack against the wall." Then she cupped her hand once more over the edge of the table next to her thighs and looked at the others. She swung one leg like a pendulum. "As I was saying, we're going to have to somehow work in our event between now and the town's Winter Faire in December."

Dismissed.

He walked behind the assembly of volunteers to retrieve a folding chair from the rack. He unfolded it behind the others, but directly in front of the aide, and sat.

He'd never been a fan of feeling dismissed.

Something in her gaze glinted a little when it collided with his. He smiled slightly and propped his ankle on his knee.

Maybe it was his imagination, but he was pretty sure the flush rising in her cheeks wasn't due to excessive heat in the room.

She didn't look his way again, though. He quickly shifted and stretched out his legs, crossing them at the ankle this time. His knee continued throbbing anyway.

"Every weekend on the school calendar is already packed," Mrs. Cardinale was saying. "The science fair." She lifted one finger. "The combined sixth-grade dance with Edison Elementary." Another finger went up. "We also have the food drive for Thankful Friday going on all this while." Third finger. "If we're going to do an event of our own, that only leaves us with the Thanksgiving holiday weekend before we're into December and an even busier schedule. Unfortunately, it gives us very little time to plan. Plus, I have a wedding to attend that Saturday, too."

Her comment set off a long-winded discussion among the other individuals while West felt the time ticking on his watch.

He listened long enough to get the gist.

He cleared his throat and not particularly caring that he'd

be speaking over the middle-aged redhead sitting at the far right, said, "Combine your thing with the Winter Faire."

All six people sitting in front of him craned around in their seats to look at him. As if he'd suggested they jump off the cape during a full moon.

He had bigger things on his plate to be judged over than stating such an obviously simple solution, though, and he spread his hands. "Nobody wants to pack another thing on their calendar at this time of the year. Particularly when they know they'll be hit up for money in the process."

A bearded guy on the far left timidly raised his hand. "I agree with the doc."

There had been no introductions and West didn't recognize him. Proof that Cape Cardinale—for all of its growth in the last two decades—was still small-town at its heart. Everyone who lived there still seemed to know everyone else's business.

You knew what to expect when you moved home, West. Don't expect them to change just because you did.

I didn't change, he mentally argued with Janine's voice inside his head. *And if you're going to hang around, at least give me some useful tips.*

Buy low, sell high? Oh, wait. You already know that one.

The redhead's passion had brought her to her feet and he realized she was glaring at him. "The Winter Faire involves the whole town! We can't just intrude on their event."

"Then don't." West had zero interest in the fundraiser. "Schedule your shindig right after Thanksgiving. Just don't expect anyone to show up who isn't hoping to win—what was that grand prize again? A golf bag?"

"A golf bag equipped with a new set of clubs," the middle-aged guy sitting next to Red snapped defensively. "My uncle is donating them. Only used 'em once!"

"Very generous," West observed.

Whatever happened to the golf clubs I gave you?
Back when you were trying to make a silk purse out of me?
You're still a pig. How's that for a tip?

West had used the clubs exactly twice before shoving them into the dark recesses of a closet. He hadn't wanted to be on the path to hospital administration like her father. Hadn't wanted to trade his patients for chalking up deals over golf.

He realized robin's-egg eyes were focused on him again. And they were narrowed in speculation.

"The Winter Faire is the middle of December," she mused. "It *would* give us a few more weeks for planning something really special. My sister's idea was a silent auction. If we can gather more items in addition to your uncle's golf bag, Rod," she added hastily.

"I think that's a good idea. It's a street fair. No worries about finding an indoor venue at such a late stage," another woman said. "It already seems like every place in town has something going on from now through New Year's."

"That's the way it is at the Highland Pub," another person said, giving the redhead a pointed look.

West shifted slightly in his chair at the mention of the comfortable pub located at the equally comfortable old Highland Hotel. His father had claimed the clam chowder there had miraculous healing powers.

Unfortunately, not healing enough to save his dad from the cancer that killed him. The fact that West Sr. had succumbed to the disease only days after West had told him he didn't want to take over the clinic was beside the point.

In reality, West hadn't been to the pub in the decade since. He'd visited Cape Cardinale occasionally. But not the pub. It was too vivid with memories of his dad. Most particularly his disapproval of West's entire way of life.

And you already have one ghost.

Enough already, Janine.

"Tell me what the Faire gets in exchange for us horning in on them, Benny," the redhead was responding. She was obviously challenging the bearded guy opposite her, though she'd resumed her seat.

West mulled the name. Benny's name was no more familiar than his face.

He wished someone would address Mrs. Cardinale by *her* first name. Then he could stop wondering.

"We'd be just one more vendor, Donna," Benny retorted, as if the answer were obvious. "We'll pay our registration fee the same as everybody else, so why would they care?"

"Hold on." Mrs. Cardinale hopped off her perch and began pacing in front of them.

Her striped sweater only reached as far as her trim hips and West looked down at his hands, feeling like his retinas had been seared with the plaid-covered perfection of her rear end.

"I know my brother's involved with the Faire," she was saying. "Or, JCS Aviation is."

"They're a sponsor." Donna dug around in her oversized purse and yanked out a colorful brochure emblazoned with "Winter Faire" across the front. She flipped it around with a Vanna White flourish and tapped a square on the back panel. "Says so right there." She waved it with the unmistakable air of someone who knew it all.

The woman next to her snatched the flyer out of her hand. "Lemme see it."

Donna didn't lose steam. "There are a dozen more companies listed on there. We get them to bring some pressure on—"

"Pressure wasn't exactly what I had in mind." Mrs. Cardinale was pacing again. And while she paced, she twined a slender finger through her hair, coiling, coiling and then—

boing. The hair sprang free; the blond waves seeming to have a life of their own.

He blinked away the image of her hair spread out against a white sheet that suddenly popped into his head.

Desperate for a distraction, he pulled out the messages from his pocket. Even another snarky comment from his ghostly wife would have been welcome.

"I was thinking that instead of just registering like any other vendor," she was saying, "we go to the organizers. See if they like the idea of adding us as more of a collaborator. You know. Give their attendees an opportunity to contribute a little back to the community when they're busy scarfing up holiday fudge and handmade gifts. Maybe they'd even do a little sponsoring of their own by waving our vendor fee. Particularly considering we don't really have the money for it in the first place. Meanwhile, we work on getting items donated. Whether we raffle them off or have a silent auction, we'll need more stuff."

The brochure was still being passed along in the front row. The Winter Faire had been an annual tradition for as long as he could remember. Only, from what he saw printed on the front of the brochure, it now brought in people from as far away as Portland.

He'd thought his mother had been exaggerating the popularity of the event. She volunteered every year and, over those years, he'd gotten very practiced at tuning out her chatter about it.

"How much is it?" West had shuffled and prioritized his messages twice and his abrupt question brought several pairs of eyes around again to look at him. "The registration fee to be a vendor," he clarified just in case it was in question.

"A thousand bucks."

He managed to keep from snorting, but only just. "For a *craft* show?" He pocketed the message slips again.

"It's a lot more than a craft show nowadays," Benny said.

"It'd have to be to garner a fee that high." As far as West could tell, the conversation had all the earmarks of regurgitating itself over again without ever coming to some sort of actionable plan.

He could sit there and be plagued with unwelcome—not to mention inappropriate—urges, or he could get moving.

He pushed to his feet. "I'll make it simple and just pay the fee if they don't waive it." He pulled out a business card and extended it over the heads in front of him toward Mrs. Cardinale. Emphasis on Missus. "They can bill it to me at the clinic address. Send it to Ruthie's attention. She'll make sure everything is taken care of."

She pinched her fingers around the card as delicately as if she were extracting a splinter from a viper. "Wouldn't that make Cardinale Community Clinic our sponsor instead of you?"

She was heading the wrong way down a one-way road if she believed that mattered to him. Much better for people to believe the Clinic was supporting the community than for him, personally. Which didn't explain why he didn't just release the card to her but held on to it. His fingertip was half an inch away from hers. "You want the money or not?"

Her eyes narrowed to slits. "If they waive the fee, will you still make the donation?"

The ultimate goal was for the school students to get some long-needed playground equipment and West was a big believer in physical activity.

So, of course he would still make the donation. It would come from his own pocket and he'd probably double it, but he didn't exactly feel like announcing it.

"I'll think about it." His fingers finally got the message his brain was sending and released the business card. She placed it on the library table behind her with noticeable precision.

Get moving, West. You have things to do, remember?

His feet finally moved. "I'm sorry. I have a meeting to get to." He reached out to push through the glass doors.

"Hold on!" She grabbed up some papers and chased after him. The door slammed shut behind her and they were suddenly standing alone in the empty school corridor. "I've divvied up the parent roster. We all have a list to call." She thrust the papers at him.

She didn't wear any rings. But just because she didn't wear a wedding band didn't mean she wasn't married.

He shook himself. Looked at the papers, but still didn't take them. "And tell them what exactly?"

Her eyebrows lifted slightly. The superiority filling her small smile should have detracted from the perfect shape of her lips, yet it didn't. "We talked about it at the beginning of the meeting. Had you not been late, you'd know."

"I guess you'll have to give me the information another time then." He reached out, not to take the papers at all but to curl her fingers around them.

To make a point?

Or just to actually make contact?

He didn't know if the sudden bemusement in her eyes was because she wasn't used to being thwarted or because her fingers were tingling as much as his, but the only sound that followed him down the hall to the exit was the echo of his footsteps.

Chapter Four

"So now I have to find enough funding to replace our longest-standing grant." West sat back on his haunches, ignoring the snap-crack-pop in his knee and gently lifted Otto Nash's forearm above the edge of the cast. "Any pain when I do this?"

Otto shook his head. His shock of long white hair was tied on the top of his head with what looked suspiciously like a leather shoelace. "No," he said, though the way his lips thinned said otherwise. "How much were the dunderheads giving?"

"You been talking to Ruthie?"

Otto's eyebrows pulled together. "Who's Ruthie?"

"My office manager." He'd come straight to Otto's from the frustrating presentation with the foundation representatives. He didn't think he would've unloaded the news under normal circumstances. "Never mind. The Dunterwood Foundation has been supporting us for years. We have patients who travel by bus halfway down the coast just because we're the only place they can get into regardless of their means to pay. Without Dunterwood support, we'll have to cut some of those patients or cut staff. Which is going to end up being both in the end, because we can't do one without affecting the other." West's investments were still entwined with the practice in Chicago but even if they weren't, it wouldn't be enough of an endowment to ensure the clinic could operate indefinitely. And he'd already put the bulk of Janine's money into a trust for Jason.

Otto's lips were pursed in a silent whistle.

"Anyway. Enough whining." There was no cure-all for the clinic's state except to do what his father had always done. Depend on the largesse of others. West carefully lowered Otto's arm again. The man was sitting in a straight-backed armchair positioned in front of a telescope aimed out of the windows that lined one wall of his lavish third-story bedroom window. Beyond the windows, the night sky was blanketed with stars. "Want to tell me why you canceled your appointment this morning when you knew you'd aggravated your injury?"

"Not particularly." Holding his arm gingerly against the front of his unfastened purple-and-green shirt, Otto pushed off the chair and walked across the room to the mirrored wet bar. He selected two short glasses from one of the gleaming glass shelves and pulled the stopper out of a crystal decanter. He poured a finger into each glass and carried them both in one hand back to West.

West took one. "What're we drinking to?"

"The general suckiness of getting older," Otto said. Then he gave a rusty-sounding laugh.

"Suckiness. Technical term. And at the moment, apt." West knocked the base of his glass against Otto's and they both lifted their glasses to drink.

West wasn't much of a drinker, but the scotch had a welcome burn. "Were you hoverboarding again?"

Otto laughed again. "If only." He pushed at one of the glass panes and it slid aside, letting in the chilly night. Another telescope was set up on the balcony and he stopped in front of it, looking through the eyepiece.

West set his glass on an art deco table and followed Otto outside. He was still wearing his suit from the Dunterwood meeting, but Otto was wearing only a pair of fraying cargo shorts and his shirttails flew around like some garish bird in the stiff wind.

"You want a jacket?"

"What for?" Otto straightened and spread his arms wide, as if welcoming the onslaught of wind.

The effect was ruined when he quickly cradled his casted wrist against his waist.

"I can't force you to have another X-ray," West said. "But I wish—"

"Son, I've been busting these old bones longer than you've been alive. I'm just bruised up again. Let it go." Otto tossed back the rest of his drink and then threw the glass out over the balcony as if he were aiming for the stars.

West immediately stepped to the edge of the balcony. The only thing directly below was shrubbery that clung to the cliffside. Further out was a view of both Cardinale and Friars beaches. "You could give someone a concussion, beaning them with that leaded crystal."

"The glasses get caught in the shrubs before they can make it that far down. Gardener picks 'em out routinely."

"Did you fall?"

Otto wasn't tripped up by the sudden question. "You're not going to let this go," he surmised.

"Wouldn't be much of a physician if I did."

"Met your father once," Otto said. "You're a lot like him."

West grimaced. "You're one of a select few who think so." His mother being the other half of that few. And when it came to Dunterwood? There'd been a decade of other clinic directors between West's father and him. And now it was on his watch that they'd decided they'd done enough?

He wasn't entirely an egotist. The timing didn't necessarily mean he was the cause even though it felt like it.

He turned away from the view and rested his elbows against the waist-high parapet. "I thought you'd only lived here a year or so. When did you meet my father?"

Otto shrugged. "I was young when I lived here. Long time ago now. Your dad was dating a pretty little filly in town, causing quite a stir with her being a mite younger than he was. Marjorie, as I recall. It was probably the most scandalous thing he ever did."

"Until he married her," West said. "Marjorie Clements is my mother."

"No kidding." Otto let out a huff of laughter. "Didn't think she was the settling sort. Not back then at any rate. Your old man was a decent fella, though. For an idealist." He looked through the eyepiece of his telescope again and fiddled with a few knobs. "Your funding will work out."

West sure in hell hoped so. "We'll see. I'm no idealist. And I never aspired to taking over a nonprofit clinic." The concierge practice he'd had in Chicago had been significantly different. Which was why his business partner wanted to open more just like it beyond Illinois altogether. "But I don't want it going under on my watch, either."

"Have faith. Life is also unexpected." Otto raised his head and, when he gestured to the eyepiece, West took his place next to the scope.

He lowered his head and then let out laugh and straightened. "I thought you were looking at the stars." Instead, the old man had his telescope focused on a yacht barely visible with the naked eye. Thanks to the telescope, however, the nearly nude woman on the deck surrounded by spotlights and a camera crew might have been just two feet away.

"She used to *be* a star," Otto drawled. "That's Gwendolyn Hightower."

Despite himself, West took another look through the eyepiece. Gwendolyn Hightower had been the stuff of fantasies when he'd been a teenager. Posters of her had bedecked his walls along with the walls of every friend he'd had. The long, unruly black waves looked the same, as did the long, very shapely limbs draped languidly over the sleek lines of the bow as if she were basking under a warm summer night. Out on the water though, West figured the temperature had to be close to freezing.

You always did like brunettes. Was that what attracted you to me, West? Did I remind you of your adolescent fantasy woman?

"How do you know it's her?" West asked over Janine's mocking voice. Through the telescope, the model's face, was turned away and hidden by her artfully upraised arm that thrust her breasts upward, testing the limits of the tiny triangles of fabric covering them. Back in the day, she'd rarely bothered with even that much. Her penchant for nudity had been as famous as her supposedly voracious sex life.

Otto leaned his good arm atop the parapet. "Heard talk that she was in the area, doing a photo shoot for some online thing. If you ask me, she looks damn good for a woman her age."

West watched long enough to see the model finally change positions. Someone rushed forward with a long jacket and that famous body disappeared beneath it. He straightened again. "And you just *happened* to find the photo shoot with your telescope?"

A faint smile hovered around Otto's mouth. "I have a lot of time on my hands. And I may have gotten an inside scoop from the kid who delivers my lunch from the Highland Pub every afternoon. Film crew's been staying there at the hotel."

"That sounds more like it." West went back inside and Otto followed him, closing the door once more before they crossed the room toward the elevator. "If that pain in your arm doesn't go away in the next twenty-four hours, call me."

Otto pushed the call button for the elevator and the doors immediately slid open. "I'll probably be out of town."

West knew his skepticism was showing. "You hardly ever leave the house, but you expect me to believe you're going on a *trip*?"

"I've left this place plenty," Otto argued. "After I first bought it, it was years before I even lived here."

"What changed?"

Otto made a face. "Broke my leg."

He made it sound simple. But along with the neurological evaluation results, West had also seen the records from Otto's broken leg. It hadn't been simple in the least. He'd been nearly incapacitated while recovering. Had endured two complicated surgeries. After which had come the months of physical therapy that had only ended a few months ago.

"If you must know, I have some investments that need seeing to," Otto added. "I don't know how long I'll be away."

West stepped into the elevator. "Just don't overdo it," he warned. "And watch where you toss your crystal tumblers."

Otto hit the button again. "Sounding like a nursemaid, Doc," he accused just before the doors closed once more, leaving West alone in the car staring at his reflection in the gleaming gold elevator walls. He was grateful that he didn't also see a translucent image of his wife standing with him.

He'd met a lot of unique individuals in his field of work. Otto Nash was definitely one of them. He could just imagine what Otto would think if he knew his new neighbor had a unique quality, too. Namely a ghost that came and went whenever she damned well pleased.

In seconds, the elevator opened again on the ground floor and he walked through the empty foyer and let himself out the front door. He knew Otto could watch the security cameras from his third-floor sanctum, but he figured the guy was probably back at his telescope, waiting for another glimpse of Gwendolyn Hightower.

He got in his car and drove down the hill to his place. Unlike Otto's property, which managed to blend itself in with the magnificent setting despite its size, West's rental stuck out like a sore thumb. Particularly with those lampposts.

He parked in the garage and went through to the sound of the washer and dryer both running.

The mountain of laundry that he could never seem to conquer was still there, but it had been halved in size.

A large, covered pot was on the stove with an empty bowl

sitting nearby. His stomach growled, but he only stopped long enough to lift the lid to see the steaming chili inside. He replaced the lid and followed the sound of the television to the living room where his mother was sitting on the couch watching reruns and Jason was sprawled on his stomach on the floor, a pencil in his hand.

"Are you drawing or doing homework?"

Jason rolled onto his back, his face splitting into a smile. "Dad!"

This. For the first time all day, West felt peace flood through him.

This is what made everything worthwhile.

"You're earlier than I thought you'd be." His mother had snatched her stocking-clad feet off the coffee table as if she'd been caught doing something wicked. "How'd the meeting go?"

"It went." The Dunterwood matter would still be there in the morning. Otto could spout off about having faith, but West wasn't putting stock in that. He'd go back to the well again and again. And if he had to, he'd start digging a new one. He'd just have to learn how to deal with philanthropists rather than venture capitalists.

But right now, what mattered was his family. His son.

He sat on the coffee table and looked at the papers spread on the floor. Close up, he could see that it wasn't a home-work versus drawing situation, but a mix of both.

He picked up the nearest sheet of paper and held up the trio of zombies for his mother to see. "Have anything to say for yourself?"

His mother patted her stylishly short hair. She wore one of her endless pastel cardigan twin sets and coordinating slacks and looked more like she was prepared for a ladies' tea than an evening watching zombie television. "I think he inherited my artistic skill," she said. "I was quite good with watercolors in my day. Your father, on the other hand, couldn't draw his way out of a paper bag." She rose from the couch. "The chili is still hot. I'll fix you a bowl."

Jason had already turned his attention back to his thick pad of paper and West set aside the sketch, following his mother back to the kitchen. "You don't have to serve it to me, you know."

"I know that." His mother gestured with the clean wooden spoon she pulled from a drawer. "Sit."

He pulled a small icepack out of the freezer and sat down at one of the island stools, dropping the pack on top of his knee. It was mildly soothing. "Anything else go on today that I need to know about?"

"How long are you going to ignore that knee?" She raised her eyebrows, waiting.

"I'm not ignoring it."

"Could have fooled me." She began filling the bowl. "Jason's school called."

West felt a jolt. Thanks to the busyness of his schedule, he'd managed to tuck that afternoon's committee meeting into a tightly-lidded box. Yet how easily the lid flew off with just a little provocation.

"Why?"

"It's time for parent-teacher conferences."

He frowned. "Already?"

Marjorie sprinkled grated cheese on top of the chili and handed the bowl to him. "Already." She pulled a bottle of water from the fridge but before she could pour it into the glass, a soft buzz came from the laundry room. She set the glass and bottle in front of him and followed the buzz. "School started for everyone else more than two months ago," she reminded him from the other room. "They're scheduling the conferences for next week and this is one thing I shouldn't be handling in your place. Will you be able to make it?"

"I'll talk to Ruthie tomorrow to make sure I do," he said.

"Well, good. That's a relief."

He heard her. But didn't really hear her. He was too busy wondering if the conference would mean another face-to-face with the classroom aide. Would she even *be* there?

Janine had been cheating on him for the last two years of their marriage. Why did *he* feel guilty for being attracted to another woman, particularly after all this time?

He shoved his fingers through his hair and picked up the bottled water. "You don't have to keep ordering this."

His mother appeared in the doorway, a T-shirt of Jason's in her hand. "What's that?"

He held up the water. "We're fine with tap."

Her blink was almost owlish. She finished folding Jason's T-shirt and placed it precisely on the counter. She lowered her voice to an almost whisper. "It's money, isn't it. Chicago was just too expensive after Janine died. That's why you moved home and put Jason in public school instead of Tuppersford."

The implication was that his wife had been the one bringing in the "real" money into their relationship. Not inaccurate considering the family money she'd inherited, but West was the one who'd been out there bringing in the paycheck that had paid for her million-dollar tastes. "This doesn't have anything to do with money. I went to Edison, remember? Public school didn't hurt me any. It won't hurt Jason, either." Unlike Jason's exorbitant private school in Chicago, the reputation of Cape Cardinale's lone private school was less about educational excellence and more about catering to the eclectic whims of the wealthy. West might be wealthy, but he was far more concerned in giving Jason normalcy. "I just don't like mineral water as much as I do tap." He set the bottle down on the counter.

Her brows knitted together. "But Janine—"

"Didn't listen to me on the matter, either."

His mother smoothed her palm over the folded T-shirt. "Well, of course, I'll stop ordering it, honey. All you had to do was say so."

"I'm saying so."

She lifted her hands peaceably. "Okay then." She went back into the laundry room.

"You don't have to do our laundry, either."

"Someone needs to," she said a little tartly. "Because your son is out of clean socks." She returned to the doorway long enough to wave several socks in the air. "Eat your chili. It'll get cold."

He stuck his spoon in the chili that was still hot enough to sterilize his taste buds. When it came to spiciness, though, the stuff was downright tame. "Does the Highland Pub still serve all those chowders?"

His mom floated back into the kitchen with another armload of T-shirts that she dropped on the kitchen table. Maxwill's cage was covered for the night, but he still let out a sharp squawk in response to being disturbed. "There would be public protests if they ever stopped. Why?"

"Someone mentioned the place today." He tossed the icepack in the sink. It wasn't doing anything and it kept slipping off his leg. "Do you still volunteer at the Winter Faire?"

"Every year." She gave him a surprisingly mischievous smile. "Want to come pass out hard candies and point out where the Porta Potties are located?"

"I'd rather poke needles in my eye."

She chuckled then suddenly cocked her head, listening for a second. "Jason," she raised her voice, "who are you talking to?"

"It's just the TV, Grandma!"

His mother made a suspicious face, but she let it go and continued folding shirts. "Was someone talking about the Winter Faire today, too?"

"At that fundraising thing I went to at the school."

Marjorie smiled. "Your dad would be so proud of you, honey. Getting involved at the school the way you are."

It would be the first time his father was proud. Just because West had gone into medicine didn't mean West Sr. had approved of his son's direction. "I'm not involved."

"But you're on the fundraising committee, aren't you?"

West wished he hadn't brought it up. "I went to one meeting. I'll make a donation. Sometimes that's enough."

"You know best, I'm sure."

An assurance that was anything *but* assuring, particularly when delivered in that dulcet tone.

He finished eating the bland chili, by which time his mother was done with the laundry.

He walked her out to her car.

"Be sure to move that last load from the washing machine to the dryer when it's ready," she said. "Don't forget. Otherwise, it'll sit there wet until who knows when and everything will have to be washed all over again."

"I won't forget." He pulled open the car door for her and she slipped inside the vehicle. She smiled up at him and he thought about what Otto Nash had said. That she hadn't seemed the settling sort.

To West, she'd always been supremely settled. Not even finding herself widowed at the youthful age of fifty had changed her. "Do you remember knowing a guy named Otto Nash?"

"Hmm. There *was* a family by the name of Nash," she said. "I think that was it. They lived in that big house down by Friars Beach. The one that was turned into that big surf shop? You worked there one summer while you were in high school. Oh, wait. That wasn't Nash." She clucked her tongue. "*Bash*. Didn't you date one of the Bash girls?"

He was getting a headache. "Otto Nash," he repeated patiently. "He knew Dad before the two of you even got married. Now he owns that property at the peak of Seaview."

"Oh, well." She swept her hand in the air. "Who knows? Your dad knew everyone. And everyone was his friend."

She started the engine. "Try to get an early night, honey. You're looking tired."

The suckiness of getting older, he thought. "Be careful driving home."

"Always." She tugged the door and he stepped away, waiting until she'd driven off before he went back inside.

He rinsed his dishes, added them to the dishwasher and started the cycle. Then he went out to the living room again, catching Jason hovering over his laptop. He jumped guiltily the second he spotted West, though, and slammed the laptop closed.

"It's two hours later in Chicago than it is here." West began picking up the scattered papers that were obviously not homework. "Tell Luc you'll have to talk to him tomorrow."

Jason's shoulders fell. He raised the laptop lid and Luc's face reappeared. "I gotta go," he said. "Dad says it's late."

"Not for me," Luc boasted then ruined the effort with a yawn he couldn't hide.

West squared the papers together, noisily tapping them on the glass-topped table. Jason quickly ended the video call and slid the computer onto the table next to West. "Can we get a puppy?"

He ought to be used to the lightening-swift thought patterns of his son by now. "Where'd that come from?"

"Luc's mom got him a puppy."

"Hope it's a small one." Their present rent-a-mansion could accommodate a dog more easily than the Mai's overpriced yet cramped luxury condo.

"I dunno. Luc said he's just a mutt. They got him at the animal shelter. So, can we?"

West directed Jason up the stairs. "I already have enough on my plate keeping up with *you*."

"I'd take care of everything."

"So says every kid since the dawn of time when they ask their parent for a pet."

"But I *would*."

"We'll see."

Jason's feet dragged as they neared the top of the staircase. "That's what Mom always said. It just means no."

Jason was eight. His mother had died when he was six. He couldn't know how effectively he'd shot his arrow right through West's gut. "Maybe. Maybe not. I'll think about it. Right now, you need to brush your teeth and hit the sack."

"Promise?"

West ruffled Jason's hair. "I promise."

"Yes." Jason pumped his fist, then seeming charged with energy, he jogged down the hall and into the bathroom.

West left him to it and turned through the doorway of the oversized master bedroom. In a style vaguely similar to Otto Nash's, a wall of windows opened onto a balcony that, in West's case, ran around the corner of his room. One side offered the distant view of the Pacific and the other looked over the massive yard where the grass was so overgrown, it climbed up the legs of the three life-sized Greek statues positioned "artfully" among a koi pond and gazebo.

He shrugged out of his jacket, remembered the phone messages and pulled them out. Ruthie didn't pass on junk messages. He knew better than to ignore any of them, though the temptation was there all the same.

He called the mayor's assistant first, glad to get a voice-mail system instead of an overly dedicated public servant still at his or her desk at that hour. He thanked them for thinking of him, but he wasn't interested in running for town council. The next three were just as quickly dispatched since they'd all come from Sean. The last was from Doc Hayes, who picked up West's call almost immediately.

"Poker night. You've already agreed, so don't try to back out now." Doc was succinct. "Friday."

West still didn't know why he'd agreed. Stu and a few others met once a month for poker. And practically the first day that West had hung his lab coat on the hook at the clinic, Doc called and told him to put the next game on his schedule.

"And here I thought you were calling to say you wanted to move your practice back to Beach Medical."

"Not likely. No offense, but last I saw, you were still in a mess of construction.

"Completion's scheduled before Christmas. Whenever I have time to talk to the head of the construction, though, she's already gone for the day, and after the conversation I had with the CEO of Cardinale Cares, I know she's more informed than he is. Where's the game again?"

"We use the back room at the pub. Don't be late." Doc hung up.

Almost as if he knew how close West was to canceling.

He added a reminder for the card game on his phone before tossing it aside. He showered, spent ten minutes debating the likelihood of vampires while tucking in Jason, and finally crawled into his own bed.

Exhaustion flowed through his bones. He wanted nothing more than sleep. Preferably the dreamless variety.

Laundry, West. You don't expect me *or Jason to deal with it, do you? He hates the chore as much as you do.*

He opened his eyes again. Stared into the darkness.

Leave the damn clothes where they are? Or deal with it now?

He heaved out a sigh and threw back the covers.

Exhaustion would have to wait.

Chapter Five

"This was delivered for you earlier." Ruthie dropped an oversized manila envelope on West's desk.

He barely glanced up from his laptop. "What is it?"

"For you," she said pointedly. She swung her coat around her shoulders and left.

It was Friday and the week had passed in a typical blur. With Ruthie's departure, he was the last one left in the office. Everyone else had already gone. It was only three weeks until Thanksgiving and the unofficial start to the great Christmas race was already going strong. These days, nobody hung around work a second longer than necessary.

He finished reviewing the lab report, added his notes to the patient's electronic file, and opened the large envelope.

A wrinkled packet of pages slid out. It was a list of names and phone numbers with a big blue note stuck to the front of it. The handwriting on it was slanted. Slightly looping. Definitely feminine.

This is your list.
Please call and ask for their support. No amount is too small. (Although large amounts won't make us run screaming in the other direction.)
An "exact" script is attached.

He smiled slightly and needlessly repositioned the sticky

note. It was signed simply "AC" and West had no trouble at all imagining who'd written it.

He set the papers aside and turned back to the next patient record.

AC.

The C was for Cardinale, of course. But about the A?

He shook his head, clearing it.

The next record was Otto's. He wondered if Otto had left town. If he'd returned. Barring complications, he was scheduled to have his cast removed before Thanksgiving. Physical therapy would follow.

Ann? Andrea? A lot of names began with the letter A.

Get your mind where it belongs, West.

Even though he knew that Otto would receive automatic reminders of his appointment, West picked up his cell phone and sent a personal text as well.

The words just hung there, though. No sign that the message had been seen by Otto. No bubbles indicating a response being typed.

He turned his phone face down on the desk and walked over to the lone window that his small office possessed. It wasn't late yet. Not even five o'clock.

His mother was on Jason duty for the duration, thanks to Doc's poker game later at the pub.

Outside, a wind was blowing through the trees that lined the perimeter of the property. Beyond them, the gray sky loomed close to the horizon of sparkling water.

Alice? Amelia? Janine's voice was mocking. *Doesn't matter what Blondie's name is. She won't come close to me.*

"Who'd want her to?" One of these days, someone would hear him conversing with a dead woman and his career would be toast. "I've had one cheating wife already."

Janine disappeared with a pop.

He turned away from the window and picked up his phone again. He searched for the directory on the school's website but there was nobody listed by the name of Cardinale. The only name listed for the fourth-grade class was E. Tone.

Websites. What good were they when they weren't maintained with complete information?

He phoned Ruthie.

When she answered, there was music and voices behind her. "What'd you do?" he asked. "Go to a party?"

"Some of us get invited to such things," she said. "But I'm at the pub with the mayor, if you must know. Unless the building is on fire, why are you calling me?"

"When you scheduled my conference with Jason's teacher for Monday, did you talk with her or the aide directly?"

"No. The school secretary was doing all the scheduling. Why?"

Because he had an unreasonable compulsion to know what Mrs. Cardinale's first name was? He could feel his neck getting hot just acknowledging the fact. "I'm looking for a way to reach his teacher." It wasn't quite the truth, but not entirely a lie, either.

A burst of background laughter almost drowned out Ruthie's voice. "Isn't there some online portal for his class?"

Was there? "I should know these things," he muttered. The realization was enough to derail further descent down a pointless rabbit hole. It didn't matter what Mrs. Cardinale's first name was. Had West known the first names of *anyone* at his elementary school?

"Ask Jason," Ruthie said. "Our table is ready." She hung up.

The last thing he wanted to do was ask his son and let Jason know just how oblivious his father really was.

The teacher conference was scheduled first thing on Monday morning. It would be soon enough to find out more about Mrs. Cardinale.

He picked up the list of names again. Realized that he recognized more than a few of them from his youth.

He flipped to the script.

He'd asked her what exactly he was supposed to say.

And she'd told him.

He didn't know if he admired the in-your-face response or not, but there was no denying it was effective.

He had two hours to kill before the poker game.

He might as well make use of them.

He sat down at his desk again and set to work.

There was no line of cars for drop-off at the school the following Monday morning for the simple reason that the students were off while the parents were on.

Jason was with West's mother again, and perfectly happy about it because the two of them were on their way to Portland and a bookstore where one of the authors of Jason's favorite graphic novels was doing a book signing. They were making a day of it, and West didn't expect them back until evening.

He found a spot in the half-full parking lot and walked through the drizzle toward the school. He'd grown up with this weather. The only reason he'd ever used an umbrella since then had been because of Janine. She hadn't minded if he got damp but had minded a great deal if she did.

He swiped his hand over his hair when he entered the school. He'd been inside exactly twice. The day he'd registered Jason for school. And the first day that he'd dropped him off for classes. That was the first time he'd met Jason's teacher. She hadn't offered to introduce her pretty blonde aide who'd been busy doing something at the back of the classroom.

Two young women, who looked all of sixteen years old, staffed a large check-in counter. On either side of the counter, double doors led off to two different wings.

Jason's classroom was through the doors to the left.

He checked in and headed off to the left, passing another barrel. It had a big sign taped to the front: "Thankful Friday." And, like the barrel at the other wing, was already half full of canned foods.

He made a mental note to add to the contributions. A lot of the people who would be receiving the food were clients at the clinic.

The classroom doors were all open, but the corridor was almost eerily quiet without any students around.

Whether he wanted to acknowledge it or not, anticipation was building with every step he took. He hadn't thought about Mrs. Cardinale all weekend.

Just most of it.

He stepped into the doorway, his gaze immediately landing on the utilitarian desk sitting in front of the classroom. Jason's teacher, Mrs. Tone, sat there. Her back was ramrod-straight and her hands were folded on top of a yellow folder. Her unsmiling profile was pointed toward the back of the room.

The desk there was unoccupied.

No Mrs. Cardinale.

Disappointment wasn't something he wanted to admit. He was there because of Jason. Shouldn't matter whether she was there or not.

He cleared his throat and the teacher's head turned. She looked at him over the tops of her eyeglasses then pointedly checked the watch hanging from a thick necklace.

"I apologize," he said. "I know I'm a few minutes late." She hadn't invited him inside, but he walked into the classroom anyway. She didn't stand or offer a handshake, so he indicated the straight-backed chair positioned closest to the desk. "Should I sit here?"

"Yes." She adjusted her eyeglasses and opened her folder. "Since we have so little time left," her voice held a censorious edge, "I'll just give you Jason's progress report." She slid a sheet of paper with a detailed chart on it filled in with red ink. "Any questions?"

West looked over the list of categories on which his son had been graded. Since Jason had been in preschool, he'd excelled in nearly every subject. Seeing a column of marks ranging from below average to well below was an unwelcome shock.

"*Fails* to meet expectation?" He looked at the unsmiling teacher. "Even in math?"

"Even in math," the teacher returned. Her gaze flickered to the door and West wondered if she was hoping her next parent would be early. "Perhaps he'd be capable of better performance if he spent less time with his—" she fluttered her fingers dismissively "—inappropriate doodling and more time with his textbooks."

West felt his jaw tightening. It wasn't so much her actual words but her dismissive tone. "Maybe he doodles because he's bored. He says most of the work is the same stuff he's already had back in Illinois. It's easy for him. He blows through it and ends up with time on his hands." He felt like he was stating the obvious.

Color had flagged her cheeks and she was clutching the big pendant like she wanted to hurl it. "Since he's had the material before, he should be earning perfect grades, shouldn't he?"

It was like having a discussion with someone on a different plane of existence. He could almost say he missed Jason's private school back in Chicago. Nearly everything had been tailored to fit his needs.

But it was also the school Owen Mai had run.

And growing up with everything tailored to fit meant not learning how to adjust when something didn't.

He tried again. "Principal Bowler and I spoke about this when I registered Jason for school. She said students who need special placement—advanced or otherwise—receive the individual attention they need, and yet—"

"Perhaps you should talk with Principal Bowler about moving him into the *fifth* grade then." She cut him off in a voice that was even more waspish than usual. "So that he'll have new material to learn from Mrs. Maitland."

West had been reluctant to move Jason up to the fourth grade in the first place. His son already had plenty of interactions with kids and adults who were older than he was. He'd experienced the death of his mother. He didn't need more maturity. He needed the opportunity to just be a kid! But if he was bored in fourth grade, it would be even worse sending him back to third.

He also realized he wasn't getting anywhere by antagonizing the teacher more than he'd already done.

"Not that his inattentiveness would be solved," she added in her snippy way. "Considering his lackadaisical attitude."

"He's *eight*," West snapped back.

She ignored him. "Education is my field of expertise, Dr. D'Angelo. You need to teach your son to focus. Or I'm afraid I'll have to consider talking to Principal Bowler myself about his suitability to be in my class."

Howell Elementary School had only one fourth-grade class. If a change was in order, it would mean a change in schools, too.

"My son is *my* field of expertise," he countered evenly.

Regardless of how things had ended, he wished for Janine's opinion. She'd always known what to do where Jason was concerned. Her ghost, however, remained stubbornly silent.

But one thing he did know about Jason was that he had no problem focusing on a task. His ability to concentrate had been fierce from the time he'd been a toddler. Yes, Jason was struggling to fit in and moving him around wouldn't help that any. But West had his eye on Jason's well-being. If

Mrs. Tone thought he'd be intimidated by the threat of moving Jason out of her class, she was sadly mistaken.

"I'll talk to Jase about the appropriateness of his doodling," he told her. "In the meanwhile, I'll also be thinking about *your* suitability for *him*."

He took the progress report and folded it in two. Parent-teacher conferences had always been Janine's territory. He knew if he didn't put an end to this now, he was going to tell the teacher that the mediocre grades were much more a statement about her "expertise" as an educator than they were a commentary on his son's ability.

And that would definitely burn a bridge he wasn't quite ready to torch.

He tapped the folded edge of the report on her desk and stood. He could see a young couple standing together just outside the doorway. Their heads were angled closely, their murmuring voices too low to decipher.

"Your next conference is here," he told the teacher. "But this isn't over. We'll be talking more."

On that particular promise, he walked out. His head was so full of steam that he just wanted out of there altogether.

It was only by chance that he happened to glance through an opened door as he strode back down the hallway and spotted a tousle-haired blonde.

She was on her hands and knees on the floor.

He stopped so abruptly, he practically skidded.

She was wearing mustard-yellow jeans, glittery gold tennis shoes and a skinny scarlet turtleneck patterned with turquoise stars.

If he'd glimpsed only her clothing, he would have still known it was her.

Mrs. Cardinale.

AC.

She was crawling around, running a sudsy sponge over the large beige banner spread out on the floor, her head bobbing slightly to whatever she was listening to on the purple earbuds he could see peeking through her wavy hair.

He leaned his shoulder against the doorjamb, feeling his ire with Jason's teacher fade. A little.

She reached out for the bucket nearby and spotted him.

Robin's-egg blues widened and she sat back on her heels. Water dripped from the sponge in one hand, and she pulled out her earbuds with her other. "If you're just getting here, beware. Mrs. Tone's even worse about timeliness than I am."

"And Mrs. Tone has already given her assessment." He straightened and waved the folded progress report. "What's the A stand for?"

Her forehead crinkled slightly. Janine—lover of every cosmetic procedure ever designed to stave off the progression of time—had never allowed her forehead to crinkle. To show any hint of expression at all. "What do you mean? A's the top, F's the bottom."

"*AC*. You signed the sticky note you left on the call list with just your initials."

The crinkle smoothed. Something flickered in her vivid eyes. Curiosity maybe? "Alexa," she said. "My name is Alexa."

Alexa. He silently repeated it. Committed it to memory, though he doubted he was likely to forget it. Not with the way she preoccupied him. "It suits you." He nodded toward the sponge. "Don't you have janitors for that sort of thing?"

"You'd think, right?" Her lips took on a wry slant. "Just one more menial task that has landed on my list of highly critical duties." She tossed the sponge into the bucket and wiped her hands down the front of her jeans, leaving behind wet prints. "How'd the conference with Mrs. Tone go?"

"You don't know?" He unfolded the report and held it out.

She rose from knees to standing with admirable ease. No snap-crackle or pop. Her fingers—still damp and cool—brushed against his when she adjusted the paper so she could see it.

He felt more than heard her faint sigh.

"You're in his classroom," he said. "Do you disagree with her grades?"

She let go of the paper, looking up at him.

Something inside him tightened and, for a moment, time froze.

At least it did for him.

She just ducked her chin and stepped back over to the bucket, leaning down to pluck out the sponge again. "Mrs. Tone is an experienced teacher." Her tone neutral.

"Who obviously doesn't understand Jase at all." His gaze drifted to her hand and the sponge that was heedlessly dripping water thanks to the way her ringless fingers had tightened around it. "If I'm acting like one of those parents who can't stand hearing something less than perfect about their kid, just say so. If Jason's grades are earned, they're earned. So, what is this?" The progress report crumpled in his fingers.

She chewed her cheek for a moment. "I don't think you're one of those parents," she finally said.

He exhaled heavily. "I'm putting you in an awkward position. Maybe I should put him in Tuppersford after all."

She frowned slightly. "I'm sure you'll figure it out." She looked like she wanted to say more. But she didn't.

He gestured at the wet floor, suddenly needing practicality in the worst way. "Want something to clean that up?" The room Alexa was working in was clear of desks and chairs, though the perimeter was lined with cabinets. They looked industrial enough to house janitorial supplies.

She looked down at the puddle that had formed near her feet as if surprised. "No, I... I'm—it's fine." She straightened the edge of the off-white banner with the toe of her gold shoe. "I don't think you need to worry about Jason. He's a great kid. He'll learn how to navigate around teachers like—" She stopped at the sound of footsteps.

He glanced over his shoulder. One of the young women

from the front desk was scurrying down the hall. She didn't give them so much as a glance.

He turned his attention back to Alexa Cardinale. Mrs. Cardinale. Who didn't wear a wedding ring.

He was as bad as Jason. Becoming fixated on some small point to the exclusion of everything else.

All he had to do was ask her. But for some reason he couldn't get the question out of his mouth.

I remember how you were shy in the beginning with me, Janine whispered in his ear. *It was surprisingly sweet.*

Sure, he thought. *Now you show up.*

He focused harder on the wholly alive woman right in front of him. He'd never been shy. Janine had just been bolder. "I took care of the call list," he said abruptly.

"The call—oh." Alexa moistened her lips. "You did? The entire thing?"

"Entire thing. It was simple. Since I knew exactly what to say," he added deadpan.

Her lashes swept down, hiding those bright blues. A small smile hovered around her lips. "That's good. Great, actually."

"I caught more voicemails than I did live bodies," he warned.

"Same here." She moved suddenly, tossing her sponge back into the bucket as she crossed the room to one of the cupboards. "I'll have to check the website. See if there's been a sudden jump in credit card donations." She glanced at him over her shoulder. "Nobody has finished their call list except for you. I'm impressed."

"You haven't finished *your* list?"

"Well, yeah." She pulled a long-handled mop from inside the cupboard. "But I'm running the committee. Kind of have to set the example." She carried the mop over and flopped the gray ropy strings onto the sign.

"What *is* that for, anyway?"

"The banner? Mrs. Tone wants to hang it in the gymnasium for the sixth-grade dance this weekend." She swiped the mop back and forth. "It's only been stored in the back of a cupboard for a millennium," she muttered.

He stepped into the classroom so that he could see the entire length of the banner. "Excel at Howell Elementary" was printed in block letters.

"Fun stuff for a dance," he said. "Does she plan to paint over it or something?"

"I don't think so."

"Whatever happened to Under-the-Sea or Rockin' to the 80's themes?"

Her lips quirked again. That appealing half smile made him wonder about the full-on version.

One part of his brain reminded him he had a full roster of patients to see. The other part was busy noticing that Alexa hadn't taken another step away from him to maintain the distance between them.

"Is this what teacher's aides always do?" He toyed with the crumpled progress report. Curling the paper into a tube. Uncurling it again. Anything to keep his fingers occupied and a metaphorical mile away from her. "Chores?"

"They do in Ernestine Tone's classroom." She propped her arms over the mop handle. "When I had my own instructional aides, we all worked together to improve our effectiveness where my students were concerned."

"*You're* a teacher?"

She raised her eyebrows. "Don't sound so surprised."

"I'm not."

The eyebrows went even higher.

"You seem too young," he offered, feeling like a dolt in a way that Mrs. Tone couldn't have achieved in a million years.

"Obviously not." She spread her arms, the mop handle held in one hand. "Just a teacher without a class to teach. At least in this town."

A bell rang, startling them both.

"I've got to get all this cleaned up."

"I've got patients," he said at the same time.

She pursed her lips slightly, hiding that intriguing half smile.

He backed out of the classroom. He knew her name. Task complete. "Have your next committee meeting scheduled yet?"

"Not until the Monday after Thanksgiving." She wielded the string mop with the air of someone who'd done so many times before. "One of the organizers of the Winter Faire is going to be there." Her blue gaze slanted his way. "Will you?"

"We'll see." He thought about Jason. "Maybe." The answer wasn't any better. "My schedule's pretty busy."

"You're a doctor. Schedules are everything."

"Not everything. Not all the time."

Her gaze met his and then flicked away. Skepticism had replaced the humor in that corner curl of her soft pink lips. She dropped the mop handle on the floor with a racket and picked up the bucket. Then she sidled around him through the classroom door. "We'll see."

He watched her walk away from him. Her hips swaying in the mustard-yellow jeans.

She'll break your heart.

Janine's voice behind him was so startlingly clear that he actually turned to look down the empty corridor.

You already took care of that, he answered silently. *Remember? No heart left for that sort of thing.*

He turned around again, and his knee twinged. Hard.

How do you expect to keep up with Jason if you're getting decrepit?

He grimaced. Yanked out his phone and sent a message to Ruthie to make an appointment with Roger Fox.

Chapter Six

Ten minutes. If he didn't show up in ten minutes, she was out of here.

Feeling better after her decision, Alexa stopped wiggling her foot and looked away from the door of Tanya's restaurant. It was Saturday afternoon, the restaurant was typically crowded, and for some reason that she had yet to figure out, she'd agreed to meet West D'Angelo there for coffee.

To hammer out things.

Or so his text message had said.

What things, though?

West would need to deal with Ernestine or Regina Bowler where Jason's grades were concerned, which left the fundraising committee.

If he wanted off the committee, he didn't need to meet with her face-to-face to tell her. Though he'd made all those phone calls, he hadn't made an actual commitment to be on the committee.

We'll see.

She wiggled her foot again and checked the time on her cell phone. Knowing how busy the restaurant usually was, she'd come straight from her yoga class to get a table. It was still early. Which meant West wasn't actually late. Yet.

She knew she was harping on his habit of tardiness but couldn't seem to make herself stop.

Or perhaps it was that she didn't *want* to stop.

There was safety in keeping one fault at the forefront. Ever since she'd seen him at the school on conference day, she'd found herself having to push the man out of her thoughts.

And he didn't go very easily.

The bells over the restaurant door tinkled and she looked toward the entrance again.

A trio of laughing teenagers practically tumbled inside and the door swung shut after them, closing with yet another trill of the bells.

"Refill?"

Alexa startled, looking around at the server who'd stopped beside her table. "Ah, sure." She moved her hand away from the sturdy white coffee cup and saucer. "Thank you."

"You bet." The waitress poured. "Are you sure you don't want a menu? Or the special. It's killer today. Over-the-Border Egg Rolls. Roasted corn, black beans, tomatillo salsa. Can't go wrong with them. They have a cashew dipping sauce that's an absolute miracle, plus you can get them with or without the southwest chicken."

Her mouth watered. But she shook her head. "I'm just meeting someone here for coffee." She glanced at her cell phone again. She wasn't entirely sure if she was checking the time or looking for a text message calling off the meeting as unexpectedly as the one requesting it.

"Okay." Fortunately, the waitress didn't look overly upset that one of her tables was being occupied during a busy lunch hour by someone who wasn't going to order food. "I'm Valerie. You let me know if you change your mind."

"Thanks, Valerie." Alexa turned her cell phone face down on the table. Then decided that wasn't good enough and stuffed the glittery pink case into her purse.

The bells tinkled again, just as they'd been doing every few minutes for the past fifteen minutes.

Without any particular hope that it would be West, Alexa angled her gaze toward the entrance.

But this time, it *was* the man himself who filled the doorway.

Her mouth actually dried.

Annoying, that.

He wore sunglasses, but it seemed obvious that he hadn't spotted her yet. Her eyes, however, were having a field day, taking their sweet time roving from his rumpled, overgrown dark hair to the unexpected casual gray sweatshirt and down to the faded blue jeans that fit with sinful perfection.

She belatedly noticed that Jason was with him, and instantly felt foolish for not having expected that West would bring his son.

He was a single father, for Pete's sake.

What *had* she been thinking?

Truthfully, since she'd gotten the text message from West asking her to meet, she *hadn't* been thinking.

Just reacting.

He'd texted her during her yoga class. When she'd read the message after the class had finished, she'd responded before she could think better of it with the suggestion of Tanya's.

And here they were.

She quickly got the attention of the young couple occupying the table next to her. "Mind if I use your spare chair?" She barely waited for their assent before she tugged it around to the small circle that was her table.

Then she stood and waved, and finally garnered West's attention.

He pulled off his sunglasses and leaned over slightly, speaking to Jason. The boy immediately grinned and waved with so much enthusiasm, he nearly knocked the tray out of a passing server's hand.

She smiled in return and waved back.

It didn't take them long to work their way through the busy restaurant, but it was still long enough for something inside her to flit around not...unpleasantly. The same thing that had been flitting around inside her that day at the school. When he'd been a man caring about his son.

An immensely attractive man.

She took a quick sip from her water glass, feeling suddenly parched.

"Hi, Mrs. Cardinale!" Jason was the first one to speak when they reached her. "I told my dad that you would be here, but he didn't believe me."

Alexa's gaze flickered up to West's. "I don't text and lie, Dr. D'Angelo."

"No offense intended, Mrs. Cardinale."

"It's Ms., actually. No husband anymore." She waved at the other two chairs as she took her own and caught the quick look that West gave Jason. "Jason wouldn't know," she told him. "Mrs. Tone addresses any female over twenty that way, including herself. And *she's* never been married at all."

"I knew you didn't have a husband," Jason said. He was busy rearranging the condiments from the side of the table to the center and missed the second quick look from his father.

Alexa prayed the flush she felt wasn't showing on her face. "Oh really? And how did you know that?"

"'Cause I heard you tell the lunch lady that you weren't married." Jason plunked his Stephen King novel in the spot previously occupied by the sauces and local honeys and flipped it open.

Seemingly oblivious to the bemusement he caused.

"You really want to read, Jase? Right now?"

Jason looked at his father as if he'd said something ludicrous and West shook his head slightly, looking about as chagrined as Alexa felt.

She toyed with her coffee cup. She noticed that Jason had progressed to the middle of the book. "Look around," she told West. "Every other child in here is looking at one device or another. I think a book is preferable." She waited a beat. "Even if it is one that could keep a seasoned adult awake at night."

His wide shoulders seemed to lose their hint of stiffness. "I can't keep him from reading everything he got his hands on and I can say I've read every word first." He tossed his sunglasses on the table and scooted his chair closer to the table. His knee nudged hers beneath it and quickly moved away. "Not much room, is there."

"No." Her half laugh sounded breathless because she was trying to move away from him, too, with an end result of just knocking their feet all over again. Regardless of how they shifted, they still made contact. And now she imagined that she could feel the warmth of him right through his jeans and her yoga pants. "Tables are really small. I hadn't thought about it much before now."

"There are worse things." He nodded his head toward Jason and the book. "I blame my mother for his taste in reading." The corner of his lips lifted. "We call her the horror queen."

"Good thing I know about her penchant for vampires and zombies," Alexa managed. She was flustered by the "worse things" comment. "Might not be flattering."

"Grandma calls herself that, too," Jason assured her. He was looking around at the crowded tables surrounding them. There wasn't an empty table in the place. "Can I have waffles with strawberries and whipped cream?"

"I think you're a bottomless pit," West said. "Considering you had two bowls of cereal and half a package of bacon already. But if you're really hungry enough." He caught the attention of their waitress, who immediately headed their way with a couple of menus in one hand and a coffee carafe in the other.

"I'm always hungry," Jason told Alexa, as if he were imparting some big secret.

"I think it's a common problem at your age," she told him just as seriously. "So long as it isn't turkey, though. Right?"

He grinned. "Grandma says I'll be as tall as my dad someday."

Despite herself, she looked through her lowered lashes toward West.

Tall.

Handsome.

She grabbed her water glass again.

Valerie stopped next to their table and her smile took in the newcomers.

"Fancy seeing you here." She set the menus on the table next to West and lifted her carafe questioningly.

"Please." He flipped over the upside-down coffee cup. "Is it too late for an order of waffles?"

"With strawberries and whipped cream?" Jason added.

"Not too late at all."

Jason beamed at her. "Thank you."

Valerie was clearly charmed not only by Jason but by his father. Equally obvious was the fact that they knew one another.

She immediately wondered just how well they knew each other and the fact that she wondered at all was entirely annoying.

"Special is the egg rolls today, right?" He barely waited for the waitress's nod. "Make it a double order." He looked at Alexa. "The cashew sauce is—"

"A miracle?" Her smile felt stiff.

His teeth flashed and she was even more annoyed when her stomach actually swooped.

There were many reasons why she didn't want to be attracted to West D'Angelo. He was a student's father, for one thing. Whether he was involved with one woman or one hundred, it was none of her business. For another, she wasn't interested in romance.

Been there. Done that.

All she'd gotten to show for it was a divorce decree and a bank account that was still gasping for air three years later.

"They usually deliver to the clinic." West's deep voice pulled her from the mausoleum of memories. "This is only the second time I've come here in person. It was just as busy that day, too."

"The doctor works too hard," Valerie told Alexa confidingly.

"Valerie's sister works at the clinic," West added.

"She's studying to be a nurse." Valerie beamed. "Since he got to town, Doctor D has already helped her qualify for a scholarship." She touched West's shoulder with unmistakable familiarity. "We'll have your food right up." Then she quickly headed away, stopping at two other tables along her way toward the kitchen.

"She's pretty," Alexa commented.

West raised his eyebrows. He looked from Alexa to the departing Valerie and back again. "Are you interested? I don't think she dates women, but—"

"I didn't mean for me. I meant you." And she wanted to kick herself for failing to keep her irritatingly intense curiosity about it under wraps. "You're obviously friends."

The faint smile playing around his lips grew and she felt that flush start to rise again.

The only saving grace was Jason. However, now that his food order was assured, he had practically buried his nose in the pages of his book. His lips were moving sound-lessly as he read. If he was giving them any attention at all, it wasn't apparent.

She toyed with the saucer beneath her coffee cup. "So, what am I doing here... Doctor D?" She drawled out that last. Proving that she truly had no self-control at all where her tongue was concerned.

Curiosity glinted in his eyes. "You tell me. You're the one who wanted to meet."

"Uh-hmm...*no*." Nerves prickled at the base of her scalp. "You sent me a text message this morning."

"Because you called my house and left me a message yester—" He gave his son a sudden look. "Jase?" His voice was low. Filled with suspicion. When he didn't get a response, he reached over and slid the book away from Jason's hands. "Don't pretend you weren't listening."

Alexa looked from Jason's suddenly set expression to his father's and back again.

A whole new level of humiliation was dawning inside her.

She had been the one to text him Tanya's. Eleven o'clock. Whereas he'd only said they ought to hammer this thing out.

A text he wouldn't have sent in the first place if he hadn't believed that Alexa had phoned him first.

"Strawberry waffles on tap!" Valerie's bright tone sud-denly cut through the yawning silence and she reached be-tween them to set a large plate laden with a beautiful, golden waffle piled with fresh strawberries and fluffy cream in front of Jason.

Another server helping her followed up the waffle with two more plates, both containing the southwestern egg rolls.

By the time they'd finished, there was barely any room for Alexa's cup of coffee that had also been refilled during the process.

Meanwhile, Jason was tucking into the waffle as if he hadn't had food in days.

"I think," West said slowly, "that someone—" he inclined his head toward his son "—is guilty of some machination." His teeth weren't flashing with his smile now. His mouth was set. "Jase. You owe Mrs.—*Ms*—Cardinale an apology."

Alexa instinctively wanted to shield the boy. "I'm sure he didn't—"

"And I'm sure he did." West cut her off. "Jason?"

The boy looked up, his eyes the soul of innocence. Whipped cream clung to his lip and his tongue snuck out to catch it. "What?"

"Did Ms. Cardinale actually call our house yesterday? Or did you make it up?"

"I made it up." Jason shoveled another piece of waffle in his mouth.

West looked like he was holding on to his patience with an effort, and Alexa shocked herself when she reached out and touched his forearm, right below where he'd shoved up the sleeves. The contact tingled and she quickly withdrew her fingers.

"Want to tell us why, Jason? We're not mad. Just…curious." She ought to win an award for that calm tone. It totally masked her desire to race out of the restaurant as if her head was on fire.

"'Cause you're nice," Jason said around his waffle. "Really, really nice. And my dad thinks you're pretty."

Alexa sat back in her chair.

West sat back in his.

He didn't seem any more able to look at her than she could look at him.

Jason licked his lips again, his gaze going from one adult to the other. "I think you should go on a date."

"Jesus *Jason!*" West shoved out of his seat. A dusky color

suffused his sharp jawline. He yanked his wallet from his pocket and pulled out a wad of cash that he tossed toward the table. It scattered across the untouched southwestern egg rolls. "My apologies, Ale—Mrs.—Miz—" the correction was made through his teeth "—Cardinale." He practically dragged Jason out of his seat. "I'm sorry we intruded on your Saturday."

"It's not that—" She didn't even have a chance to finish.

Jason barely had enough time to grab his book with one hand and the remains of his sticky waffle with the other before his dad frog-marched him through the restaurant and out the front door.

Their exit didn't happen without notice, and Alexa's cheeks felt hot when the attention swung back in her direction.

"Kids," she said to no one in particular. "They say the darnedest things."

Then she shoved a southwestern eggroll into her mouth and wished the ground would swallow her whole as well.

"*What* were you thinking, Jason?" West was beside himself. Knowing he was overreacting didn't mean he could stop it.

"I told you. I think you should go out on a date together."

"Since *when*?"

"Since always," Jason said around his mouthful of waffle.

"And then what?"

"And then you…you know."

He stomped on the brakes for a red light. "I really don't."

"You get married and I get a puppy."

West stared. What was the logical progression from marriage to dogs?

"Luc's mom is getting married. And he's got a puppy."

Comprehension hit at last.

"Carla Mai is getting married?"

Jason licked his fingers and dried them down the front of his shirt. "That's what Luc says. They got a puppy *and* they're moving to the Burbs. He said it wasn't far, but they'd still have good internet so we can still be friends and play ZombieCart."

Considering Carla's state of mind the last time West had seen her just a few short months ago, he'd have thought she'd never entertain the idea of marriage again.

Shows what he knew.

"The Burbs isn't the name of a town. It just means they're moving out of the city. And I told you I'd think about the puppy. I damn sure don't need to exchange a bunch of I do's along the way!" He strangled the steering wheel a little harder. "You shouldn't have lied about her calling us." He couldn't believe he'd been so easily duped.

By an eight-year-old.

Again. Janine's ghost was suddenly sitting on his shoulder, clucking her tongue. *Don't forget he changed the pickup calendar without you* even *noticing.*

"But you wanted to meet her." Jason's reasonable observation helped pop the invisible bubble on West's shoulder. "You texted her and everything. And she texted you back. I don't see why you're all mad about it."

The driver behind them tooted his horn three times in impatient succession and West realized the light had turned green.

"I'm not mad." Clenched teeth to the contrary. He worked his jaw to loosen it and took his foot off the brake, offering an apologetic wave at the car behind. The gesture he wanted to offer was another thing entirely. "And I've already met Ale—Ms. Cardinale, Jase. More than once at your school."

"That's different."

"Nooo." He drew out the word. "It's not."

"She doesn't wear her yoga clothes to school."

"I'm not talking about her clothing!" Forget old Gwendolyn Hightower posters. His brain would forever be etched with the sight of Alexa Cardinale's pocket-sized perfection displayed in purple spandex glory. He raked his fingers through his hair. "How'd you even come up with the idea to say she'd called?"

"One of the characters on Grandma's lovey shows did it."

"Of course," he muttered. Zombies. Vampires. And his mom's daytime soaps. Was it any wonder that Jason's doodling always had such a vivid bent?

He drove past the medical building where a work truck was parked next to the dumpster. The place was typically unoccupied on weekends. The sign that construction work was still continuing was welcome. Maybe they would hit their targeted completion date after all.

"Are you still mad?"

He let out a long breath. "I told you. I'm not mad, Jason." He gave his son a stern look. "That doesn't mean I'm thrilled with you lying about anything, much less getting someone else involved, too. Ms. Cardinale didn't deserve it."

Jason slouched in his seat, looking dejected. "Do I gotta apologize to her?"

It hadn't even occurred to West.

And it should have.

"That's probably a good idea," he said.

Jason blew out a loud puff of air. But he didn't protest.

West was so wound up that driving anywhere seemed preferable to going back to their house. So, when he came to the next intersection, instead of heading home, he turned in the opposite direction. Merged into the congestion behind an ancient Volkswagen bus that was plastered with stickers touting every iteration of "Save the fill-in-the-blank," and remembered the same Beach Road some twenty years earlier.

Times had definitely changed.

Cape Cardinale still possessed the same two beaches. Friars and Cardinale. And traffic had always been busier close to Friars for the simple reason it was larger and more easily accessible. To get to Cardinale, you either had to hike down one side of the cape or you had to drive down a road filled with more hairpins than his grandmother's handbag. He didn't know if there'd been as much development over there, but there'd certainly been a lot near Friars.

High-dollar boutiques and jewelry stores sat comfortably alongside an ancient, chain convenience store and an even older laundromat. There was a wine shop and a barbershop. An art gallery and a chewing gum museum.

You name it and it was there.

He passed the surf shop where he had once worked until Felicity Bash's father had found her and West having sex in the barbershop where she worked.

West hadn't gone back to work at the surf shop after that.

To this day, he didn't know how that particular piece of gossip hadn't found its way to his mother's ears. It said a lot about his father's influence, because West Sr. had most definitely known.

The surf shop was still operating, but very few people were renting gear at that time of the year. The waves were too wild and only diehards dared to brave them. The only things they'd need from the surf shop were new boards when they ended up getting pummeled against the rocks.

West had always preferred surfing at Cardinale.

The waves were dicier, but because the beach was smaller and harder to access, there were fewer crowds. Even in the dead of summer when scores of people flooded the town, a person could count on catching a wave there.

"D'you want to learn how to surf, Jase?" West hadn't been on a board in decades. Considering everything, he'd be lucky if he could even pop up, despite the all-clear he'd gotten that week from Roger about his knee.

"Get a massage. Learn how to stretch, for God's sake." They'd been just a few of the suggestions from the orthopedist before he'd handed over his exorbitant bill.

"If I learn to surf, can I get a puppy afterward?"

Despite everything, West felt a laugh rise in his chest.

He reached over and scrubbed his hand over Jason's head. Noted absently that he needed a haircut.

Which probably meant that West needed one as well.

He turned again on the spur of the moment at the next corner.

"Where are we going?"

"To get haircuts," he told Jason. "I know a place not far from here." Though he doubted that Felicity Bash still worked there.

Chapter Seven

"What're you wearing to Meyer's wedding?" Dana sank down onto the one side of the sectional couch where Alexa was stretched out with a book.

Not that she was particularly reading. The words on the page kept disappearing thanks to Alexa's preoccupation with the way the morning had ended with West walking out of Tanya's.

Talking with her sister was preferable to thinking about *that*.

She drew her legs up beneath the soft throw that artfully coordinated with the upholstered couch. All Dana's doing, of course. The blanket was probably made of wool originating from virgin goats living on some remote Himalayan peak.

It was warm. It was light. It was heavenly.

Too bad the throw was only there to enjoy because of Dana.

If it had been up to Alexa to furnish the beach house, they'd have been sprawling on second-hand furniture and eating off dime-store dishes.

Not because those were Alexa's preferences, but because that's what her budget would have stretched to.

"I haven't decided what to wear yet." She wasn't ashamed of the admission but nevertheless offered it with a heavy dose of wariness. "Why?"

"I haven't decided, either." Though she'd just sat, Dana rose again.

She paced around the furniture that really was too large

for the small living room of the beach house. But since the fireplace had been deemed unrepairable and blocked off with plywood, they'd been able to push the couch against a wall that otherwise would have been unusable. She stopped in front of a large, glossy, framed photograph and adjusted the corner of it.

Alexa pretended that she hated the thing. The swirling photograph of blues encompassed the ocean and the galaxy and had been dubbed by the public as *Pietro's Last* because it had literally been the last thing her father did. While on one of his endless voyages, his ship had gone down in the Mediterranean during a storm. His three crew members had survived. But Pietro had been lost. His body never recovered.

Fitting that he'd died in the Med when he'd spent so much of his life there, hunting for yet one more perfect shot of the universe around him rather than caring about the fractured families that he'd left back on dry land.

Alexa didn't really hate the photograph.

She just hated the man who'd died practically while taking it. In his last moments, he'd still managed to transmit the digital file. One last gift of artistic genius to the world.

At least that's the way Lotus had marketed the photograph. She might have been left out of the will—same as all of the wives who'd preceded her, including Alexa's mother—but she wasn't suffering too badly as a result. She was living in a fancy Manhattan apartment, after all.

Not a run-down little house on an Oregon beach.

"I think we should paint the walls again." Dana suddenly looked back at Alexa, catching her midyawn.

She covered her mouth. "Sorry." It was a good thing she wasn't on duty for the school dance that evening when she was yawning in the middle of the afternoon.

"We painted the walls when we moved in." She waved her hand, taking in the cramped living room and the adjacent kitchen, separated by a narrow pass-through. The white paint had been an improvement over the dingy faded walls that probably hadn't changed in forty years. "Another coat isn't going to magically transform this place. If anything needs to be done, it's the deck, and I don't think either one of us want to tackle that." She narrowed her eyes, studying her sister. "And back to the wedding, by the way. We don't have to dress up a lot. Right?"

Dana stopped fiddling with the photograph's frame, which had been hanging perfectly straight in the first place, and moved to the dinky breakfast bar between the living room and the kitchen. Alexa had put a basket on the counter months ago to contain the growing collection of shells they'd all been finding up and down the beach. Dana began poking through them. "It's a church wedding," she said. "A certain amount of formality is expected."

"Even if the reception is being held at one of Meyer's hangars out at the airport?" The idea of having to dress up gave Alexa a headache. No matter what she did, she could never compete with her clotheshorse sister, so why even try? "A hangar hardly evokes formality."

"Depends on the circumstances." Holding a swirly-green shell between her fingers, Dana wandered to the window that overlooked the unfinished end of the front deck. It, along with the small windowpanes in the front door, was the only window that looked out to the ocean.

No spectacular wall of glass offering an equally spectacular view for their little beach house. Nope. They just had a boarded-up fireplace, a kitchen the size of a postage stamp and a bathroom full of hideous pink fixtures.

Seven months, she reminded herself. A shorter period of time than gestation.

She yanked her feet off the couch and planted them on the floor.

She scrubbed her hands down her face and eyed Dana through her spread fingers. "Admit it. You're afraid I'll

wear something to the wedding that is wildly inappropriate. That's why you brought it up." She dropped her hands.
"And what you really want to do is tell me exactly what I
should wear."

"You're never *wildly* inappropriate." Dana balanced the
shell on the narrow windowsill and stood back, watching.
As if waiting for it to fall. "But, actually, I thought maybe
we could go shopping together."

"For *dresses*?" The most shopping together that they ever
did was for groceries.

"Yes, for dresses." Dana sounded exasperated. "The
shops are open for hours yet. And don't say you can't afford a new dress. I've seen your paycheck. It's small, but you
hardly have *any* bills and you're tighter with your spending than anyone I've ever known, including my husband!
I'm sure you can spare a little change for a decent dress."

Naturally, Dana figured none of her clothes were decent.
Big surprise there. Alexa didn't focus on that, though, because it was nothing new. "Tyler's tight?"

Dana huffed, as if she didn't appreciate the side rail.
"Anyway. What do you say? Can we pretend to be sisters
who enjoy one another's company long enough to get our-
selves something appropriate for Meyer's wedding?"

"I'll bet your closet—" Alexa gestured at the bedrooms
located shotgun-style behind the kitchen "—already has a
half dozen dresses that would be appropriate."

"Our bedrooms don't *have* closets," Dana reminded. "I
had to arrange for armoires, remember?"

"I'll even prove it." She pushed to her feet and headed
around the couch.

"Stay out of my room."

"Why? Afraid I'll see all the boxes of shoes you've never
even worn?" She quickened her step, darting into Dana's
room before her longer-legged sister could block the doorway.

She threw open the gleaming wood wardrobe that took

up one wall of the unimpressively-sized room. Clothing hung on the rod from padded hangers, arranged both by color and length. Even Dana's purses were stored in fancy quilted fabric boxes lined up on the inner shelves.

"You always have to be magazine perfect." Alexa pulled a white dress off the rod and dangled the hanger from her finger. "Why can't you just wear something like this?"

"Don't be ridiculous." Dana snatched the hanger and returned it to the armoire. "We're guests. We don't wear white to weddings unless the wedding couple has requested it as a theme or something. Which Sophie and Meyer have not done."

Alexa noticed then that Dana's hand was actually trembling. "I'm just yanking your chain, Dana."

"You think I don't know that?" Dana slammed the armoire doors shut and leaned back against them. She was actually pale.

"Are you sick?"

"No, I'm not sick!" Dana's voice rose.

So did Alexa's eyebrows. "Um, you're not exactly the usual cool-as-a-cucumber." Look how far they'd come. There'd been a time when Alexa would have said that her sister's usual was "cold fish."

Dana brushed her hair away from her face and sank down onto the foot of her immaculately made bed. "Tyler's planning to come to the wedding," she said abruptly.

Alexa blinked. "So?"

Dana huffed. She spread her palms. "So, I haven't seen him in a…a while."

"You're always running back and forth to Corvallis," Alexa argued. "And you talk to him on the phone all the time."

Dana smoothed back her hair. The gigantic diamond ring on her wedding finger blinked in the sunlight coming through the underwhelming window. "I don't talk to him all the time. And Ty hasn't been at the house in Corvallis."

Alexa hastily got control of her dropped jaw and pressed her lips together. If Dana wasn't talking to her husband at night, who *was* she talking to? "Where has he been then?"

"Up in Seattle. Olympia. Wherever." Dana worked her knife-edged jaw back and forth. "Doing God knows who," she added under her breath.

Alexa still heard and her breath left her like she'd been punched in the chest.

Those emotions she knew only too well.

She sat down cautiously beside Dana. Careful not to encroach on her space but still wanting to do more than just hover in the doorway. "Are you sure?"

Dana flattened her left hand over her right. She spread her fingers. The rings were slightly loose and the weight of the diamonds listed slightly to one side. She carefully centered them again with the tip of her perfectly manicured index finger. "Well, he's not sleeping with me." Her brusque comment didn't quite mask the raspy undertone.

Alexa slid her arm around Dana's shoulders. "That doesn't necessarily mean—"

Dana shrugged Alexa's arm away and propelled herself off the bed.

Alexa tucked her hands under her thighs. So much for offering some sisterly comfort.

She watched Dana pace the short length of the bedroom. When she reached the end, she turned on her heel and paced back.

In any other setting, in any other circumstance, it would have been like watching a model walking a very short runway.

"If things are bad between you, why's he coming to the wedding?" Until their father died, Alexa could have counted on one hand the number of times they'd all been together.

She wasn't sure she'd even recognize Ty nowadays if she mowed him down on the street.

"My *husband* has actually kept in contact with our brother. Can you believe that?" Hand on her hip, Dana whirled to face Alexa. Her long blond hair swirled around her shoulders and fell perfectly into place. Her smile was brittle and tight. "Meyer invited Ty himself. Because *I* certainly didn't."

Alexa tucked her tongue between her teeth. For the first time in her life, she felt for Dana. She truly did. She knew how awful it was to suspect your spouse of infidelity.

But *why* did her sister have to be physically so freakishly perfect?

"He's not going to stay *here,* though." Alexa pointed to the floor. "As in the beach house." Not really a question. But more like a hopeful assumption. There wasn't any room to spare inside the beach house. Just because Meyer was getting married, didn't mean the terms of their father's will would miraculously change. If anything, it meant they'd get even more cramped if Sophie couldn't tear herself away from her new hubby at night.

"Stay here?" Dana snorted. "As if." She threaded her fingers through her long hair as if she wanted to rip it out of by the roots. "But, *oh*—" her teeth bared "—I am going to want Ty to *want* to. I'm going to want him to *ache* for it."

She snatched open the doors of her armoire again. "All those?" She swept her hand along the garments. Every single one toned in neutral colors like some decorating palette of the nudely kind. "None of them will do."

"That's really why you want to go shopping? Not to make sure whatever I wear isn't an embarrassment but to find yourself a smokin' outfit guaranteed to make your husband's jaw drop?"

"I don't want it to drop." Dana's voice was low. Almost feral. "I want it to hit. The. Floor. If he's going to cheat on me, he can damn well show some painful appreciation for what he's throwing away."

Alexa sank her teeth into her lip. "I get it," she said after a moment. She might have entertained fantasies of having Dom come crawling back just so she could tell him to go to hell. But she'd never done anything to bring those fantasies to life.

He'd rejected her.

She'd been so demoralized she'd been certain that any such attempts would have ended in yet more evidence that proved what had already been proven.

Her worthlessness as a woman.

She wouldn't wish that feeling on her worst enemy.

And certainly not on her sister, who had the ability to bring men right to their knees.

She pressed her hands against the silk bedspread and stood. "Well, all right then. Let's get shopping."

Dana narrowed her eyes. Obviously suspicious. "Really?"

Alexa spread her arms wide. "Wives who've been cheated on. The Saturday edition."

"I really don't understand you sometimes," Dana admitted.

"Same goes." Alexa felt a stab of unfamiliar regret. "And why would we? It's hard to understand someone we've never really gotten to know."

Dana's lips curled downward. "I tried."

"You did." Alexa led the way out of the bedroom. "You kept us on speed dial. And then an email loop. And then a text group. You're the only reason I know all of your birthdays. It was better than nothing and a lot more than he ever did." She jerked her head at *Pietro's Last* as she walked past it to retrieve her purse from where she'd left it in the living room. She pulled out her keys and jangled them. "Now. Whose vehicle are we taking?"

Dana let out an unexpected laugh. "What do you think?"

Alexa tucked her keys back inside her purse. "I was hoping you'd say that," she admitted as they walked back down the length of the small house and out to the equally small paved area barely covered by the metal carport.

Poor dinky Betty with her patched-up yellow paint and mismatched tires looked like a sad little country mouse next to Dana's gleaming black Escalade.

"If you end up pulling the plug with Ty, who gets the Escalade? Did you have a prenup?"

"Prenup? For what? Ty didn't have anything when we first started out." Dana clicked open the SUV doors and they climbed inside. "We got married against my mother's wishes. She cut me off then and there. Said he was after the family money and she'd never give us a cent. She took a heck of a lot of pride living right up to that vow, too. Until Ty made his first million and she suddenly began acting like everything had always been sweetness and light."

"Whereas our father waited to die before he gives us that." Alexa gestured at the beach house.

"He paid for your college tuition."

"Because he had to."

"Regardless, he did it." Dana deftly backed the big vehicle up the narrow driveway until she reached the road and put it in Drive. She didn't race up the hairpins but neither did she have to coax a temperamental engine up the side of the cliff, either.

Nevertheless, for the first time, Alexa realized Dana didn't like the ascent in her SUV any more than Alexa did in hers.

Who'd have thought they'd have that in common, too?

"I never even finished college," Dana said once they were on level ground again and she cruised past the church before turning toward the center of town. "I was just the regular devoted little wife, helping out my husband with the books while he worked fifteen-hour days trying to make a living."

She made a disgusted sound. "My mother knew what she was talking about. 'He'll ruin your life,' she said. 'You're giving him too much control over your life.'" Dana looked at Alexa. "That's what sex does to us." She was strangling the steering wheel between her hands. "Makes us lose our minds," she muttered.

"It's been so long since I've even had sex, I can barely remember *what* it did." Alexa swatted away the mental image of West D'Angelo. Now was *not* the time.

"Well, if that's the case—" Dana flipped on her windshield wipers when a barrage of raindrops suddenly struck. "Then I think I'd have to say someone wasn't doing it right!"

"Dad! You're not doing it right."

West thumbed a different toggle on the game controller and watched his cartoon zombie on the television go screaming off a cliff into a roiling river of lava and flames. He didn't want to admit to the frustration he felt. It was a video game, for crying out loud. It had a rating that said it was designed for youth up to the age of eighteen. He was thirty-eight. But so far, he'd sent his character, Vern, into the lava a half dozen times at the same exact spot in the game.

"Sorry, Jase." He tossed the controller aside and managed to push his way up and out of the chair that was little more than a bean bag on the floor. "I think this dog is too old to learn." He stretched out his legs, trying to ease the stiffness. "At least this particular trick."

Jason just shook his head, looking disgusted.

He picked up West's controller and, on the wall-mounted television, the miraculously resurrected Vern hopped onto his motorcycle and began racing with a hoard of other zombies toward the highest peak of the mountain where they were supposed to sail across the lava-filled crevasse to another mountain. Just before Vern reached the edge of the cliff, Jason hit a button that popped the motorcycle up into a backward somersault that catapulted him across the chasm.

He held up the controller for West. "Now you can keep playing."

One zombie life saved by an eight-year-old.

West took the controller but only to set it on the bookshelf next to the worn paperbacks already crowding the space. "We've been playing for half the day," he said. "I think we both need a break. It's Sunday. Go run around the backyard. Breathe some fresh air."

"But we're finally on the fourth level. That's where the dragon lair is."

"We'll pick it up at this spot next time, won't we? The game saves our spot?"

"Yeah, but—"

"Yeah, but." West spoke over Jason's favorite protest. "Jase. I can't sit on the floor anymore."

"You need to do yoga," Jason said. "Luc's mom does yoga. He says she was always complaining until she started taking lessons."

Since he'd discovered that Carla also happened to be marrying the yoga studio *owner*, West figured that the lack of complaining had more to do with romance than it did with anything else.

"Fine. I need to do yoga," he repeated just to bring an end to the subject. "I'm going upstairs." Maybe a shower would help get the kinks out. "Next time I see you, I expect you to be out of this basement and outside."

To his surprise, Jason turned off the gaming console right then and there and followed West up from the basement. In the kitchen, he yanked open the refrigerator door and stared inside as if waiting for inspiration.

West pulled out a bottle of cold water for him and pushed the door closed. "You're wasting energy."

And you're trying to turn into your father. How's that going?

He ignored Janine even though she wasn't exactly incorrect and headed for the staircase to go upstairs. When the doorbell rang, he changed course and went for the front door instead. It was a massive beast, complete with sidelights that were etched with an ivy vine pattern.

As a result, he could see the blonde standing on the other side of the door even before he opened it.

Her hair was pinned up in a haphazard way and she wore a shapeless lemon-yellow dress that reached to her ankles beneath a hairy-looking purple-and-green sweater.

Talk about what not to wear, Janine said.

West was more interested in Alexa's face than her admittedly colorful choice of clothing.

He ignored his annoying personal ghost and pulled open the door. "Hey."

Smooth, West. Real smooth.

Alexa looked up at him, her gaze so wide and entrancing, he felt like Vern plummeting off a cliff. Only it wasn't lava at the bottom. It was a sea of robin's-egg blue.

He didn't even realize at first that she'd also lifted her hand. Or that his sunglasses were sitting on her palm.

"You left these at the restaurant yesterday," she prompted.

Something else he hadn't realized.

"Thanks." Beyond that, he didn't know exactly what to say. So he plucked the sunglasses off her palm and a spark of static electricity stung them both.

He wasn't sure who was startled more by it.

He tossed the glasses on the foyer table and when he turned back, she was tugging the sleeves down over her fingers as if she were cold.

"Want to come inside?"

She looked over her shoulder at the little car parked at the curb. It looked forlorn at the end of the row of post lights. "Thank you, but I should probably be getting back home."

"You could have put the sunglasses in Jason's backpack tomorrow."

"Yeah." She sucked in her upper lip then let it out again. "I know. I don't know why I brought them today." She looked again over her shoulder.

Her restlessness was coming off her in waves.

"You sure you don't want to come in? My mother left us with a vat of clam chowder from the pub. I was just thinking about fixing some for our lunch."

It was like the flip of a light switch. Sudden interest made her brows lift. "The *Highland* Pub?"

He checked a smile and stepped back in invitation. "Is there any other?"

She chewed the inside of her cheek then seemed to end whatever internal debate she'd had and stepped inside the house. Her blue gaze flitted around the ornate foyer.

"We're just renting," he said, and felt like an idiot as a result. "Not really our style." Add another heaping layer of idiot.

She stepped past him, trailing her fingertips along the scalloped edge of the gold-leafed foyer table. Her gaze went from the symmetrical brocade side chairs flanking the massive staircase to him. "But you rented it anyway."

He couldn't tell what she was thinking. Her expression was too neutral.

He hoped his expression was equally neutral considering he couldn't stop thinking of what Jason had told her at the restaurant. *My dad thinks you're pretty.*

West did. Eclectic clothes and all.

But he'd never told Jason that.

She was still looking at him. Eyebrows raised ever so slightly in a faint show of interest.

"We needed somewhere to live," he said. "I didn't want

that to be a hotel, and this place came mostly furnished. So. Here we are. Kitchen's this way." He led her past the formal dining room with the ginormous dining table. He noticed a stack of Jason's books on the floor by the windows. He was constantly leaving them lying around. He detoured long enough to pick them up and set them on top of the table. "You're new in town, too, aren't you?"

That brought a distinct flicker in her eyes. "Since last June. I'm staying with my, uh, my sister and two brothers."

She seemed to hold her breath at the admission, though he couldn't imagine why.

"I don't have siblings. A bunch of them would come in handy to fill up this place."

Her lips stretched slightly. "Our house is a tad smaller," she said dryly. "Although it is—" she sketched two air quotes "—*beachfront.*"

"Yeah?" He looked at her again. Too easily imagining her strolling from her door down to the beach in something a lot less shroudlike than the yellow dress. "Which one?"

Her hesitation was almost unnoticeable. "Cardinale," she said.

He wondered again about her connection to the town's founding. "I used to surf down there. How do you like it?"

She lifted her shoulders. "Too soon to tell." She followed him into the kitchen.

The second they stepped foot in the room, Maxwill Sing started hopping from one perch to another, his vociferous squawking filling the room.

And whatever reserve Alexa had felt melted away like magic. "You have a canary!" She immediately walked around the breakfast table to stand closer to the birdcage. It was taller than she was, yet it still only occupied half the area in front of the bow windows. "We had a canary when I was growing up. His name was Toddy Bird." Her smile glowed. "He lived nearly twelve years. And he sang *all* the time."

West absently noted that her dress was about the same shade as the canary. "Maxwill's five. All he does is squawk."

"Max*will*?" Alexa raised her eyebrows. "With an *i*?"

"Yeah. Maxwill Sing. Even though he doesn't."

"Aww." Alexa looked up at the bird. He'd flown up to the highest perch, well above her head. "That's okay, Maxie," she cooed. "Your squawk is beautiful. If that's your song, you sing away."

Maxwill dove to the side of the cage right in front of Alexa's nose and wrapped his claws around the black metal. He puffed up and flapped his wings.

She laughed, clearly not startled.

West pulled bowls out of the cupboard and set them on the island. "He's showing off."

"I'd show off, too, if I was as beautiful as you." She addressed the bird directly, earning another feathery display as Maxwill flew to the floor of the cage, splashed water from the saucer, then flew back up to squawk raucously in Alexa's face again. "Do you let him out?"

"Occasionally." He dumped chowder into a saucepan and turned on the flame. "He doesn't like going back in his cage." He joined her in the nook, but only so he could see out to the backyard.

There was no sign of Jason, and he walked over to the stairs that led down to the basement. "Jason," he yelled. "Get up here."

A second later, footsteps pounded up the stairs. "I wasn't playing ZombieCart—" Jason's eyes nearly bugged out of his head at the sight of Alexa. "Mrs. Cardinale! What're you doing here?"

Chapter Eight

*W*hat was *she doing here*?

Even though the question plagued her, Alexa couldn't help but smile at Jason. He wore slouchy black pajama pants patterned with orange jack-o'-lanterns and a short-sleeved red T-shirt with the word "Hollyview" printed on the front.

The pants looked too big. The shirt too small. And he was positively endearing.

"I brought your dad's sunglasses," she told him. The excuse was just as thin as West had already pointed out. She could have put the sunglasses in Jason's backpack. Wouldn't have even needed to see West in the process.

She'd wanted an excuse to get out of the beach house, but she could have just gone to the store. Nobody would have thought twice about it for the simple reason that nobody had been at the beach house at all.

Sophie and Meyer were off doing wedding stuff.

Cutter had driven to Portland in search of some sort of specialized equipment and Dana had gone to Corvallis, certain that Tyler would be nowhere near there.

Would Alexa have been so willing to show up at West's door with his sunglasses if even one of them had been at the beach house?

The question was pointless, of course.

She was there and she could count on one finger at least one person whose happiness about that fact was unqualified.

"I see you got your hair cut," she told Jason. So had his father, but commenting on West's haircut was a far different prospect.

Jason preened. "D'you like it?"

Gone were the wavy locks that were perpetually untidy. Now his hair was cropped close at the nape and around his ears. Longer at the top to hint at the waves that still existed if his hair grew only a few centimeters more. "Very much," she said, even though she felt a hazy sort of sorrow at the change.

He looked older. More like he belonged in the fourth grade with kids a year older.

"Do *you* like it?" she asked in return. It was patently obvious that he did. No kid ever grinned that hard if he was unhappy.

"Yeah." Barefoot, he paced around the kitchen island with pent-up energy. "I even had a shave." He slapped his palms against his cheeks. "Just like my dad."

She couldn't keep from imagining the two D'Angelo males sitting in twin barber chairs. Or halt the frisson running down her spine when her gaze strayed back to West again and it collided with his.

"There was no blade in the razor for Jason." As if she'd needed to know, even though all she'd been thinking was that she missed Jason's father's overlong locks, too.

Not that his new all-over short look was unattractive.

West D'Angelo could have had a shaved head and he'd still stop traffic.

The question wasn't *what* she was doing there, but *why* she was there at all. Logically, she had no business being there.

Logic, however, had never been her finest subject.

She gestured at the birdcage, resolutely keeping her focus on Jason. "I had a canary when I was your age, too."

Jason dragged out one of the nailhead-trimmed barstools and she realized a little belatedly that it was for her. "Thank you."

His smile was so wide it was a wonder his face didn't split into two. He climbed on the barstool next to hers just in time for West to place a bowl of chowder in front of him.

"It's hot," West warned. "Don't burn your tongue."

Jason picked up his spoon. "We got Maxwill when I was a baby."

"Three," West corrected. He set another bowl on the island and slid it toward Alexa. "A very precocious three. We put a lock on Maxwill's cage to stop you always letting him out to play."

She could envision it so easily.

What wasn't so easy was imagining the woman who had completed the rest of West's "we."

His wife.

She knew Jason's mother had died a few years ago. She realized now just how sketchy that information was. What were the circumstances of his mother's passing? An illness? An accident?

And why was she asking? For Jason's sake? Or because of Jason's father?

That was pretty pointless, too. West D'Angelo was a single father. Even if Alexa were the sort to dally around, she wouldn't choose to do it with a single father.

Sure about that?

She picked up her spoon and plunged it into the chowder. Better to burn a layer off her tongue than to continue debating herself into insanity.

Then West pulled out the barstool next to her and sat down with his own chowder, sandwiching her between himself and his son even though there were three more barstools arranged along the enormous island.

All of her good intentions flew right out the window.

Feeling suddenly too warm in her mohair sweater, she began pulling her arms out of the sleeves, and when West's hand brushed hers as he tried to help, heat rushed through her veins with the frenzy of a giddy schoolgirl.

She'd been married, for Pete's sake. And before Dom, there'd been other boyfriends. Relationships.

Someone wasn't doing it right.

Her sister's words circled around her mind. Taunting.

Alexa finally got her arms freed and the sweater draped haphazardly over the back of the barstool and she plunged her spoon back into her chowder. "Did you have other pets?" Surely that was an innocuous enough question.

"No," West answered.

"But we're gonna get one," Jason said confidently. "A puppy. Aren't we, Dad?"

She sensed West's sigh more than heard it.

"I said I'd think about it."

"Did you have a puppy when you were growing up, too?" Jason asked her.

"No. My mom was allergic to dogs." That was Nadine's story anyway. "And we couldn't have a cat because of Toddy Bird. He was our canary."

"'Cause cats like to chase birds?"

"Something like that." Alexa's mother had been so convinced that a cat would *eat* Toddy Bird that Alexa used to tense up every time she saw a cat. "What kind of puppy do you want?"

"It doesn't mat—" West didn't finish, probably because Jason didn't give him a chance to.

"The best kind," he said with such certainty she couldn't help smiling.

She swallowed another spoonful of the hot chowder. The temperature had already done its worst, though the taste was just as wonderful as it had been the first time she'd eaten it at the pub, shortly after they'd all moved into the beach house. Everyone had already been at each other's throats and Fitzgerald Lane had suggested the outing to help break the tension.

None of them had expected it to succeed. But it had.

They'd even developed a habit of all going there every few months. They'd eat chowder and drink beer. Sometimes argue. Sometimes not. Usually, Cutter would end up finding some woman to leave with. Then their group, broken from four down to three, would hit their separate ways again.

Funny that she was just now recognizing the habit.

As if they couldn't function as a family group unless they were all involved.

All or nothing.

Just like the terms of Pietro's will.

"Bad clam?"

She looked at West. "What?"

He gestured with his spoon. "You looked like you tasted something sour."

"Oh." She blinked at her bowl. "No. It's fine. I just—" She shook her head and looked at Jason again. "'The best kind of dog,'" she repeated. "What does that mean? The best kind of breed? The best size? The best color?"

"I don't care what color." Jason's tone made it plain he thought such details were beyond trivial. "Or how big. I mean the kind of dog that's *smart*. I can teach him tricks and he'll sleep on the foot of my bed and never go away."

From the corner of her eye, Alexa caught a flash of something hollowed out on West's face.

Connecting these particular dots was simple enough.

Jason's mother was the one who'd gone away. She'd left a hole that they were still trying to circumnavigate.

"That sounds like a pretty special puppy," Alexa told him gently. Then she started to shift on the barstool but caught herself just in time. She wasn't sure she wouldn't get heart palpitations if she brushed against West again. "I meant to tell you—" she deliberately brightened her voice "—that we've gotten some new donations for the playground fund. Nearly two thousand dollars now."

West's spoon paused midair. "Already?"

"Already. We still have a lot of call lists that haven't been completed, too. So hopefully that two thousand is just a start." She tapped Jason's shirtsleeve. "Was Hollyview your school in Chicago?"

"Yeah."

"My school in California where I used to teach was called Holly*vale*."

"You're making that up."

She ignored West's comment. "It's a pretty large school. We even had four different third-grade classes."

"I wish you were the teacher here."

You and me both. "Come on now," she said aloud. "Mrs. Tone isn't that bad."

Both generations of the D'Angelo males gave her looks.

"Okay," she allowed, "I know she seems a little old-fashioned."

Maxwill let out a sharp squawk. He flipped his feathers and shook his head.

Make that three D'Angelo males.

"A lot old-fashioned," she amended. "But she has good intentions. She wants her students to succeed." She hoped.

"How long did you teach at Hollyvale?"

"Since I was credent—" She broke off. West had shifted

slightly and his upper arm was grazing hers. Warm. Distracting.

She couldn't make her frame any narrower. And it wasn't as if that contact was unpleasant…

She jerked herself together. "I was there for eleven years. They couldn't guarantee I'll have my same third-grade class when I go back home next year, but I'm keeping my fingers crossed."

She immediately realized her mistake.

Jason was staring at her with horror. "You're not staying in Cape Cardinale?"

She opened her mouth but she wasn't sure how to soften the facts.

She didn't have a chance to say anything, though, because Jason pushed his bowl so hard it slid off the other side of the island and landed with a geyser of thick white soup and the crack of crockery breaking. He jumped from his barstool, left it wobbling, and shoved the one next to it for good measure before he ran out of the room.

Like two dominoes, the stools toppled and the crash reverberated.

"I'm so sorry," she whispered. "I didn't expect—"

"You couldn't have." West's tone was short. Not accusatory like Jason's, but not absolving, either.

He went around to the other side of the island. He picked up the two halves of the bowl and tossed them into the sink. His face was grim, the line of his jaw sharper than ever. He opened a cupboard and yanked out a mile of paper towels.

"Let me." She hurried around to his side. The tile floor was awash with clam chowder. "You can go after him."

A muscle in his jaw flexed. After the briefest of hesitations, he pushed the stream of paper towels into her hands and righted the upended barstools on his way out of the room.

She chewed the inside of her lip. The silence was deafening.

Even Maxwill was still. Perched on a lifelike tree branch, his head, black eyes unblinking.

She should have put the damn sunglasses in Jason's backpack.

A quick search yielded a stack of rags beneath the sink and Alexa used several to clean up the floor. Then she turned her attention to the spatters on the cabinets and used West's mile of paper towels to dry and polish everything when she was finally done.

Silence still reigned, but no longer so completely. Maxwill was tossing around seeds, entertaining himself as he hopped from perch to perch. The hands on an enormous wall clock ticked. The built-in refrigerator hummed quietly and she traced her finger over the notes written on the calendar hanging there. Then she sighed and pulled on her sweater. "Bye, Maxie," she whispered, before leaving through the kitchen door.

It let out into the back yard and she followed the brick footpath through the overgrown grass, hoping there wouldn't be a locked gate to the front where she'd left Betty parked on the street. The house was imposing from the front. But from the back, it was even more so, and she stopped in her tracks when the brick path broke away from the perimeter of the house to circle around three larger than life-sized statues.

She recognized two of them—*Venus de Milo* and *The Winged Victory*. The third statue stood on the opposite side of the koi pond that separated them. It was also female but Alexa didn't know her art history well enough to recognize it.

And probably, somewhere, Pietro Cardinale was rolling over in whatever watery grave his soul had finally found over her lack of artistic sensibility.

She circled the koi pond, noticing the mottled orange-and-white colors of the fish nearly obscured by the green fronds of underwater plants that swayed in the ripples from a small waterfall. At the end of the meandering pond was a gazebo sheltering a stainless-steel grill. She hoped it worked better than the one at the beach house.

The model that Meyer and Cutter had assembled was attractive but entirely inoperable. Dana's latest round of overpriced steak had once again been cooked up at Sophie's place on her ever-reliable gas grill.

A raindrop plopping on Alexa's forehead hurried her along the brick path. She passed under an arbor laced with vines that had turned mostly brown in the chilly autumn weather and went through a gate that was—miracles of miracles—already pushed ajar.

The skies opened then, and she grabbed the folds of the linen dress that she'd gotten on the sale rack the day before with Dana and ran to her car. She was sopping when she slid behind the wheel and turned the key in the ignition.

Nothing.

Not even the *tic-tic-tic* of a dying battery.

She sagged. "Come on, Betty. Help a girlfriend out."

She pumped the gas once. Let off it entirely and turned the key again.

Betty chuffed. Huffed. Finally caught.

Alexa's relief was bone-deep. She patted the steering wheel. "I knew you had it in you."

Shivering, she fastened her seat belt and looked at the house. She'd gotten their address from the class roster, but she'd never expected to find a minor mansion.

The brick sidewalk leading to the front door was lined by ornate lanterns atop metal posts. Some of them had already come on.

She looked to the massive front door and up to the Juliet balcony.

Jason stood in the window and her chest ached. *I'm sorry.*

She wished he could hear her thoughts. Know how deeply she meant them.

She knew children easily became attached to their teachers. Even though she wasn't technically one at the moment, they'd formed a bond in Ernestine Tone's class. And he clearly felt she'd betrayed that.

West appeared in the window behind Jason. She could see his head angled down toward his son. Speaking to him.

Jason turned away from the window and disappeared.

After a moment, West lifted his hand. Acknowledging her.

Then he, too, turned and disappeared from view, replaced by the filmy white curtain that drifted back into place.

She still couldn't make herself look away. Not until the curtains puffed out again and she held her breath, waiting to glimpse either one of the D'Angelos one more time. But the filmy curtain merely settled again.

No one was there at all.

Eyes stinging, she pulled Betty away from the curb and drove away.

Chapter Nine

"Pack these up." Ernestine Tone handed a stack of worksheets to Alexa. "Jason D'Angelo's grandmother will pick them up at some point. Not that they'll matter. That boy won't be back to this class again. I can see the writing on the wall." She sniffed. "They'll just buy the boy's way into Tuppersford."

Alexa's jaw tightened. It was lunch hour on Wednesday and they were alone in the classroom. Though Jason hadn't been in school at all that week, she wouldn't believe he'd stayed out for three days because of what had happened on Sunday.

"He's had a fever," she reminded Ernestine. "And he isn't the only one." A dozen kids throughout the school were out sick. She pulled an oversized envelope from her drawer and slid the worksheets inside. "It's not as if he's playing hooky."

"How do you know? His grandmother watches him, and *she* never cared about following the rules."

The woman made no sense sometimes. "What are you talking about?"

Ernestine's rubber-soled shoes squeaked as she returned to her desk. "Jason doesn't belong here," she said dismissively. "His grades are too poor. He'll fit right in at Tuppersford."

Alexa shot to her feet before she could think twice. "His grades are *not* too poor." She slapped her desk in emphasis. "He's an exceptional child and you know it."

Ernestine looked incensed. "How dare you!"

Alexa plowed on. "For *some* reason, you—" she swished her hand at Ernestine "—can't stand the idea of helping him succeed." She'd run over the line, far over it, but there was no hope of reining herself in. "Why is that, Ernestine?" Her breath was charging in her chest. "You didn't like him putting your face on some of his drawings? Even though you are constantly finding fault with him? *He's* the child. You don't have to be his best friend! But you're *supposed* to be his best teacher!"

Ernestine pointed her shaking finger toward the door. "I will *not* tolerate your disrespect. Get out and do not come back."

"Ever thought about trying to actually earn some respect?" Alexa swept up the envelope and stormed to the classroom door. "You know the interesting thing here, Ernestine? You didn't hire me." She yanked open the door. "Pretty sure you can't fire me." She pulled the door shut after her so hard the windows rattled as she strode down the corridor.

Regina Bowler, standing down the hallway with another teacher, watched with obvious shock. "What on earth?"

"That woman—" Alexa jerked her thumb over her shoulder "—shouldn't be allowed to teach. Maybe she was great in her day and maybe that day has lasted a long time." She gestured wildly with the envelope for Jason. "But not anymore."

"Let's go to my office." Regina tucked her hand around Alexa's arm as if she were afraid Alexa would bolt back to Ernestine.

That was the last place she wanted to go.

"We'll finish this later, Becky," Regina told the other teacher and, with her usual speed, hauled Alexa along the hallway.

They plowed through the doors to the administrative area

and Alexa dropped off the envelope at the secretary's desk. "Jason D'Angelo's grandmother is picking that up," she told her. "But I'd like to see her before she leaves."

"Sure." The secretary wrote on the envelope, nodding.

Regina pulled Alexa into her office and closed the door. "Now." She folded her arms. "*What* was all that about?"

Alexa told her. Everything. From Jason's unintentionally hurtful doodling to the progress report that had been wildly unfair, and a host of other little things that painted a picture of slights against many of her students, and Jason in particular. "I know Ernestine's had a long career, Regina. But she's completely unreasonable when it comes to Jason."

"Are you sure this doesn't have something to do with her attitude toward you?"

Alexa plopped into the plain chair in front of Regina's desk. She spread her palms. "I don't know. I'm her instructional aide but she treats me like a lackey. Is it just me or is she like that with everyone?" She raked her hair back. "It doesn't even matter. The students are the ones who matter. Jason matters."

"Your contract runs through the academic year. I can reassign you to another class, but if you preferred to go to the district office, I know there's a position available that would fit."

"I don't want to leave Howell. For that matter, I don't want to leave the class. Jason is one of many. All of them deserve more than Mrs. Tone is giving them." She peered at the principal. "She wasn't always like this, right?"

Regina sighed. "I taught alongside her at Edison for the first ten years of my career. It was the only elementary school we had in town back then. I remember she was engaged for a while, but that ended badly, and if she ever had a personal life outside of teaching, I never heard about it. Lots of educators say teaching is their life, but when it comes to Ernestine, it's true."

"I get it. She's an institution and I'm just a one-year hire. So, what happens now?"

"I'll speak with Ernestine if you want to remain in her classroom."

"I meant with Jason D'Angelo."

"I'll speak with Ernestine," Regina repeated with a weary smile. "We'll work it out, Alexa. If Jason isn't thriving, maybe a move to Mr. Geraldo's third-grade class would benefit him. Socially at the very least."

Alexa shook her head. "Take a look at Jason's work, Regina. His school records from Chicago don't even cover the half of it. I think he's truly exceptional. How many kids do we come across like him? At the very least, he should be tested for the gifted program."

"I don't disagree. But his father was very clear when he enrolled Jason that he didn't want to push him too fast. He barely agreed with the grade level and that was only because of the influence his previous school had."

"So, he approved the skipped grade with the result that Ernestine gives him abysmal marks on his first quarter report?"

"We could table gifted testing for a year. Dr. D'Angelo struck me as a caring father. He could have a completely different outlook in a year."

"Excuse me." The secretary opened the door after a quick knock. "Jason D'Angelo's grandmother was just here picking up his homework."

Alexa half rose. "I was hoping to see her."

"I know. I told her and I thought she intended to wait. But the next thing I knew, the bell rang and she was booking it out of here. I thought you should know."

"Thank you, Gerta," Regina said, and the secretary bowed out again, pulling the door shut behind her.

"I guess I'll be making a phone call to Jason's home as

well," Regina said. "Unless you…" She trailed off, raising her eyebrows.

"That's a conversation that's better coming from you."

"Are you sure? Seems like you've been developing a connection with his father."

"I wouldn't call it that. And how would you know anyway?"

"You're forgetting where you are, my dear. This is Cape Cardinale. Donna Blankenship is not only on your fundraising committee, but she's the biggest gossip in town and seemed to think sharing your exchanges with Dr. D'Angelo would be riveting. And then I heard about you meeting up at Tanya's restaurant from four different sources. You can't make a move in this town without someone noticing." The second bell rang and she opened her office door. "Something you may want to remember the next time you see our handsome Doctor D."

West looked from the address Ruthie had written to the building beyond his windshield.

Not really a building, though.

An airplane hangar. Located in one corner of the Cape Cardinale Airfield.

The oversized bay doors were closed, but a standard-sized door to one side stood open. He tell if there was actually anyone inside, much less a bunch of participants for a beginner's yoga class. But there were a bunch of vehicles parked outside the hangar, at least. He took it as a good sign.

He parked near a light that sent a wide glow through the night and pulled the yoga mat out of his trunk.

Ruthie, evidently tired of nagging him, had purchased the gear for him and practically pinned the address to the front of his lab coat. "I registered you for a month of classes," she'd said. "The clinic is paying for it, too. I'm hoping that'll guilt you into actually going. First session is tonight. Your mom's in league with me, too. She's on Jason-watch."

He really did have too many bossy women in his life.

A powder-pink Jeep roared past him, screeched to a stop close to the hangar, emitted two women who dashed through the opened doorway, and drove off again.

Yoga, he thought. *Of all things, why yoga?*

Because it was my favorite?

He closed the door hard on his wife's ghost and walked into the hangar only to be met with a blast of heat.

He immediately understood why Ruthie had told him to take a towel. The interior of the hangar—which didn't seem to house anything related to aviation—felt like it was a hundred degrees.

Yoga mats were spread out like a rainbow. A good twenty of them. Most occupied by women.

He wasn't the *only* man, but he still felt conspicuously out of place, which wasn't helped by the tall brunette at the front of the attendees who greeted him the moment he walked in. She wore a sports bra and a pair of yoga shorts that barely covered her rear. Her sleek limbs already had a sheen of sweat that only emphasized the perfection of her form.

If she'd been cast in cement, she would have fit right in with the statues in his backyard.

"Dr. D'Angelo?" She didn't wait for him to respond. "Thank you for filling out your paperwork online. It saves so much time." She gestured, taking in the wealth of real estate before her. "Find a spot anywhere. You'll want plenty of space to stretch out."

The cavernous space had been reduced by half its size thanks to a series of large rolling heaters. They were positioned in a big semicircle, glowing red and heating the space to a level just shy of hell.

Really, Ruthie? Regular yoga wasn't bad enough?

He found a spot as far away from the red eyes of death

as he could and flipped out his mat as if he knew what he was doing. Nearly everyone else had water bottles sitting near their mats. He'd left his in the car.

Big mistake.

Too bad Janine couldn't bring it in for him. Her ghost would have been doing something useful.

"Here." The instructor appeared in front of his mat, a tall disposable bottle of water in her hand. "You'll want to bring your own next time."

He took the water and she returned to the front of the room. Her yoga mat was plain gray. Like West's.

She hit the button on her phone and pressed her hands together below her chin. Everyone who hadn't been standing at attention suddenly did so as ambient music from hidden speakers filled the air.

"Welcome to the Wednesday Wash." Her tone took on a mesmerizing lilt. "I'm Olivia Hartwell. For those of you who are new—" her gaze didn't touch only on West, which was a little heartening "—it's important to give respect to your body. To the heat. Staying in this room through the next hour is a success, whether you simply lay in Savasana on your mat or follow our flow. Listen to your body," she stressed. "Everyone, remember this is a time to wash away the mind and focus on the now."

Immediately, *his* mind began wandering. To the patients he'd seen that day. To the funding they'd lost from Dunterwood. To Jason, who had picked up a fever on Monday morning.

West knew his son couldn't conjure a fever just because he was upset over learning that his adored Mrs. Cardinale wasn't planning to stick around after the school year. The timing was coincidental.

His fever had broken that morning, though. If it didn't spike again, he'd be able to return to class tomorrow.

To Alexa.

West realized everyone around him had their fingertips interlaced under their chins. Their elbows rising upward. Stretching.

"Remember your breath should be controlled. Relaxed and *deep*." Olivia's voice melded with the music. Peaceful. Relaxed. "Stretch upward with your elbows. Stretch your lungs. Your mind."

She was moving soundlessly now around the room. A suggestion here. An adjustment there. Naming poses.

He watched the others, following along. He'd been married to Janine for too long to be unfamiliar with it all. Warrior pose. Tree pose. Balance. Hold. His mind wandered further. He wasn't washing anything away. He'd have to work on that.

They went to the floor next. His muscles were so warm and loose, his knee didn't crackle or pop once.

"Straighten here." Olivia's finger lightly touched his shoulder. "Lower there." Another light touch.

Sweat pooled.

He'd allowed the stresses of the last few years to build up. He knew it. Doc Hayes knew it. Even Jason knew it. So, West filled his lungs with the hot air. He breathed it out again. Absently followed along with Olivia's instructions. Arms out now. Lengthen the fingertips. Forearms. Spine.

More sweat flowed. His mind drifted even further. Had Alexa's fundraiser gotten any more donations?

Did she do this yoga stuff? She'd been dressed for it that day at the restaurant, but that didn't mean anything.

Is that why you went along with Ruthie so easily? Did you hope you'd see Blondie here?

I'd rather see her than you, he thought.

Ouch! Tell me how you really feel.

You don't want to know.

The music that filled the hangar wasn't exactly music. More an amalgam of nature sounds layered with singular musical notes that hung on for long stretches before slid-ing into some new slow and simple melody that eventually faded away into another lingering note while ocean waves just pushed and pulled and pushed again.

If it wasn't for the tangible sensation of muscles releas-ing and flexing, he might have thought he was dreaming.

Or that he had passed out in the heat.

Nice plank.

He should have known Janine hadn't gone anywhere for long.

He ignored her and grabbed the edge of his towel. Wiped the sweat from his brow before it ran into his eyes. He turned onto his back. Pretended to be a happy baby and that he didn't feel like a spectacle in the process.

He fought to get back into the lullaby of the music.

Olivia led them into a twist that felt so freaking good he could have cried. Maybe he did. Or maybe it was just more sweat. His towel was damp. His shirt soaked. Who knew?

"And last, we enter Savasana," Olivia said. "The corpse pose. Relax your entire body. Legs. Arms. Face."

Inch by inch, he managed to let go. Felt himself start to sink—really sink—into the thin mat.

He almost made it.

Yoga was my thing, Janine complained.

Maybe it's mine now. Why don't you let go, Janine?

Why won't you let me, West?

He opened his eyes, Janine's question echoing through his mind.

Around him, some were still lying prone. Some were sitting. Drinking water. Toweling off. Rolling up mats and exchanging quiet whispers with someone else.

He rolled to his feet.

"What did you think?" Olivia stopped next to him.

She had another bottle of water in her hand that she ex-tended to him, and he realized he'd drunk all of his along the way. He took the offered water and, by some stint, managed not to guzzle half of it down like a man dying of thirst. "I haven't sweat this much since my first day interning." He dragged the towel over his head. Draped it around his neck. "But I'm glad my office manager insisted."

"Ruthie's nothing if not insistent."

He gave her another look. "You know Ruthie?"

Olivia smiled. "I'm a physical therapist with Cardinale Cares. But before that, I worked with one of the physicians whose practice used to be in the same building as your clinic. She's one of kind, that's for sure." Her gaze ran over him, assessing. "The gift membership she gave you is for a month. Will you be back?"

"Weeknights aren't easy for me. I have an eight-year-old son I need to make arrangements for." Despite Ruthie and his mom's collusion.

Olivia clearly wasn't one who gave up easily. "We do a similar class on Saturday mornings. We meet at the park in town near the gazebo. Bring your boy. It's just regular yoga. Not hot. Unless it's raining and then we come here to the airfield." Humor filled her face. "We save the heaters for the weeknights. And if that still doesn't work for you, we do a Thursday class at eleven. Of course, you can do all of them every week if you like."

He chuckled. "Let me work on one week at a time for now." He lifted the water bottle. He'd nearly killed it, too. "Thanks. I'll replenish your supply next time."

"That's what they all say," she laughed as she reached up to turn off one of the heaters, and he realized she'd turned off the others while he'd been damn near asleep during that last pose.

As hot as the hangar had been, it was already cooling noticeably. "How hot do you get it in here?"

"We try to keep it up 100 to 102. It's hard. Particularly

during the winter. The hangar's so large. But Meyer Cartell hardly charges us anything for the rent, so it's worthwhile."

"Meyer Cartell!" The name was a blast from the past. "I can't believe he's still around."

"Been running the airfield for years now, along with JCS Aviation." She began rolling the heater across the concrete. "How do you know him?"

"I was in high school with a friend of his." He took hold of another heater and followed her.

"Then you should definitely come to the class on Saturday. He's almost always there with his fiancée. She's a friend of mine." Olivia pushed her heater into a corner below a catwalk that traversed the upper third of the hangar on one side of the building. She took his and worked it closely to the first. "Do you know Doc Hayes?"

"Play poker with him." He grasped the stands of two more heaters and started moving them.

"Sophie—she's his fiancée—is one of Doc's nurses."

He handed off one of the heaters so she could position it exactly the way she wanted. "You said Meyer runs JCS?" At the fundraising committee meeting, Alexa had mentioned her brother worked for JCS.

"Has for as long as *I've* lived here. You're smiling."

"Just thinking it's true that it's a small world."

The heaters were all stored away. He returned to his mat and rolled it up. He'd already finished the extra bottle of water she'd provided.

"So, I'll see you on Saturday?" She gathered her belongings as well and walked with him toward the door.

Another brunette, West? You're so predictable.

"Yes, I'll see you on Saturday," he told Olivia.

Janine, he ignored completely.

Chapter Ten

Alexa shifted, trying to keep some warmth flowing through her toes while she waved on the vehicle that had just dropped off a load of students in front of the school. She'd only been on the morning drop-off crew for ten minutes and the damp cold had already seeped through everything she wore.

The SUV in front of her was taking forever to move along; the driver more interested in his cell phone than the line of cars he was holding up.

Alexa tapped on his closed passenger window, gesturing that he should move. She earned an exasperated wave of the cell phone, as if it should be obvious that his phone was of primary importance.

She knocked harder. "Just pull ahead out of the line," she said through the window.

He gave her a middle-finger salute.

"Morning to you, too," she muttered and waved to the car behind him, gesturing to pull up alongside instead.

Becky Newberry was the other teacher on duty and she lifted her hands in a "Really?!" sort of way at the oblivious driver as she hurried as fast as her pregnant state allowed to the other car, where she opened the door for the kids. She ushered them around the SUV and to the sidewalk and, like water flowing around a rock, the rest of the cars followed suit, surrounding the SUV driver and his precious phone, blocking him right in.

When Alexa saw Jason's grandmother through the windshield of the next car, she braced slightly, but Jason didn't give her so much as a glance when he got out and jogged into the school, his backpack bouncing against his back.

His grandmother pulled right in front of phone-guy, who was clearly fuming at this point. She rolled down her window, wagging a beringed finger at him. "Serves you right," she yelled then smiled benignly at Alexa before driving off.

Alexa agreed. Served the driver right for getting stuck, but she also didn't want the situation escalating. She walked into the driveway again, physically preventing the next car from going around him, and waved the SUV along. She didn't earn any gestures of thankfulness for the effort, though, and his tires chirped as he roared away from the curb.

"Jerk," Becky said breathlessly as she jogged forward again to open the next car door.

Drop-off at Hollyvale had been well orchestrated, but it had nothing on the process at Howell Elementary.

There were only a few cars remaining in the line when the first bell rang and Alexa gestured for Becky to go in for her first-grade class. "I'll finish up these folks." Ernestine wouldn't be impressed whether Alexa was in the classroom on time because Ernestine was out with whatever bug was going around and had arranged for a substitute teacher to fill in for her.

By the time the cars were gone and she went inside, herself, Alexa's feet were numb. She stopped in the lounge for hot coffee on her way to the classroom.

The substitute was a woman who looked old enough to be Ernestine's mother. But despite her age, Mrs. Cuthbertson was friendly and actually welcomed Alexa's involvement as they got started with the day. Even though Jason ignored Alexa for the most part, the day still passed quickly with none of the tension that was usual under Ernestine's lead.

Even the kids seemed more animated than usual, and Alexa couldn't help but feel pleased when Jason was included with a small group of boys who ran out as soon as the class was dismissed.

Maybe there'd be a silver lining if his dismay with her prompted him to finally find a place for himself among his classmates.

She stayed after school to help with another gymnastics meet. After that, she and the custodian emptied Thankful Friday bins into the storage unit and when she finally got home to the beach house, Cutter's truck occupied Dana's usual spot and Alexa assumed he was holed up inside the camper working. Meyer was undoubtedly with Sophie and Dana was gone as usual. Ever since her revelation about the state of her marriage, she came in late and left early, barely speaking to anyone.

The wind was howling and Alexa wished the fireplace wasn't boarded up. It would have been the perfect evening for a cozy fire.

The thought snuck in that West's house had a fireplace. More than one.

Lost in *that* particular thought, she startled when her cell phone pinged with a text message from Sophie reminding her about her wedding dress fitting. She sent a thumbs up, then sat there a while, just holding her phone.

She finally just punched in the number that she hadn't even realized she'd memorized.

West's voice was deep when he answered, and it took a moment of shivers before she realized it was just a recording.

She rubbed her forehead, annoyed with herself. "This is Alexa," she said after the beep. "I just wanted to ah, let you know we've received another few thousand in donations for the playground." She chewed the inside of her lip. "Anyway, that was. . .all. Oh. It was good seeing Jason back, too. Good night." She hung up. Dropped her head onto the counter and groaned.

Way to make an impression.

Eventually she straightened. Went out for a run on the beach and finally fell asleep reading.

She awoke to her cell phone ringing and her first thought was *West!*

But it was just Regina Bowler.

"Ernestine is in the hospital," she greeted baldly.

Alexa rolled onto her back, willing her adrenaline to calm the heck down. It was still dark and her alarm wasn't set to go off for another hour and a half. "What happened? How is she?"

"She had the bug that's going around only it's worsened into pneumonia now. She'll be out for sure through Thanksgiving next week. Maybe longer. Are you up to subbing?"

She sat bolt upright. "What about Mrs. Cuthbertson?"

"She won't do more than a day here or there."

"Ernestine doesn't know that you're asking me, I assume."

The principal's silence was answer enough.

"Obviously, I'm more than happy to take the class. I'm just not sure how well I'll survive the fallout once she's well and back on the job."

"We'll deal with that when we have to. See you at school."

"See you at school," Alexa echoed, but the principal had already hung up.

She swung her legs off the bed and turned off the alarm clock. There was no point in trying to get another hour's sleep. Not when she could use the extra time in the classroom to get ready for the day.

She could hear Meyer's snore through his closed bedroom door and was more than a little shocked to find Dana's door open. She peeked inside. The bed was undisturbed.

Annoyance burbled inside her.

The beach house hell was all or nothing. If any one of them didn't stick to the terms of the will, they all lost out. And though Fitzgerald Lane wasn't so militant that he did a bed check every day, he *did* have a propensity for dropping around a few times a week ostensibly to see if there was anything he could do to make their stay more comfortable.

Not even the prospect of leading her own classroom for the next several days was enough to quell her irritation, and she stomped into the kitchen, not caring if she did wake up Meyer.

She started a pot of coffee, slamming around a cabinet or two when she realized that Dana was curled up in the chair in the dark living room. So sound asleep that not even Alexa's cantankerous clatter had disturbed her.

Irritation fizzling, she circled around the breakfast bar and moved the heavenly throw from the to spread it lightly over her sister. Dana still didn't stir, and Alexa tiptoed back down the hall to the bathroom. She showered quickly, worked her hair into a braid, and then armed with a travel mug of coffee, a protein bar and her messenger bag, let herself out the back door.

Betty started right up and even did an admirable job of climbing the bluff without sputtering even once.

There were a few cars in the staff lot at the school when she arrived and Alexa parked in her usual spot at the far end of the lot even though she could have used Ernestine's.

Never let it be said that Alexa was "taking over" not only Ernestine's class but her parking space as well.

The school doors were all still locked, but she found the custodian in his office, drinking coffee and pecking at a computer keyboard with two fingers. He let her in and flipped on lights as she walked down the corridor to the classroom.

She sat at Ernestine's desk and pulled out the center drawer where she kept her lesson plans. She would stick to the sensible plan, but that didn't mean she couldn't mix it up just a little.

She was going to enjoy it for every second that it lasted.

Soon, the bell rang and she greeted them as they tumbled through the doorway, only to gape at the sight of her sitting on the edge of the desk at the front of the room. "Don't stand there." She waved them in. "We have a full day ahead of us."

"Where's Mrs. Tone?" Jason was the first one to actually ask.

Her pleasure that he'd addressed her directly was wildly out of proportion. "She's out sick for a few days."

"And *you're* our sub?" Aidyn Savage was the self-appointed king of classroom superiority, and he jostled Jason out of his way. "I'll be your sub until she returns, but that doesn't mean we're going to forget manners."

She glimpsed a grin on Jason's face as he turned to dump off his backpack in his cubby.

After announcements and attendance and the Pledge of Allegiance, she closed the classroom door and picked up the workbooks she'd assembled that quiet early morning hour before the school came to life and passed them out before sitting on the edge of Ernestine's desk.

"Mrs. Tone wouldn't like you sitting on her desk," Netta whispered.

"I think she'd like me sitting in her chair even less," Alexa confided in return.

Aidyn hooted in laughter.

"What're these for?" Duwan Wood, Aidyn's second-in-command, held up his workbook.

"Until Mrs. Tone returns, we're going to have time every day to wear our creative caps. You can draw or doodle or write in your workbooks." Her gaze strayed to Jason's corner of the classroom. "The only rule is that you follow the theme we're working on in our lessons." The announcement earned as many groans as it did whispers, and she went to the whiteboard. "Today's theme is *connection*." She wrote the word in huge green letters across the top of the board.

"I don't get it," Aidyn grumbled.

"You will," she said cheerfully. She capped the marker and set it in the tray behind her. "Duwan, will you collect everyone's homework from yesterday?" Since he'd never been asked by Mrs. Tone to help, he looked uncertain as he slid out from behind his desk. She selected another colored marker. "What do you suppose the definition is of the word *connection*?"

"Look it up on the internet," Aidyn said.

He was trying to be smart, but she just smiled. "We could do that. But I think we'll come up with our own definition instead." She turned to the board. "Tell me all the words that you think help describe 'connection.' Just call them out."

After a slow start, the kids were soon yelling out all sorts of words. She wrote them on the board and when the contributions petered out, she moved to the middle of the room and studied the board along with the kids. Most of the words were literal. Descriptions of one thing touching another. A link. A physical connection.

She strolled closer to the desk at the front of the classroom, stopping short of it by a foot or so. "This morning, I ate a protein bar on my way to work." She bent her knees then jumped straight up in the air, landing neatly on top of Mrs. Tone's desk.

Adrenaline pumping, she turned and faced the kids.

They were staring at her as if she'd painted her face in Howell Elementary purple.

"Is there a connection between the protein bar and the fact that I can jump straight up onto a desk?"

"Protein gives you energy and energy helps you jump?"

"Exactly." She jumped down and propped her hands on her hips. "It might not be visible, but there is pretty much a connection between everything," she said breathlessly. "Between music and math. Math and science. Science and imagination. Imagination and physical reaction. You name it and you'll find it will always relate to something else." She gestured at the paper turkeys taped on the walls. "You made all those to decorate the room and they make me think about the roasted turkey my mother makes every year and my tongue thinks…yuck."

"My tongue thinks yum," Netta said.

Alexa caught a wisp of a smile on Jason's face. "So, what do you suppose all this—" she grabbed another colored marker and circled the word cloud on the board "—has to do with the empty pages in your workbooks?"

"We can write about anything we want," Netta said loudly. "And I'm going to write about my puppy!"

"Boring," Aidyn said. "I'm writing about ZombieCart."

Jason's head came up again. "Who's your favorite character?"

"Gordo." Aidyn sneered. "Duh. He's the main dude."

"There is no main dude in ZombieCart," Duwan said. "They're all equal."

Aidyn rounded on his friend for failing to fall in line. "No, they're not. Gordo has special powers!"

"I like Vern," Jason said.

"Vern's a nerd," Aidyn scoffed.

Netta turned around in her seat and beamed at Jason. "No, he's not. I like him, too! He doesn't have special powers but he's the only one who can do flips with his motor-cycle." She smirked at Aidyn. "It's always the fastest way to level up."

"You all have thirty minutes to work on the first page in your book," Alexa said before the exchange could go any further. "Then we'll do spelling after that."

Duwán was frowning. "What if I don't finish my drawing?"

Alexa smiled. The energy flowing through the classroom was palpable. "You'll have more time throughout the day."

"What if I run out of pages?" Netta's sentiment was echoed by several others.

"We'll make more," she assured. "Anyone need colored pencils or markers?" Hands shot into the air and she carried the plastic containers filled with the art supplies Ernestine so stingily allowed around the room, letting them take their fill.

Then she sat back to enjoy them all bowing their attention to what was obviously a novel way of starting their day.

"And then she let us draw!" Jason thrust a bundle of newsprint over the seat at West. "I didn't even have to hide it behind my spelling workbook!"

West automatically took the booklet and set it on the passenger seat. A purple windbreaker was waving for them to move along and he hit the gas. The school fell behind in his rearview mirror and even though he hadn't seen Alexa outside the school with the other teachers, he couldn't help looking one more time.

She wasn't there, though. Which just left him with the weight of his phone and Alexa's message that he'd already listened to more than once. Examining every word, every tone, looking for an excuse to return her call and finding none. "You don't seem mad anymore that Ms. Cardinale plans to move back to California next summer."

"She's not gonna move," Jason said confidently.

West braked at the stop sign and looked over his shoulder at his son. "Did she tell you that?"

"No. But I just know."

"Wishful thinking doesn't make it so, Jase. She has plans."

Jason shrugged. "Plans change."

A quick toot of a horn prompted West and he drove out of the parking lot. "We're meeting Grandma later for dinner, but I have stuff to take care of at the clinic first. You'll have to hang out there for the duration."

"Why isn't she fixing us supper like she usual?"

"Because it's time for us to do something nice for *her*."

"What restaurant?"

"Someplace called the Cliff." Ruthie had confided the restaurant was one of Marjorie's favorite places, and judging by his mother's reaction when he'd told her, Ruthie had been correct.

"Aidyn Savage says the clinic's gonna close 'cause it doesn't make any money."

West jerked. "Who's Aidyn Savage?"

"He's in my class. If the clinic closes, we'll move back to Chicago, right? I think Mrs. Cardinale would like Chicago. There are lots of teaching jobs in Chicago."

"How do you know that?"

"Luc and I looked it up on the internet."

His head was starting to pound. "The clinic isn't closing and we're not moving. Regardless of whether or not she likes Chicago."

"Okay, but I hope Mrs. Tone doesn't come back to school. Then Mrs. Cardinale could be our teacher all year long."

"One thing doesn't necessarily mean the other."

"It's a connection," Jason said with certainty.

West rubbed his temple. "Okay. Whatever." At least Jason wasn't on the get-married-get-a-puppy track. But West was still surprised that some kid in Jason's class had talked about the clinic closing. Kids didn't come up with things like that in a vacuum. He would have had to have heard it from somewhere.

The construction dumpster was still in place when they got to the clinic. They went inside the empty clinic and West installed Jason in the conference room where he could spread out his things and connect his video game to the wall-mounted television. "No games until your homework is finished."

"We didn't get any homework today 'cause we finished everything in class. We even worked ahead in the math book and did a whole science center. We made *slime!*" Jason was already spreading out his wrinkled newsprint papers. They were covered with his extraordinarily detailed drawings. Usually, he just drew with his pencil. But now they were filled in with vibrant colors.

"Your class worked ahead *and* you had time to draw all of that?"

"Mmm-hmm." Jason fumbled inside his backpack and came out with a handful of colored markers that he let rain on the conference table. "She even let us bring home classroom supplies. Mrs. Tone will be *mad* when she finds out," he said with relish.

"You'd better be sure to return everything you borrowed then," he said. "I'll be in my office. Drinks and snacks are in the little fridge under that counter there so don't go wandering."

"I won't." Jason tucked his tongue between his teeth, surveying his drawing.

West turned to head for his office but hesitated. He

watched Jason tuck a marker behind his ear. "Want to go to a yoga class at the park tomorrow morning?"

Jason didn't even look up. "Okay."

If only West had a fraction of his son's ability to concentrate.

He continued to his office and the stack of pink message slips Ruthie kept stacking on his desk. But instead of responding to any of them, he just replayed the message that Alexa had left him and wondered how he'd turned into the sort of man who needed an excuse to call a woman.

Muttering an oath, he pressed the dial button. It rang several times before her voicemail came on.

He grimaced. "It's West. Congrats on the donations." He flexed his fingers around the phone. "I think Jason's gonna use up all the ink in the markers. You made him a happy kid." *Ask her out, you stupid idiot.* "Anyway…ah…thanks." He ended the call. Groaned and tossed his phone aside. "Pathetic, West. Truly Pathetic."

Chapter Eleven

"There's the gazebo." Jason's finger jabbed the air in front of them.

West had just spotted it himself. He hitched the strap around the yoga mat higher on his shoulder and nudged Jason along. They were already late and a lot more people milled around the park than he'd expected. "Are you warm enough?"

"I'm sweating," Jason complained. "How come I have to wear a coat but you don't?"

Because West was showing as much logic as his mother did when it came to Jason. Always assuming a child had a different thermostat than everyone else. "You can ditch the coat when we get there."

"What if I don't like yoga?"

"Then you can play on the playground or read." No doubt, Jason had a book tucked somewhere in the too-big puffy coat Margaret had gotten him.

"Jason's growing out of everything," she'd claimed. A valid excuse, but West still felt like he'd fallen down on his parenting when she'd handed over the shopping bag full of clothing when they'd picked her up the night before for dinner.

They passed a row of shrubbery bordered by a chain

link fence and he stopped short at the sight of the yoga mats strewn all over the park alongside the bright white gazebo.

"Puppies!" Jason breathed.

"Puppies," West echoed.

Every kind. Every color. Every size.

They were bouncing over the people occupying the yoga mats, tails wagging. Tongues lolling. Yapping. Nipping.

Who cared if the class started on time or not? At least forty people were there, engaged in varying levels of concentration as Olivia did her best to keep the yoga going, and nobody noticed their tardy arrival at all.

Jason shucked his coat and dumped the provisions he'd brought to occupy himself on the grass and giggled wildly when a white mutt with a black pointy ears latched his teeth on his paperback and started to drag it off. West scooped up the pup and detached it from the book, then set him free.

Olivia stood at the front of the chaotic assembly. A wireless mic allowed her voice to carry over it all.

It was a lot different than the session at the airport.

Jason hopped around, pulling off his tennis shoes and impressively falling into lockstep with the rest of the class even though he had a brown-and-black spaniel in his arms that was licking his face like it was covered in his mama's milk.

Why hadn't Olivia mentioned there'd be a zoo of dogs?

It wasn't the only thing different about the class. The temperature in the low fifties and the occasional gust of wind would have been a lot more bracing if a person didn't have to stop what they were doing every ten seconds just to deal with an overload of cuteness.

By the time they got to the end pose—basically sprawling on your back staring up at the sky—even West was resigned to the wriggling masses of canine mischief. The button-nosed beagle stretched over his windpipe was at least warm.

"And let's thank the folks from Puppy Harbor for another

successful puppy yoga event," Olivia said through her loud-speaker, earning cheers. "Puppy Harbor has locations in Lincoln City and Cannon Beach and they're coming soon to right here in Cape Cardinale." She had a white fluff ball in her arms that kept knocking her mic askew. "If you're interested in adoptions or want more information, just visit the folks in the gazebo!" She was laughing when she turned off the loudspeaker.

West looked over his neck scarf of beagle at Jason, who was sitting with his legs spread wide, keeping two match-ing mongrels more or less corralled.

"Dad. *Please?*"

He looked up at the sky.

He couldn't even blame Janine for this one. He cut his gaze over to the gazebo where a dozen people were busy setting up crates and another dozen were handing out forms to the people—not just those who'd obviously come for the yoga class—lined up halfway across the park.

"Get your shoes on." He capitulated. "And we will go over and see—*see*," he emphasized, "what the adoption process involves."

"Yes." Wiggling with as much excitement as any of the dogs, Jason began stuffing his feet into his tennis shoes while West displaced the beagle. He was a cute guy. More interested in sleeping at this point than playing, because he snuffled his nose into the towel West hadn't even needed, curled up and closed his eyes.

West pulled on his own shoes then rolled up their mats and fastened the tangle of straps around them. "That line is long, buddy," he warned. "It's going to take a while."

"I don't care how long it takes." Jason made a face when a white-haired woman came by with leashes, trying to cap-ture a few that way. He kissed the two puppies he'd been playing with on the heads and then helped the shelter volunteer fasten the leads.

She beamed at him. "Thank you, honey. They don't know how to behave on a leash yet but at least I don't have to chase them around." Her crinkled gaze met West's. "I just usually work in the office," she said breathlessly. "These events take it out of a person."

"I could help." Jason bounced on his toes. "I can catch puppies. Right, Dad?"

"Long as you stay in sight."

"Well, all right." The woman handed over two of her nylon braided leashes. "They get tangled easily—oop. He's already off. Thank goodness for the fence. We'd never keep them all contained."

West chuckled. "My son's in heaven. Here." He scooped up the two pups who were twining around her legs and handed them to her. "I'll take the rest of the leashes for you."

She beamed even more. "Such a nice family. All you have to do is bring the puppies up to the gazebo. They're already sorted by their collars and tags." She walked away, her pace rolling a little.

It felt like half the town had descended on the park. He figured that the Puppy Harbor folks must not care too much if a puppy or two just happened to find their way out of the park with a new family without the proper t's crossed and i's dotted first.

He left their jackets and yoga gear against a tree. With the beagle in one arm, he worked his way through the crowd, every now and then spotting a pup that was catchable. He had three more tangling together on their leashes when he nearly ran into Olivia.

"I have been looking for you." She tugged him toward the spot where she'd stood while leading the class.

"Wish you'd have warned me about the dogs," he told her. "I'd have worked harder to leave my son at home."

"There's no way you can be as grouchy as you sound. Not with a dozen Puppy Harbor leashes hanging around your neck. Here." She took the beagle from him. "Meyer!"

A tall ruddy-haired man turned at her call and West grinned. He approached the man, extending his hand. "Meyer Cartell. I'd have recognized that hair of yours anywhere."

Meyer chuckled as he shook West's hand. "I couldn't believe my ears when Olivia told me about you. I don't want to think about how long it's been. What is it? Twenty years? How the hell are you?"

"Good. Really good." West realized the words were almost true. He bent down to untangle the puppies who'd wound themselves up so tightly they couldn't even move. "My son's around here somewhere, playing Chase the Pup." He straightened, lifting his two palmsful of dog. "Pot calling the kettle, apparently."

"A son." Meyer rubbed one of the puppy's heads and her eyes rolled in pleasure. "Congratulations. Sophie and I are just getting started."

Olivia had been watching them, her attention bouncing back and forth between them. "Obviously I'm not needed for this little bromantic reunion, so I'm going to head out." Her gaze skated over West. "Hope to see you at yoga again."

"As long as it doesn't involve anything on four legs, I'll work on it."

She laughed. "Here. I'll turn these two in for you."

"As an apology, it's pretty weak. How many were there? Five hundred dogs?"

She laughed again. "Fifty-two is what I was told." She nuzzled the puppies against her cheeks and set off.

He would have had to be dead and buried not to appreciate the sight of her dressed in formfitting white from neck to knee until he realized the person she stopped at next was Alexa Cardinale.

His gaze slammed right into hers.

Like Olivia, her figure was lovingly outlined in tight fabric. Unlike Olivia, her outfit was candy-apple-red-and-white stripes that left her arms bare and ended midway down her thighs. All she needed was a bow, and she'd be a candy cane left by Santa.

She said something to the blonde on the other side of her before heading toward the gazebo alongside Olivia where they were swallowed among the crowd.

It was probably a good thing that Jason hadn't seen her. The combination of puppies and his favorite teacher would have been too much to bear.

Fortunately, West could see Jason crawling around a tree nearby trying to coax a puppy into his arms.

He dragged his attention back to Meyer. "Olivia told me you run the airport."

Meyer nodded. "Yeah. I left the Air Force a while back. John—you remember John Skinner?"

"I'd have asked Meredith to the prom if she'd have had eyes for anyone besides him. They got married as soon as she graduated high school. You still in touch?"

Meyer's expression sobered. "Might say that. Unfortunately, John died a while back in a plane crash. Left Meredith with their two kids to raise."

West grimaced. "I'm sorry to hear that. We lost my wife a few years ago, too." After so many times of repeating the words, they came more naturally if not more easily. "How's she doing now?"

Meyer bent down and caught a tiny poodle as it raced past. His expression lightened. "She's good. She and the kids moved recently to Colorado with her new husband. Nice guy. Lawyer."

West was tracking Jason's progress. He had three puppies now. All leashed; none of them tangling because he held the end of one in each extended arm and a third between his teeth. He was making his way to the gazebo, stopping every few steps to let the pups catch up. West looked at Meyer again. "There's such a thing as a nice lawyer?"

"A few." Meyer grinned. "My fiancée's father is one of them. What about you?"

"Since Meredith never gave *me* the time of day, I ended up in Chicago with a medical degree and a woman who did give me some time." Until she hadn't. "My mother's still here in town. I brought Jason back home a couple months ago. She's a lot of help with him."

"I can imagine. How's he doing?"

"Better than his old man, generally. Never thought I'd end up back in Cape Cardinale running the same clinic that my father established."

"I'm with you there. I never thought I'd end up here, either." Meyer's face split into a smile and he held out his arm. "But this beautiful woman makes it all worthwhile. Sophie—" The blonde who had been talking to Alexa joined them, slipping into Meyer's outstretched arm. "This is West D'Angelo. He went to high school with Meredith. West, my soon-to-be bride, Sophie Lane."

Sophie eyes were warm and smiling. "Meredith's my dearest friend! She'll be here for the wedding next week. She and Olivia are my attendants." She looked from West to Meyer and back again. "You should come!"

West immediately shook his head, but Meyer latched onto the idea.

"You *should* come," he added. "Bring your boy."

The last wedding West attended had been his own. He

had no real interest in attending another one, despite this not unpleasant trip down memory lane. "My wife ran our wedding like a five-star general. I know adding guests at the last minute is a high crime."

"Don't be silly!" Sophie waved her hands as if shooing away the idea. "If we could have the entire town there, we would. Two o'clock at Oceanview Church. If you can't make the ceremony, at least come to the reception afterward. We're having it out at the airfield."

It was too hard to give an outright no when she was so sincere in her invitation. 'I'll see what I can do." That left plenty of opportunity to bow out.

Which he would.

"Had I known all this was happening—" he angled his head toward Jason "—I'd have skipped the park and taken him straight to Tanya's for breakfast."

"An excellent choice before *or* after puppies. Tanya's waffles are divine," Sophie said. "If I didn't have another wedding dress fitting this afternoon, I'd be dragging Meyer there, too." As if they were longstanding friends, she gave West a quick hug and a peck on his cheek. "Two o'clock. This general—" her eyes sparkled as she poked her thumb at her chest "—has spoken."

Then she turned to Meyer and gave him a little more than a quick peck. "The girls and I should be home around four if you want to throw something on the grill." She batted flirtatious lashes. "Weather's supposed to be nice all weekend and you know how I love it out on the deck." She laughed and bounced off again, her honey-colored ponytail bobbing.

"Wedding prep," Meyer said ruefully. "Every time I turn around, there's something else to be done. All I want is to put my ring on her finger and get on with the honeymoon. Not that we're having much of one right now, but come next summer? Two weeks in French Polynesia with nothing around us but blue skies and blue water."

Remember Tahiti?

"Janine and I had a week in Tahiti for our honeymoon," he told West. Effectively answering his wife's unwelcome apparition at the same time. "Wear sunblock. Everywhere," he added pointedly.

Meyer laughed. "Good advice that I already know too well." He sketched a salute and followed in the direction that his fiancée had taken.

Were the sex vibes between us ever that palpable?

If they had been, you wouldn't have landed in bed with Owen Mai.

Nitpicker. Janine pouted and dissolved into nothing again.

West strode over to Jason and took the leashes from him. "I've got these. You crawl under this bush here. I saw something white a second ago."

Jason dropped to his belly and snaked half his body beneath the bush. In moments, he was wriggling back out with a muddy-pawed white Frenchie. The dog was cleaner than Jason, though. Mud streaked from his chin to his knees and he had leaves stuck in his hair.

He also looked happier than he had in months.

He hopped to his feet and rubbed his hands down his long-sleeved T-shirt, leaving more dirt behind. "Can we get in line now?"

A puppy was going to be in their future, like it or not. And at least there were plenty to choose from right here and now.

"Yeah," West said, resigned. "We can get in line."

"Yes." Jason fist-pumped and he raced toward the back of the line. Far as West could tell, it hadn't shortened any in the last fifteen minutes. People were crammed six-deep around the gazebo. He took a side detour long enough to scoop up their gear before joining Jason.

"Who was that guy you were talking to? Did you know him before?" Jason had found a twig from the downtrodden grass alongside the sidewalk and tucked it between his nose and upper lip. A little wooden mustache.

"His name's Meyer Cartell."

Jason sneezed. The twig fell and Jason just glanced around, looking for another. "He's Mrs. Cardinale's brother." He pounced. But it wasn't a twig he'd found. It was a rolypoly. He nudged the bug that had curled into a ball around his palm, perfectly oblivious to the way West was staring at him.

"How on earth do you know he's her brother?"

"It's not a common name. Mine is. It's in the top fifty of every list I looked at on the library computer."

"Yeah, but we named you Jason because it was your mom's maiden name."

He rolled the bug from one palm to the other. "I know. Janine Jay Jason. JJ. She was talking about him with Mrs. Newberry during lunch once." Jason squatted down and poured the bug off his hand into a pile of mulchy leaves near the base of a tree.

It took West's brain a second to catch up. No, Janine's ghost hadn't been talking to Mrs. Newberry at lunch. Alexa had been. Which was how Jason knew her brother's name. That wasn't in a typical top fifty list.

And once again, his son's powers of observation felt staggering. "You shouldn't eavesdrop," he told him. "It's not polite."

"That's what Grandma says, too, but they were the ones talking right in front of me."

Who could argue with that?

He nudged Jason forward in the line. They'd progressed

all of three feet. "I am apparently oblivious to what's going on in this town."

The old guy in front of them in line looked over his shoulder. "That's what my wife tells me." He gave a cackle of laughter and turned back around.

"Not me," Jason stated seriously. "I know the custodian gets to the school really early so he can use the computer before anyone else gets there."

"Do I want to know why?"

"Mr. Meacham's not weird or nothing. Except he writes lady books."

The old man looked back again. "What's a lady book?"

"You know. The lovey smoochy kind. Where the ladies wear the big dresses like in *Cinderella*." Jason giggled and propped his hand on his hip, jutting out his butt one way and his skinny chest the other and lifting his chin high. He minced around on his toes like that; his apparent impression of what ladies in Cinderella dresses looked like.

West had a hard time not laughing. The old guy didn't bother trying. "My wife reads those lady books," he told Jason when he was done guffawing. "Think you got it nailed, but I'm not sure *she'd* agree." His eyes twinkling, he turned forward again.

"Do the teachers talk about Mr. Meacham's hobby in front of you, too?" West asked when Jason finally fell back in line. "Is that how you know about it?"

"Unh-unh. The lunch lady is friends with Mr. Meacham. He comes in and helps her clean up after the lunch line. She keeps telling him he needs a sudomin 'cause nobody'll buy his lady book if he uses his real name."

"Pseudonym." West deciphered aloud.

"Yeah. That's what I said. I don't see what's the big deal." There were chalk marks on the sidewalk where they stood and Jason hopped from one colored square to the next. "Shakespeare's a good name."

The old guy's shoulders were shaking. He was clearly laughing again, though was exercising a little more control.

"Yeah," West agreed. "Sort of taken already, though."

"But that's his name. Shakespeare Meacham."

West rubbed his chin. "Buddy, I don't know anything about writing lady books or any other kind of book. But I think maybe your lunch attendant might have a point with Mr. Meacham."

He lifted his arms and dropped them again at his sides. "I wish he wrote something more interesting. Like zombies or dinosaurs."

"There's a wide world of books out there, Jase. Something for everyone."

"I guess." Jason delved in his bag of amusements and pulled out West's old copy of *Jurassic Park.* It had several sharp dents, courtesy of puppy teeth. "I'm glad *you* didn't used to read lady books, though." He stuck his tongue out the side of his mouth and made a choking sound. "Bo-ring."

"You could write your own story. I'll bet Ms. Cardinale would like that."

"I like drawing better."

"You just went with your grandma to see Tom Pendragon in Portland. I know you like his graphic novels. Try that."

"His books are for little kids, though."

West remembered when eight *was* little. "Little kids need books, too."

Jason was quiet for a moment, his expression screwed up in thought. "Could we bring back mom? Like the dinosaurs?"

West winced and was glad that he'd already had the foresight to clear *Pet Sematary* from his Stephen King collection before Jason could get to it. The tale of bringing the

dead back to life was one that definitely could be put off a
few years. He knelt and squeezed Jase's hands. "That's science fiction, Jase. Your mom never wanted to leave you,
but you know she can't come back." He braced himself
for some comment from her ghost, but it was only Jason's
voice that replied.

"She does in my dreams."

West stared down at the chalk squares to stop the sudden burning in his eyes. He cleared the knot from his throat.
"Mine, too, Jase. Mine, too." He cleared his throat again
and pointed to a bench. "You can sit over there and read if
you want."

Jason immediately grabbed the rest of his stuff. Except
the coat. He was halfway to the bench when he looked back.
"Hey, Dad," he called out. "After we get a puppy, can we
still get a strawberry waffle?"

"At the rate this line is moving, it might be a waffle tomorrow morning," he muttered. "We'll see," he said loud
enough for Jason to hear.

It was enough. His son flopped his stuff on the ground
and followed it, eschewing the bench. His nose immediately
disappeared into the pages of his book.

"Kids," said the guy in front of him. "Their wants are
a mile long."

"Sometimes," West agreed. A window had appeared in
the wall of people ahead. Just wide enough to give him a
glimpse of blonde hair and candy cane stripes.

And sometimes an adult's wants went even further.

"You look absolutely perfect," Dana said.

They were at Sophie's family home where her father's
new wife, Francesca, had placed a trio of full-length mir-
rors to reflect every angle of her. "Like something out of
a fairy tale."

Alexa agreed. Sophie did look stunning. She just hoped her fairy tale with Meyer had a true happy ending. "Are you *sure* you want to marry our brother? He's kind of annoying. And he snores."

Sophie laughed. "He only snores if he drinks beer." She shook her hair back from her shoulders and turned to her reflection again. "I'm the lucky one." She tugged at the edge of her bodice where it covered her breasts before sweeping down to her waist in a deep V before angling back up again to form another triangle that met atop her shoulders in satiny braided straps. "I'm not showing any side boob, am I?"

"If you were, do you think Meyer would complain?"

Dana sent Alexa a censorious frown before she looked again at Sophie. "Your gown fits perfectly."

Sophie and Alexa were the same age and about the same height. But when the universe was handing out curves, it had blessed Sophie and forgotten Alexa altogether.

Francesca sailed into the room with several champagne flutes already filled. "Bubbly all around." She had a faint accent that Alexa only knew was Belgian because Sophie had told her so. "No spilling," she warned Sophie.

"Maybe I should take it off," Sophie said, holding the flute at a stiff-armed distance.

Dana set aside her glass after barely a sip and helped unfasten the tiny pearl buttons. "There you go," she said with a flourish and Sophie floated out of the living room holding the dress against her breasts.

"Such a beautiful girl," Francesca said fondly. "I can't wait for the wedding."

"They've definitely been in the works for the Lane family," Dana said. She resumed her perch on one of the upholstered chairs and toyed with the stem of her champagne flute. "First you and Fitz and now Sophie and Meyer."

"Speaking of Fitz," Francesca said. "I've talked to him

about Thanksgiving. And how ridiculous it is to expect all of you to stay in that little house through the holiday. Particularly with the wedding. So, he's agreed to give you all the four days *off*." She air-quoted the word. "Thursday through Sunday night."

Alexa blinked. "Seriously?"

"Wonderful," Dana murmured. Her gaze slid to Alexa's. She looked as delighted with their unexpected furlough as Alexa felt.

Neither one of them, though, said anything to Francesca, who was so clearly pleased with her success. The four days off meant Sophie and Meyer could go off for at least two nights following their wedding, which was probably the true root of Fitzgerald's unexpected lenience.

It did leave Alexa at a loss what to do on Thanksgiving Day, though. Go home to San Francisco even though her mom would be gone?

Maybe you could come with me to my grandma's. The memory of Jason's words suddenly slid into her head.

"What's *that* smile about?" Dana asked her.

Alexa jerked guiltily. "I don't know what you mean."

Fortunately, Sophie bustled back into the room wearing jeans and an oversized sweater. She picked up her champagne. "What'd I miss?"

Francesca told her and Sophie whooped. She threw her arms around her new stepmother and kissed her cheeks. "Bless you, bless you, bless you! Meyer was set to bribe Cutter for the use of his camper trailer." She snatched up her flute again. "He'd have agreed of course," she said with a laugh, "but he would have made Meyer pay dearly." She pointed her finger at Dana. "I don't know how you and Tyler manage being separated so much."

"This is the difference between being newlyweds and being married for eighteen years," Dana said dryly. She moistened her tongue with her champagne. Probably not up to her standards.

Which just made Alexa toss back the contents of her glass. Her own show of loyalty to Francesca, whose taste was every bit as excellent as Dana's.

Alexa couldn't help but be amazed at her sister's ability to turn her emotions on and off like a light switch. If Alexa didn't have several new additions to her wardrobe from that afternoon of shopping with Dana, she could have believed she'd imagined the entire thing.

"What was your wedding like, Dana?" Francesca idly toyed with her long dark hair. "You must have been very young when you married?"

"Twenty." Dana's lips twisted. "Alexa was only fifteen. Cutter, ten."

"Ever thought about that?" Alexa asked suddenly. "Pietro spent twenty years between all of our moms. One kid every five. Like he had a timer on it."

"Or an attention span that only lasted that long," Sophie suggested. "That's what Meyer said once. After your father split up with Cutter's mom, though, it was quite a while before he married Lotus." She sprawled on the couch, one leg propped on the other updrawn knee. "What *was* your wedding like?"

"Small," Dana said.

"Your mother wasn't there," Alexa recalled.

"She didn't approve , remember? We had Tyler's parents and my siblings. That was it."

Siblings who were near strangers, Alexa thought. She pointed her empty glass at Dana. "And your dress was *really* plain. I'd forgotten all about that."

"It was all we could afford." Dana's eyes were lost in memory, her faint smile weak around the edges. "I was never happier, though. We had such dreams together." She blinked once and leaned back in her chair, recrossing her ankles.

Alexa was glad her sister didn't seem inclined to mention Alexa's wedding to Dom. More specifically, the non-wedding, since they'd simply gone to a courthouse to do the deed. They'd had no guests. An official at the courthouse had served as a witness.

"Did you have a honeymoon?" Francesca asked.

"Camping, if you can believe it. Ty loved it. Me?" Dana shook her head. "Not so much," she said deadpan.

"Fitz and I are going to Belgium next year. Once all this business with your father's estate is finished."

Alexa frowned. "Why wait? It's not like Fitz has to be here or lose out on an inheritance."

"He made a commitment," Francesca said simply.

"Well, I'm just glad that my dad found you," Sophie said. "He so deserves to be happy."

"So do we all, my dear," Francesca said, lifting her glass slightly. "So do we all."

Chapter Twelve

"Who's Pietro Cardinale?"

Ruthie, who'd just dropped a stack of mail on his desk, looked surprised by West's question.

It was Monday afternoon and they were closed for the lunch hour. "You're joking, right?"

He flipped through the mail. "Do I look like I'm joking?"

She sighed noisily and tapped the computer monitor in front of him. "Google it, sweetie."

Another letter from Dunterwood. He wearily sliced open the envelope and extracted the single sheet. "I *know* he was a photographer. You've got that huge photograph of his hanging in the lobby. I meant who was he in connection to Cape Cardinale?"

"Nobody. He was just born here." She was eyeing him like he'd asked where cow's milk came from. "That's the only connection I know of. The town didn't get its name from his family. He took his name from the town."

"You're no help at all," he grumbled and looked down at the letter.

Then looked again. "Did you see this?"

"The Dunderhead envelope? Obviously."

He got up from his desk and dropped one arm around her shoulder, holding the letter in front of them both. "Read!"

She sighed mightily. "Because I so enjoy feeling beat by a club?"

When he just looked at her, she sighed yet again and adjusted her eyeglasses. She snatched the letter from his fingers. "'Due to a regretful oversight on our part, our foundation failed to renew its financial support—'" her voice lost the annoyed tone, quickening "'—of the fine services your medical clinic has been providing to the citizens of the Cape Cardinale region for more than four decades.'" She wrapped her bony fingers around his wrist; her vermillion nails digging. "'Please accept my apologies as well as the enclosed—'"

They both reached for the envelope. Ruthie beat him to it and slid out the thin blue bank check.

They stared at the number.

"That's a lot of zeroes," he finally murmured.

"More than usual," she agreed faintly.

She flipped the letter in the air and resumed reading again. "'As well as the enclosed grant, which I personally guarantee will be renewed annually for the next three years. At that time, we will review your then-present needs and make upward adjustments as necessary. Your acceptance of this payment constitutes agreement to the terms on the reverse of this letter.'" She flipped it over to look briefly at the backside. "'If you aren't able to meet these terms, please contact me directly at my personal number listed below.' Signed by the president and CEO, P.O. Nash."

Stunned, he grabbed the letter back from her. "*Nash*! As in Otto?"

She shooed him with her hands. "Let me sit."

He got out of the way and she sat in his desk chair, pulling his computer keyboard front and center. Her long nails clacked noisily on the keys. While she typed, he reread the letter then read through the terms, which were almost laughably simple.

"There're no stipulations on how we use the funds," he told her. "For all they know, we could use it to paint the building in fourteen-karat gold."

"Is that what you plan to do?" She stopped typing finally and angled the monitor so he could see it. "That's P.O. Nash." She tapped the screen where a white-haired woman wearing riding breeches and a monogrammed shirt sat atop a gleaming black horse. "Penelope Osgood Nash," Ruthie said. "Very old money. And definitely not Otto."

"Definitely not." Whether there was a connection or not was moot. The clinic had its grant—and then some—and that's what mattered. "Here." He pushed the check at Ruthie. "Get that thing in the bank."

"You don't have to tell me twice." She pushed back the chair. "I guess you got through to the dunderheads after all."

He sank down into his chair again. "You know, with that much extra funding, we can hire more staff."

"And he's already spending it," she said in a bright voice as she left his office.

He let his head fall back in relief.

You weren't really that worried, were you?

He looked toward the chair positioned in front of the lone window his office possessed.

Janine sat there. Tangible as anything, if he didn't count the fact that sunlight was passing right through her.

"What do you think?"

She was studying her manicure, legs crossed. *Well. You're welcome in any case.*

"You're responsible for this?" He flipped the letter on his desk.

It's as good an explanation as anything else, isn't it? She disappeared again.

He leaned back in his chair, propped one foot on his desk and rubbed his hands down his face. "I'm losing my freaking senses."

"There's probably a pill for that."

He sat bolt upright, knocking a stack of files onto the floor at the sight of Alexa standing in his doorway.

"Where'd you come from?"

"California, but I'm pretty sure that's not what you meant." She crouched next to his desk and reached for the scattered folders. "Your secretary let me in."

He'd reached for the folders, too, and their hands collided.

She went just as still as he did. Until he made the mistake of looking up from their fingers—damn near entwined—to her eyes.

"She was on her way out," she said faintly.

Her eyes were particularly blue in contrast to the unusually sedate black skinny turtleneck she was wearing. Her narrow pants, however, were a screaming hot-pink and her shoes were red, white and blue. Plaid.

"Who?" he asked stupidly.

Her pupils contracted and she moistened her lips. "Your um…your secretary." She suddenly pushed what she'd collected on the desk and straightened.

That ought to have been enough to break the spell.

It wasn't.

He cleared his throat and took his time gathering the rest of the files. "Don't let Ruthie hear you call her that. She strongly objects to the term." He finally dumped them on top of the others and sat in his chair again, willing his body under control.

"Sorry. Here." Alexa pulled a folded paper from her back pocket and prudently set it on his desk. "That's the tally of all the funds you raised for the playground equipment from the calls you made. I figured you deserved to see it."

He unfolded the sheet, smoothing out the creases against his desk. Imagining that the paper was warm from being tucked in her pocket against her curvy, compact rear.

Then his eyes focused on the numbers. "Forty-seven *thousand*?"

Her smile was nervous. As was the way she bobbed her head. And her eyes were skating over everything except him.

Probably knowing he was turned on as hell and wishing she was anywhere else.

"You must have been very convincing." She folded her arms. "Among the rest of us, we've only managed another three."

"Must be my day for money," he muttered. "Maybe I should buy a lottery ticket, too." He tormented himself a little more by refolding the tally sheet. It didn't really hold the shape of her butt, but his imagination was otherwise pretty convincing. "Does that mean you don't need to raise any more money for the playground equipment?"

"Hardly." She perched on the seat in front of the window but just as quickly rose again. Maybe feeling the residue of some unearthly presence.

The notion at least served as a shot of cold water. He watched her pace to the other side of his office.

"We're still proceeding with the Winter Faire plans," she said. "But it feels like there's a little less pressure now, thanks to you."

"Thank the people who donated." His gaze strayed to the chair. It remained thankfully empty. Then he realized. "Aren't you supposed to be in school? Tone's not back already?"

She shook her head. "The class has music and gym this afternoon. I also wanted to talk to you about Jason."

West froze. He knew it couldn't be that Jason had snuck

the puppy they'd adopted in his backpack or something. General Grant, as the Maltese mix had been named, was so far spending his days with Marjorie since they had yet to find a crate that he couldn't escape. "What about my son?"

"He's perfectly fine," she said quickly. "Exceptional as always, in fact. Which is the reason I'm here. I'd like to recommend him for the gifted program over at Edison."

He shook his head. "I've already told the school he's too young. I don't want him having that sort of stress. Not after the last few years. He's good in math, but—"

"Good is an understatement. I gave him a sixth-grade worksheet this morning. He flew through it." The topic of his son was apparently enough to wipe away everything else because she began squaring up the disorderly folders. "At the very least, he's ready for algebra." She tapped the ends of them on his desk then propped her hip right where they'd been sitting. She held the folders on her lap. "You recognized that he's not being challenged enough in his classwork. It showed in that progress report—"

He shook himself. "Now you're saying that load of bull was correct?"

"Not at all." She chewed the inside of her lip and slowly drummed her fingers on the manila stack. "I'm not sure any of us realized just how unchallenged he's been. I want what is best for Jason. He's advanced in more than just math. His reading skills, his language comprehension. Does it occur to you that *staying* where he is might be more stressful for him than finding a better fit?" She didn't wait for an answer. "What was his school situation before you moved here?"

"Private school. Very individualized."

"It would be similar in the gifted program. Individualized."

"I know what the testing process is like. He'll feel even

more out of place." The kids in public school who went in for gifted testing weren't always lauded.

"Have Jason assessed privately then. None of his classmates need even know about it unless Jason tells them. I have a psychologist friend in California who's done excellent work with children even younger than Jason. That sort of thing comes with a price tag, though. Which is why most parents have to work within the confines of the school system."

Confines. The word exactly fit the way his office was feeling. He pushed back from his desk and put it between them, though he didn't go so far as to sit in the chair that his wife's ghost had so recently occupied. "Money's not the issue," he said abruptly.

"One less hurdle then. There's no question he's gifted." Alexa's gaze followed him. "It's a matter of learning to what degree. There are more resources now than there've ever been for kids with his abilities. Online programs, residential—"

"Forget residential. Jason's with me. Period."

"Okay." She hesitated for a moment. "But does that mean you'll *consider* an assessment? You must know it's going to be necessary at some point."

"Some point when he's older. When he's more interested in quadratic equations than zombies."

"Don't knock those zombies. I ran one of his drawings through this program a friend of mine designed." She cradled the stack of folders against her breasts as she leaned toward him. Her mesmerizing eyes were not avoiding his now. And he felt pinned in place by them.

"They were mathematically beautiful," she said. "And he was just…doodling."

She was mathematically beautiful, he thought. Maybe that was what was so arresting about her. That whole golden-ratio thing. He looked from her wide eyes to her perfectly proportioned lips.

"Well? Haven't you noticed that?"

"No." He yanked his lab coat off its hook if only to break out of the spell that had him drifting right back down seductive mineshafts. "I have patients coming in soon." Soon being a relative term. "I'll walk you out."

"Here's your hat, what's your hurry?"

He grimaced. "Not at all."

She rolled her eyes and set aside the file folders, leaving them in a neat stack. She moved past him through the doorway. "Just agree to think about having Jason assessed, okay?"

"I'll think about it." He started to take her elbow and, realizing it, shoved his arm through the sleeve of his lab coat instead. Unfortunately, the sleeve was inside out, which made a mess of it.

"You're tangled." She tsked. "Here." She reached up and pulled down on the collar of the coat. "Dom used to do the same thing."

Her fingers had grazed the back of his neck, leaving it feeling scorched. "Dom?"

"My ex-husband. He was a doctor, too." With a deft shake, she presented the lab coat again. "In you go."

He didn't like being compared any more than he liked feeling dismissed. He took the coat from her and tossed it over the top of Ruthie's counter as they passed it on the way to the lobby. "Jase told me Meyer Cartell's your brother."

She gave a bemused blink. "Technically my half brother. So?"

"I know him from way back."

She shrugged. "It's a small world." She preceded him through the swinging door into the reception area. "Never more evident than right here in Cape Cardinale."

"After which you're named."

Her chin angled slightly. "Again. So?"

"What's the connection?"

"I figured you knew." She gestured at the wall, looking vaguely annoyed. "You've got *Pietro's Last* hanging right there. He was my father."

"You're *Pietro* Cardinale's daughter," he said. And he'd thought Janine had been born with the proverbial silver spoon.

"One of them. Don't look so stunned. He might have been an amazing photographer, but he sucked in the father-hood department."

"You and Meyer share the same mother?"

Alexa laughed humorlessly. "None of us have the same mother. Peter Cartell was Pietro's real name. Until he started to get famous and decided that was too ordinary. By then, Meyer was already born. Exit Mrs. Cartell and enter Pietro Cardinale and his endless stream of wives."

"Why are you worried about fundraising a couple thousand dollars if—"

"Let me stop you there." She turned her back on the framed print. "I live on what I make. The only thing *he* left us was the beach house. Which we have to live in together until next summer. *Then* we can sell it and *then* we can get back to our real lives."

"Your life being in California."

"Exactly."

"Must be a helluva beach house." He remembered she'd said she was near Cardinale Beach. But it was plainly obvious that she wasn't happy about her living situation.

Her jaw slid back and forth. "You have no idea." She reached out to open the entry door.

"Have dinner with me."

She went still.

He couldn't believe the words had come out of his mouth.

Finally, considering he'd been thinking about it for days. "You can tell me more about your psychologist friend," he improvised rapidly.

Her expression cleared. "Sandy. Sure. If dinner's what it takes. I know it feels like I'm rushing, West, but if everything is already in the works before Ernestine returns to school, she won't stop the process no matter how annoyed she is over my involvement. She's supposed to get out of the hospital any day now."

"She ought to be concerned with her students' success. Period."

"I agree with you completely. But anyway, the local gifted program is over at Edison. It's on the other side of town."

"I know where it is. *I* went there when I was a kid."

Her lips rounded slightly. "Oh, well. There you go then."

"Meanwhile, you're teaching the class, and Jason is suddenly re-enamored of you after you apparently did a standing high jump onto Mrs. Tone's desk?"

She unfolded her arms. Tugged at the hem of her clinging turtleneck and avoided looking at him. "Sometimes it's good to start out getting their attention." The only thing nonchalant about her was her tone.

"It would get mine."

Her lips twitched. She pushed her fingers through her wavy mop of hair. "I was just glad I didn't fall on my face," she admitted. She didn't seem to know what to do with her hands again and ended up sliding them into her back pockets. She rocked on her plaid shoes. "Anyway, unless Jason changes schools entirely, he's still going to have to deal with Mrs. Tone."

"And she's taken a dislike to him."

She opened her mouth as if she wanted to deny it. But couldn't. "I don't know why, either. Aidyn Savage is much more of a disruption in the class. Jason doesn't disrupt anything." She abruptly pulled out her hand and nudged the frame of her father's artwork. "But she doesn't like *me*, either. So maybe it's just the new kids on the block she objects to." Her gaze flicked over him. His imagination tried to tell him it lingered a moment longer than usual. "I... I better get back to the school. Thanks for seeing me."

"Did you give me a choice?"

Sudden laughter filled her eyes. "When do you, uh, want to talk more about Sandy?"

"I'll call you. I have to make sure my mother can watch Jason."

"Sure. Of course." She tugged her hem again. He was already aware of the way the thin knit clung to her lithe figure, following it like a lover's hand. The outline of her tight nipples was hard to miss. "Talk to you later then."

"Yeah." He pulled open the door himself. If she didn't leave now, he was going to do something really stupid.

She moistened her lips and gave him another half smile then hurried through the doorway. She practically skipped down the corridor before she pushed through the main entrance.

He closed the door and flipped the lock again.

Somebody looks ready to get back in the saddle.

He jerked. "Dammit, Janine!"

She was gone again in a wisp.

Alexa received the text message the next morning while she was waiting for the coffee to finish brewing.

Tonight or tomorrow? Both work.
I can pick you up at 7.

She exhaled carefully, turning her phone face down on the counter. There was no way to misinterpret *this* text message. She drummed her fingers. "It's just a meeting with a student's parent," she murmured. "That's all."

"What're you mumbling about over there?" Cutter sat on the other side of the breakfast counter, cradling his head. His hangover was obvious.

"Not mumbling." She took a little too much pleasure with the noise the metal cupboard made as she closed it and plunked her mug on the ugly avocado counter. "What's got you up so early when you were obviously out tying one on last night?"

"Have a call scheduled with a client in Paris." He propped his elbows on the counter and rubbed his bloodshot eyes. "And it's freaking cold in the camper. Can't run the heater. It overheats my server."

"Maybe you should rent an actual office for work stuff and leave the camper for actual living?"

"Don't yell."

"I didn't raise my voice at all," she said, dulcet. "You're even cheaper than I am."

"It's not cheap. It's expedience." He squinted at the coffeepot. "A pod machine is a lot faster."

"This is cheaper and friendlier to the landfill." She thumped another mug on the counter and grinned when made a sort of mewling sound of pain. "Serves you right for drinking too much."

"Like you've never done that?" He reached over and picked up her phone.

"Hey!" She slapped at his hand.

"Lookie, lookie. Someone's got a date?"

"It's not a date," she snapped. "And stop looking at my phone."

"I was just checking the time. You don't want people reading your personal business, stop disabling the screen saver on it."

"Entering a password every time I turn around is a pain in the butt."

"I've told you. Biometrics. No password necessary."

"So says the tech genius." The coffee gave a last spurting gurgle and she grabbed the pot, filled her mug first and then splashed some into his. "I've totally given up trying to get all that stuff to work. It's supposed to recognize my thumbprint? It doesn't. My face? Forget it." She dropped her phone in the pocket of her robe and turned out of the kitchen. She still needed to shower.

"Who's the guy, though?"

"Who says it's a guy?"

"You wouldn't be blushing if it weren't."

"I'm not blushing!" She stomped down the hall toward the bathroom only to find the door closed. The sound of the shower was plain, though. She knocked. "Dana, you better be quick in there!"

"Tell big brother who he is."

She looked at Cutter, who'd moved to the hallway but only to lean against the wall as if he were holding *it* up. "You're the baby around here, remember?"

"Baby or not, I think there's some vetting that's necessary."

"God." Meyer yanked open the door to his bedroom. His rusty hair stood straight up and his T-shirt and sweats were wrinkled. "Could you be any louder?"

"Share the pain," Alexa told him and went into her bedroom, slamming the door shut.

"Ow," Cutter complained. "Cruel, Lex. Just cruel."

She snorted, smiling despite herself. Both of her brothers were just big puppies.

She pulled out her phone.

"It's *not* a date," she said quietly.

So why did it feel as if it was?

She threw herself down on the bed and rested the phone against her chest.

Okay. Yes. She was attracted to West D'Angelo. More than a little. She wasn't dead, after all, and he seemed like he was similarly afflicted. At least for the moment. But he was Jason's *father*. Any more involvement than that was just not going to happen.

She could still hear the hiss of the shower through the wall, and she lifted her phone. Looked at the text message again. At the small clock in the upper corner of the screen.

"Dana," she growled. "Move it along, girl."

She moistened her lips. Centered her thumbs over the small keyboard on her screen. Debated.

Get it over quick? Or give herself another day to get her libido locked back in the deep freeze where it usually lived?

Quick, she decided and rapidly began typing.

Tonight. No need to pick me up, though.
I can meet you wherever.

Last thing she needed was Cutter offering more of his commentary if West actually came to the beach house. The shower stopped running and she started to put her phone aside, but she saw the dancing dots that meant West was responding. She was grateful only the contents of her messy wardrobe witnessed her breathlessly clutching the phone as she waited.

The Cliff. See you tonight.

The Cliff?
She threw herself down on the bed. She'd never been there but she still knew it was the fanciest place in town.

The continued silence from the bathroom sank in and she scrambled off the bed, darting out of her bedroom.

Just in time to see Meyer shutting the bathroom door.

She stomped her slipper on the floor. "Meyer!"

"Snooze you lose," Cutter reminded from the shadowy living room.

She retreated to Dana's bedroom and pounded on the door. "I actually *have* to work! You couldn't manage to wait an hour?" Then she grabbed her coat from her bedroom and shoved her arms through the sleeves.

Dana opened her bedroom door, looking at her with bewilderment. "Where are you going looking like that?"

"Up to Sophie's to use her spare shower!"

Clutching her keys, she stomped out of the house and slammed the door behind her.

She climbed into Betty and gunned the engine.

It promptly stalled out.

"Betty, Betty, Betty." She dropped her head onto the steering wheel. "What was I thinking? I could've just told him we'd need to meet at school. Nobody could mistake that for—"

The car door opened, startling her out of her wits.

Dana stood there. "Get inside, you nitwit."

"I told you! I have to shower."

Dana was only wrapped in her thick bathrobe. "Meyer's already out of the bathroom. He was only messing with you. *Well?*" she prompted, sounding perturbed when Alexa just continued sitting behind Betty's wheel. "Now what?"

"I think I might have a date tonight!"

"A *date!* With whom?"

"Someone I have no business dating, that's who! The father of one of my students." *My* students. How quickly she'd allowed herself to start thinking that way.

"Is it against the rules or something?"

"No, but—"

"For crying out loud, Alexa." Dana jiggled Betty's door. "What are you worrying about then? It's freezing. Come back inside."

She yanked her key from the ignition and got out. "He's a *doctor,*" she said through her teeth.

"As long as he's not Dom, who cares?" Dana turned toward the house.

Grumbling under her breath, Alexa followed Dana back inside. She went straight into the bathroom, pointedly ignoring both Cutter and Meyer who were standing on either side of the doorway.

They bowed deeply as she went inside. "Your majesty," they said in unison.

She slammed the door shut and flipped on the shower. The water didn't drown out the sound of their laughter at all.

Chapter Thirteen

"Excuse me. You're Mrs. Cardinale, aren't you?"

Alexa looked at the couple who'd stopped in front of her.

"We're Seth and Sarah," the woman said. "Aidyn's parents?"

"Oh. Right." Alexa stood and offered her hand. "Nice to meet you." She glanced around but saw no sign of Aidyn among those crowded around the hostess station of the busy restaurant. If the Cliff was this busy on a Tuesday evening, she couldn't imagine how busy it would be on a Friday or Saturday.

"Aidyn's with a sitter," Sarah said. She cuddled comfortably next to her husband. "We're out for our anniversary."

She smiled at them. "Congratulations."

"Thank you. I told Seth it was you. You were working morning drop-off the other day. Aidyn talks about you so much."

She couldn't quite hide her surprise. "Really?"

"Oh, yes. Even before Mrs. Tone got sick."

"He's a great kid. A natural leader."

"A polite term for bossy," Seth said dryly. "Any word on how Mrs. Tone is doing?"

"Improving. But we don't know quite when she'll be back. The class just finished making get-well cards for her."

"Party of two for Seth?" the young woman at the hostess desk called out.

"That's us," Sarah said. "Are you waiting for someone?"

Alexa nodded. "Enjoy your dinner. And happy anniversary."

The couple moved off with a smile and Alexa—who'd lost the little wedge on one of the bench seats in the lobby the second she'd stood up—returned to the little wedge of space near the front door that she'd already occupied for longer than she wanted to admit.

West was late.

She knew she shouldn't be surprised by that, yet she was.

She'd arrived exactly five minutes early.

Sixty-five minutes ago.

The door opened again and another person walked in, joining the party standing right in front of her, and she winced as one of them backed up and stood right on her foot.

The middle-aged woman turned with a profuse apology. "I'm so sorry. I didn't see you there."

"No worries," Alexa assured her. She wouldn't feel her big toe for a few days, but since her feet were already aching from standing around in the beautiful boots that Dana had talked her into purchasing, maybe that was a blessing.

She pulled out her phone again. Checked the time. Checked for a message from West. Anything. A missed call even.

But there was nothing and she dropped it back into the pocket of the trench coat she'd borrowed from Sophie. She yanked the belt together over the knitted column dress that could have been a reject from Dana's wardrobe if it had been any shade of ivory rather than pumpkin-orange and wound her way back to the hostess's station and waited until the girl returned from seating the Savages.

When she did, she gave Alexa a saccharine smile. "I'm

sorry. As I've said, I can't seat you until your entire party is here."

"Thank you," Alexa said equally sweetly. She peered over the top of the desk at the wildly messy reservation list. "What I came up to tell *you* was to cross D'Angelo off your list. I won't be waiting any longer."

The hostess raised her eyebrows slightly. "If I do, you won't be able to get added later when you change your mind."

When? Alexa nearly snorted. "I won't be changing my mind," she countered. "But if you want to leave the name and Dr. D'Angelo ever does shows up, be sure to tell him that you can't seat him until his entire party is here."

She turned on her heel and wound through the crowd yet again. It was too close inside the restaurant, which only added another layer of discomfort on top of her aggravation.

She didn't know whether to be glad or not that she'd insisted on meeting West at the restaurant. If she'd agreed to him picking her up, she would have had Dana and the boys as witnesses to her being stood up.

On the other hand, she wouldn't have stood around for an hour in the most uncomfortable boots ever created.

She was practically limping by the time she reached Betty where she'd had to park on the winding road that led up to the restaurant. It was called the Cliff for a reason. Namely that it was perched on one, with a stunning view of the ocean. But it also had a parking lot the size of a postage stamp and the owner had apparently never heard of something called valet parking.

Which meant at least half of the patrons ended up parking on the road.

The food had to be as spectacular as the setting to be as busy as it was, but Alexa knew she'd be happy to never set foot there again.

Assuming her feet ever worked again.

She collapsed in the driver's seat and peeled her feet pain-fully out of the boots before throwing them in the back seat. She should've known better than to follow Dana's fashion advice. Alexa far preferred having blood circulate through her feet over the stylish boots, even if they *had* been on the clearance rack and made her feel tall and stylish and sexy.

When she finally made it home, she parked alongside Dana's SUV beneath the metal carport and went inside. She tossed the borrowed coat on her bed and went straight to the kitchen where she yanked open the cupboard and pulled out the family-sized jar of peanut butter that they'd all agreed was nearly as important as their supply of coffee.

She further armed herself with a butter knife, a sleeve of saltine crackers and a cold can of diet cola and flopped down in the corner of the sectional couch. She dragged the heavenly throw over her legs and opened the peanut butter.

"Food at the Cliff not to your liking?" Dana, who'd been watching from a side chair, set aside her book.

"I'll never know." Alexa didn't bother with crackers for the first blob of peanut butter. She just licked it off the knife before plunging it right back into the jar.

"Double-dipping," Dana said.

"Too bad." Alexa withdrew another helping of peanut butter and sucked it off the knife. "I'll buy everyone jars untainted by my cooties." Her tongue was starting to stick to the roof of her mouth, though, and she popped open her soda, taking a long drink. "And don't," she said as soon as she'd swallowed, "offer some snark about using a glass."

Dana lifted her palm. "Snark-free zone."

Alexa managed to squelch the automatic "That'd be a first" comment. She knew she was usually the guilty party when it came to snarkiness. She dipped her knife a third time, but this round spread the peanut butter on a cracker.

Dana got up and went into the kitchen. She returned with

the roll of paper towels. "Maybe don't get cracker crumbs everywhere," she suggested. "Ants, remember?"

Alexa rolled off a few sheets and draped them over her lap. She doctored four crackers, lined them up neatly on the napkin, and screwed the lid back on the jar.

"Want to talk about it?"

"Not particularly." She licked the knife clean again, chased it with soda, then reached for the first of her PB saltines. It wasn't caviar on toast points, but then, caviar had been Dom's thing. She fitted the entire cracker in her mouth and ate it. After another chaser unglued her tongue once again, she tore off another paper towel, wiped her mouth with it and then pointed it at Dana. "Never expect people to change their stripes."

Dana set aside her book again. "Meaning?"

"Meaning just that." Alexa picked up her second cracker, admiring it for a moment. "What happened to all those peanut butter cups that I put in the glass jar?"

"Not what. Who."

"Cutter." She shook her head. A little peanut butter cup on top of her PB saltine would have been just the thing. "He hoovers up everything."

"Whose stripes aren't changing?"

"Men 's. They're all the same."

"As much the same as women are," Dana agreed. "Which is to say not at all."

"Only a few weeks ago you were crying in your soup about Ty."

"I wasn't crying—" a hint of defensiveness colored Dana's tone "—and we're not talking about Tyler."

"We're not talking about West, either. Even if he is just like Dom."

"Ah." Dana's expression cleared. "Now I see. I must be getting slow in my old age."

"Give me a break." Alexa scarfed down her third cracker. She would need another drink before long. She'd nearly emptied her can of soda, such was the mortaring power of her saltine delicacies. "You look younger than Cutter and he's still a growing boy."

"He's twenty-eight and I wouldn't let him hear that."

"I'm not afraid of Cutter."

"You're not afraid of anything."

"That's because I know the only one I can count on is *me*."

Dana set aside her book yet again but with an air of finality this time. She rested her arms on the knees of her posh-looking corduroys as she leaned forward. "I might envy your self-confidence, but just because West D'Angelo is a physician, doesn't mean he's like your ex-husband." Her tone was annoyingly reasonable. "Sharing a profession isn't the same thing as sharing the same character. Or, in Dom's case, lack of it. I don't have to have met him to know that. Are you really going to let *him* rule the way you see life? There are people you can count on, Alexa. You're living with three of them."

"Save the lecture." Alexa crunched her way through her fourth cracker and drained the rest of her soda. She pushed off the sofa. "And the pity, too."

"Who said anything about pity?"

"Please." She lobbed her soda can into the recycle bin as she passed the kitchen on her way to her bedroom. "That's the only reason you'd claim to envy me." She looked down the hall at her sister. "About anything." She closed herself in the bedroom.

From her position in the tiny living room, Dana sighed. Even after six months under the same roof, they hardly knew each other at all.

Then she looked down at the rings on her fingers and sighed even more.

* * *

"Here." Alexa thrust the trench coat into Sophie's hands as soon as she answered her door the next afternoon. "Thanks for the loan."

"Anytime. Want to come in? I'm working on the gift bags we're giving out at the reception."

"I can come back another time and help, if you want to wait. Right now, I need to go back to the Cliff." And she hoped to high heaven that the same hostess as the evening before wouldn't be on duty again. "I think I might have forgotten my cell phone there. I haven't been able to find it all day."

Sophie followed her down her porch stairs. "Had that good a time, with West, eh?"

"Hardly." She looked over Betty's roof at Sophie. "He didn't show."

"No!" Sophie frowned. "Seriously?"

"It's not something I'd joke about. Anyway, I want to stop there before I head out to the airfield. I told Olivia I would lead her class tonight," she added at the blank look Sophie gave her. "It'll take me at least an hour to get the heaters going."

"Oh, right. She's gone to Portland." Sophie threaded her fingers through her hair and held it back from her face. "I swear. I can't seem to remember anything right now."

"You do have a wedding in three days," Alexa said dryly.

"And tomorrow's Thanksgiving. I'm still so surprised my dad decided to forgo the whole traditional feast." Sophie lifted her shoulders. "I guess even he's feeling overwhelmed with the wedding." She suddenly pointed her finger at Alexa. "We should plan—"

"No." Alexa cut her off quickly. "Don't even start. You have enough on your plate with the wedding."

But Sophie wasn't listening. "We just need a place big enough to hold us all. We can potluck it. Order pizza."

"Okay. Whatever. But ask someone else to handle the details so Meyer doesn't have a nervous breakdown." She slid down behind the wheel and drove off, Sophie waving at her in the rearview mirror.

It was still too early for the restaurant to open to the public, but there were cars in the lot already and Alexa went around to the service entrance and talked her way inside. But her success ended there. Nobody had turned in an old cell phone.

She couldn't imagine someone wanting the thing. In the world of tech, it was positively ancient, but after hunting all day for the thing, she was really wishing that she'd listened to Cutter about keeping it protected with a password. Going back to the Cliff had been her last resort.

She drove out to the airfield, unlocked the hangar with the keys Olivia had given her and started setting up. With the heaters fired up, she changed into her yoga shorts and sports bra, over which she pulled a long sweater. She'd subbed for Olivia a few times in the last six months, but it was by no means normal for her to lead the class and now she couldn't even use the playlist that she'd made on her phone for music. Which meant she had to settle for a classical radio station played on the ancient boombox.

She rolled out her mat and worked through several poses on her own, and when the door opened several minutes later to her first participants, she wasn't sure if she was relieved or not. Nevertheless, at least she knew most of them and was glad she was able to greet them by name. People could be particular about who led their classes and though she'd been practicing yoga since she'd been eighteen, she didn't pretend to be on par with Olivia Hartwell.

When West D'Angelo walked in the door, though, all of that went right out the window.

Then he noticed her and smiled as if nothing at all was

wrong, and she felt her own expression freeze. Who needed more proof that what had felt like a date to her had just been an easily forgotten meeting with the temporary teacher?

She walked over to the boom box and nudged the volume up a little. Let the music mask the frog that was suddenly jumping around in her throat.

Focusing on the people directly in front of her, she thanked everyone for coming, reminded them that she was merely one of them, and assured them that Olivia would be back for the next class. "So don't judge me too harshly and let's get started." She spread her arms out. "And a deep breath in…"

Standing on his mat in the rear row, West once again wondered what he was doing there. The temperature felt hotter than it had been last time. Although maybe the heaters weren't any hotter.

It was just him.

Alexa's yoga gear was no more nor less revealing than Olivia's had been the previous week. But Alexa's fluorescent-pink grabbed his attention in an entirely new way. Concentrating on anything other than that was damn near impossible.

She knew it, too. He was telegraphing it to her across the heat waves or something. Because she wouldn't even look his way. Nor did she walk around during the interminable forty-five minutes the way that Olivia did. The rise and fall of music—Bach to Puccini—was a far cry from Olivia's somnolent gongs and flutes and nature sounds, too.

Judging by the way the people around him jumped in the middle of the corpse pose when the soprano hit her zenith, he wasn't the only one who thought so.

When the class ended, even more people hung around to talk with her. Several others helped with the heaters. And even though he did the same, Alexa continued to avoid looking his way.

Finally, though, the heaters were stored and the temperature in the hangar had dropped dramatically. Alexa had pulled on a thick oatmeal-colored sweater that reached her knees and, with the long strap of her bag slung across her body, she waited at the door, jangling a set of keys while the last few hangers-on—he among them—walked past her.

"Happy Thanksgiving, Alexa."

"Great class, Alexa."

"See you next week at school, Alexa."

When he passed her, she turned aside and flipped off the lights before pulling the door and using the keys.

It was plain that she was taking her time about it. Plainer still that he was the reason. But, finally, she couldn't pretend anymore and she turned to face him.

Her lips were thinned. "*What*?"

She's too much trouble, Janine whispered.

"It wasn't like I had a choice," he told Alexa.

Her eyebrows rose slightly. "Not showing up for our meeting, you mean?"

Meeting? Yeah, discussing Jason was part of it. But only a part. Regardless, the unfortunate events the night before would still have played out the same. "I called as soon as I had a chance."

She lifted her hand and took a wide path around him. "Whatever."

Only two vehicles were parked in the lot. Theirs.

Way too much trouble, Janine insisted.

He followed Alexa. "That's it? *Whatever* and walk away?"

"What do you want me to say?" She pulled open her car door and pitched her bag inside. "Thank you?" She followed the bag and slid into the car. "I waited at the restaurant for more than an hour."

But he stopped her from yanking the door closed by grabbing the doorframe. "Emergencies happen, Alexa."

"Particularly for doctors." She tugged on her door. "I get it. Been there. Done that, though. You could have at least sent a message."

He frowned. "I did. I even called the restaurant directly. I had a patient—"

She lifted her hand. "I don't need explanations, West."

He wasn't sure what had the upper hand. Bewilderment or insult. "Or want any, apparently."

"It's fine. The only reason we were meeting was for Jason's benefit. When you have *time,* let me know."

Insult. "Don't question my priorities, Alexa," he said flatly. "If you don't recognize them by now—"

"I recognize a lot," she said and yanked on the door.

This time he let it go.

The door slammed shut between them.

He turned and strode to his own car. Lifelong instincts didn't just get up and walk away, though. She hadn't left the parking lot yet. So, he sat there, engine humming, and let his emotions clang around inside his head if for no other reason than they drowned out his wife's ghostly commentary.

Finally, Alexa's headlights came on and she buzzed past him, her face nothing but a pale blur through the windshield.

He followed at a healthy distance until they reached the end of the road that looped around the airfield.

And when she turned one way, he turned the other.

Chapter Fourteen

The first thing Alexa did when she got home was head straight to the shower. Nobody got in her way this time, because nobody was there.

She dropped her bag on the floor of the bathroom, shucked her clothes and stepped directly under the stinging spray. To wash off the sweat. Certainly not to hide any tears that hadn't been threatening her the entire way home.

She stood there long enough for the cold water to get hot and then get cold all over again. She dragged the tangles out of her dripping wet hair, brushed her teeth and wrapped herself in a towel before bundling her belongings together and returning to her bedroom.

There, sitting right on top of the puffy white duvet, was her cell phone.

She dropped the ball of clothes on the floor and approached the bed as if the cell phone might be a snake. Set to strike.

But it merely lay there. Perfectly familiar in its sparkly pink case.

She finally snatched it up and the screen blinked to life. "Where did you come from?"

The phone provided no answer.

It did, however, indicate exactly how many calls she'd missed. And how many new messages were waiting.

Four were from West. All had arrived after she'd left the restaurant.

She chewed the inside of her cheek. Okay. He hadn't exaggerated about trying to call. If she hadn't misplaced her phone, she would have heard them.

But now what? Listen to them? Ignore them?

The fact was, she had no business indulging romantic thoughts about West D'Angelo and she knew it. Her overreaction to being stood up proved it.

A knock came on her bedroom door and she nearly jumped out of her skin. Clutching her towel, she cracked it open.

Meyer stood in the hall. "Get the phone?"

She held it up. "*You* found it? Where was it?"

"Sophie found it. In the pocket of the raincoat you borrowed."

The realization sank like lead. "It was a trench coat," she said, cringing because it was the kind of detail that Dana would have corrected, too. "I can't believe I didn't check the pockets." But of course, now that she knew, she remembered sliding her phone in the pocket as she'd left the restaurant the night before. Could remember, also, tossing the coat aside when she'd gotten home. Too upset over finding herself reliving the same kind of situation she'd experienced time and time again with Dom.

"At least you've got it back now. And by the way, thanks for telling Sophie we all needed to do something special for tomorrow."

"I didn't tell her that!"

"Now I've got to drag tables and chairs out here from the airport tomorrow morning because she's decided a Thanksgiving meal on the beach seems like a perfect idea."

Alexa couldn't help laughing. "We'll freeze."

"Not with a bonfire." He held up his hand. "You have

issues with it, take it up with her." He started to turn away but glanced back. "And you really should put a password on that phone, kiddo."

"I know, I know." She lightly tapped the corner of the phone against her forehead. "I'll get on that. And thanks, by the way. I was beginning to think a ghost had returned it to me."

His teeth flashed. "No ghosts here. G'night."

"G'night," she echoed and closed the door again.

No ghosts?

Dom was alive and well. Living his best life, no doubt, with his latest "Tiffany." Yet Alexa was still letting the relationship haunt her.

She exchanged her damp towel for her robe and, with no small sense of irony, slid her phone into the side pocket of the robe.

Then she fixed a coffee doctored liberally with cream and settled in the side chair that her sister usually occupied and fiddled with her phone settings until she had a password on the thing.

She knew what she was really doing.

Stalling.

Finally, coffee half gone, she dialed into her voicemail. First was her mother who had called the previous afternoon to tell her that she'd arrived safely in Whistler and Sergio was just *so wonderful*. Much more used to long, meandering messages from Nadine, this one was brief in the extreme and, all too quickly, West's voice came on.

"Alexa, it's West. I'm sorry I couldn't catch you earlier. Patient emergency. We'll talk later when I have more time."

The urgency in his voice sounded genuine. But then, that was how Dom used to sound, too. At least in the early days. When emergencies were more likely to be real and not an excuse.

She ended the playback and stared out the window. She hadn't realized it had begun raining. It was falling so softly she couldn't even hear it, but the glimmer was plain on the unfinished deck and lightning was flickering in the distance. It had better end soon, or Sophie's beachy Thanksgiving idea would be a soggy one.

Alexa pinched her eyes closed, wishing there was a magic pill that could take away the emotions clogging inside her. Knowing that Dana was right—that Alexa's experience with Dom was coloring her perception of everything—didn't make it any easier to change. She wasn't even sure she *wanted* to change. The lessons she'd learned had been hard ones.

Alexa was still Alexa. There was no remedy for that. Whether or not West was like Dom. Whether or not he was the most honorable man on the planet. Who she was had been forged into her a long, long time ago.

She balanced the phone on the window ledge next to the collection of small shells that Dana had arranged there and restlessly crossed the room. Stopping in front of *Pietro's Last*.

"None of us were ever enough for you," she murmured. "Not just me. It was all of us. Your kids. Your wives." She studied the galaxy of stars that merged with the ocean, the line of horizon between the two impossible to determine. "Even when you thought you might have found it, you realized you hadn't. Why did you need the rest of the world so badly, Dad?"

"Maybe he believed the rest of the world was the only thing he could do well."

Startled, she spun on Cutter, who was sitting on one of the barstools at the dinky breakfast counter. "How long have you been there?"

He had a bottle of water in his hand and he gestured with

it toward the wall where the print hung. "Long enough to catch you mooning over things you can't change."

"I'm not mooning," she muttered. "And shouldn't you be out on a date or working on some techie problem halfway around the world?"

"Date was a dud, and the latest techie problem has already been solved." He waggled his oversized phone and set it back down on the counter.

"I'm sure whoever she is would love being referred to as a dud."

"Don't get pissy. *She's* the one who left early. She's probably saying the same about me." He twisted open his bottle and took a drink.

She went into the kitchen. The caffeine was already buzzing in her system, but she refilled her coffee cup anyway. "Why doesn't that bother you? You've dated half the available population in the last six months and it never leads to anything."

"That's a matter of opinion," he said dryly.

She rolled her eyes. "I'm not talking about sex."

He took another drink of water. "I'd be a lot more bothered if it *did* lead to something."

"Why?" She eyed him over her coffee cup. "Because it puts a crimp in your bachelor sensibilities?"

"Because I know what *I* can do well," he said. No sign of his usual flippancy in evidence. "And the stuff that lasts between people is not one of them."

She lowered her cup. "He screwed us all up."

"Speak for yourself, Lex. I'm perfectly content knowing who I am."

"Implying that I'm not?"

"You're the one mooning around alone in the dark."

"I'd be alone if you'd stop sneaking up on people."

His smile flashed briefly before he chugged down the

rest of his water. Then he tossed the empty bottle unerringly into the recycle box. "I'm hitting the hay. Don't moon too long. Not good for what ails you."

"Nothing is ailing me."

He swung his leg off the barstool. "Right." He reached out a long arm and knuckled her lightly on the top of her head. "Keep telling yourself that."

She huffed and shoved his hand away. "You're the kid brother, remember?"

He just smiled and went out the front door, letting in a burst of cold wind and the sound of waves.

She went over to the door and pressed her hand against it even after he'd closed it.

Then she picked up her phone and closed herself in her own bedroom.

She perched on the side of the bed and dialed her voicemail again. It picked up right where she'd left off.

"It's West." His deep voice was clearer than on his first message. And prepared or not, she still felt a frisson dance down her spine.

"My patient is still in surgery. I promised the family I'd wait until they can get here. Don't suppose you want to drive to Corvallis and give me a ride back once they do? That medevac was a one-way trip." He said it with a wry half laugh that was appallingly appealing. "Kidding. Send a text or something so I know you're still talking to me. I should have called you earlier in the first place, but time got away from me."

The third message came that morning. Just after midnight.

"It's me. Still in Corvallis. Jason's been with my mother all night. Be prepared for extra zombieness when he gets to school."

She chewed the inside of her cheek. Jason *had* been particularly prolific with his doodles that day. Most of them now contained some version of General Grant, the puppy that he'd gotten the previous weekend.

She exhaled and listened to the last message, which had come in shortly before noon.

"I'm home."

That was it.

Sad that she listened to it at least a dozen times.

Then she sent a text message.

Can we meet?

She chewed her cheek some more while she waited. Watched the three little dots dance. After what felt an interminable wait, a response came.

Jason's in bed.

Her shoulders sagged. Naturally. Why would he want to see her now?

But then her phone vibrated with another text.

You'll have to come here.

She didn't bother with a response. Mostly because her hands were suddenly shaking way too much.

She threw on jeans and a thick sweater. No fussing about for an hour with her hair or dithering over her clothing to find something that struck the right tone for the date-that-might-just-be-a-meeting.

She scrawled a note and left it on the kitchen counter saying where she'd gone and quietly went out the back door, pulling on her shiny yellow raincoat along the way. She got inside Betty and they began their way up the hairpins while lightning strobed in the clouds above.

Finding her way to West's home was a lot easier the second time around than it had been the first, aided in no small part by the blazing lights that lined the front walk.

The rain was coming down harder than ever as she parked at the curb. She fumbled around for the umbrella even though her hair was still damp from her shower and then she made herself stop because all she was doing was procrastinating.

She pocketed her phone and keys, flipped up the hood of her raincoat and dashed up the bricks between the fussy posts toward the front door.

It opened before she reached the porch and a lump the size of Texas grew inside her chest. Her feet dragged to a halt at the base of the wide, shallow steps.

Raindrops pinged off her hood. Bounced off her raincoat. Water ran in rivulets around her tennis shoes. She was oblivious to it all, focused on West, standing in the doorway.

The highway of lights behind her did nothing to illuminate his expression. "You just going to stand there all night in the rain?"

She lifted her hands. "I lost my phone. Last night I mean. I'm sorry. I hadn't gotten any of your messages and I jumped to conclusions and… I'm sorry."

He didn't say anything to that, and she curled her fingers. Lowering her hands again. Her foot started to move backward. Away from that first step. She glanced up. The curtains in the Juliet balcony window fluttered. Maybe the window was open. Maybe Jason wasn't exactly in bed.

She moistened her lips and looked back at West. She took a step closer. Peering through the light to his shadowy face. "How is your patient?"

He shifted slightly. "Recovering."

The toe of her gold tennis shoe nudged the first riser. The deep overhang of the porch protected the steps from the rainfall. If she went up just one of them, she'd be protected, too.

"My ex-husband cheated on me," she said baldly. Even though she hadn't intended to say any such thing. "A lot. Right under my nose. He'd claim he was with patients when he wasn't."

"You want my patient's name?"

"Of course not!" But did she? Was she really wanting more proof? More reason to trust what West said? "No," she said more calmly. More certainly. "It's none of my business."

"No. It isn't." He waited a beat. "My wife cheated on me. For a long time. Right under my nose." His sigh was audible. "I don't want Jason ever knowing."

She balled her hands together. Pressed them against the ache in her belly. "Is there anyone who believes in faithfulness? Is it just a fantasy?"

"I believe. Come out of the rain, Alexa."

"I think I'm getting too used to being in it."

He stepped forward. She realized he was barefoot. Wearing jeans that looked just as worn out as hers and a sweater that was just as misshapen. He came down three of the six steps and extended his hand. Palm up.

She realized she was crying again. She'd done more of it in the last six months than she had in the last six years. "I don't want to fall in love." At any other time, in any other realm, she'd never say such a thing. "Not with anyone."

But his hand didn't move. He didn't laugh. Didn't so much as crack a smile. "Then we're agreed."

She went up the first step. Settled her palm on his.

His fingers curved around hers and his thumb brushed over the back of her hand. Warm. Slow.

"I can't stay."

"I know. You're going back to California."

"I mean tonight." She felt flushed all the way through and all he'd done was hold her hand. "Crazy as it sounds, I kind of have a curfew."

"I'm sure that'll be a very interesting story." He tugged her up the second step. "Jason's here, anyway."

"Right. Wouldn't want to give him the wrong idea."

"He's got plenty of them." He joined her on the third step. Halfway up. Halfway down. "You don't know the half of it."

"Maybe we should just stop here then."

"Maybe so." He took her other hand, too. Lifted them. Brushed his thumbs over her knuckles, lowered his head and kissed one hand.

Her stomach swooped. "West."

"Yeah?" He kissed the other hand.

"Nothing," she whispered.

He tightened his grasp on hers and pulled her closer. He lowered his head until his mouth hovered a breath above hers. "Alexa."

She was dizzy with anticipation. "Yes?"

"Nothing," he murmured and pressed his lips to hers.

It was like being struck by lightning. Less fatally, certainly. But the electricity that bolted through her was surely enough to leave her hair smoking. It definitely left her knees feeling like mush and her heart feeling like it might explode.

She realized that he was swearing and dragging her right up the steps. All the way to the front door. "Are you okay?" His hands weren't holding hers at all. They were sweeping down the back of her, smacking her through the raincoat.

"For a first kiss that was a doozy." She was pretty sure she was actually swooning when he took her shoulders and spun her around to face the runway lights that had all gone dark.

Except for the two closest to the house.

One was spitting out flames at least six feet high. The

other shot sparks that skittered on the ground with the fervor of water on a hot skillet.

The smell was acrid, and the rain was only exacerbating all of it.

"Oh," she said faintly. "Lightning *did* strike."

"Electrical short," he said tersely. "I think what hit you were the sparks. They were bouncing off the entire porch for a second there. Can you walk?"

"Of course I can walk." She took a step to prove it, and her knee buckled. From exactly which impact—West or the electricity—she wasn't sure.

"That's it. I'm calling 9-1-1." He swept her off her feet and carried her inside the foyer where it would have been dark if not for the light show only yards away. Even though he tried the light, it didn't come on. "Electricity's definitely out. Probably a good thing." He deposited her on one of the chairs near the staircase but kept his hand on her shoulder as if afraid she might slither off. "I need to get my phone."

"Here." With only some fumbling, she pulled her cell phone out of her raincoat pocket and held it up for him. "There's no— Oh wait. The passcode's—"

"Doesn't matter." He cut her off. "Think your phone's fried." He showed her the screen that was a firework in its own right, colors streaming in rows up and down what should have been a black, blank screen.

A small blessing. He need never know the new passcode she'd come up with was 1HotdocD.

She leaned forward, clasping her head in her hands. She could hardly think straight. "I'm fine," she lied. "Just go find a phone before that fire spreads and burns down your house."

"I'm not worried about the house." But he went. And even before he returned, she could hear sirens.

Then he was back. Crouched in front of her, rubbing her hands. "Are you cold?"

Her teeth were chattering a little. "N-not really." She realized somewhat dimly that he had a brown doctor's bag with him. "I used to have a purse that looked like that," she said. "I never really loved a purse before—that's Dana's thing—but I loved that one."

"You're really helping my sense of masculinity here." He flipped open the wide buckle, delved inside and came out with a pen light that he shined in her eyes. "How's your head feel? Any ringing? Tingling?"

"Just a, uh, a little woozy." Not helped at all by the way his long, warm fingers were exploring every inch of her head and neck.

He was very…thorough.

And evidently, she wasn't so far gone that she couldn't help imagining that thoroughness put to other much more pleasurable pursuits.

"Woozy how? Dizzy? Nauseated?" His hands left her neck, but only to get busy with the zippers on her raincoat. It was so maddening that she very nearly clasped his hands just to press them against her aching breasts.

But then he'd succeeded with the zippers and tossed the coat aside. In the red-and-white light that had begun strobing the interior, she saw the holes in the jacket where the rubbery yellow had melted away, leaving the white lining looking singed.

"Alexa?"

She was barely aware of what he was pulling next out of his doctor purse. "Dizzy," she answered belatedly. Though she could certainly claim a sick stomach at the sight of her raincoat. "What the heck happened?"

"Shh." She realized his hand was under her sweater. He was wielding his stethoscope.

Unfortunately, her heart just raced even harder from the feel of his knuckles against her bare skin and goose bumps prickled all along her nerve endings. She hadn't bothered with a bra and her barely B-cups were suddenly feeling way more sensitive than usual. Her nipples were so hard that just the feel of her sweater against them was painful.

What they needed—wanted—was the stroke of his finger.

But his hand slid away. Not even a facsimile of a fondle. He draped the stethoscope around his neck. "Hold on to me."

"Why?"

He didn't wait to answer. Simply lifted her right off the chair and carried her through the house, finally depositing her on a long couch in the family room.

She hadn't seen the room when she'd been there the first time.

Not that she could see much now what with the electricity out. But there was a real fire in the fireplace, and she sighed a little at the sight. "A fire. I've fantasized a little about your fireplace."

He made a sort of choked sound. "Put your head back down, sweetheart." He nudged her back in place and then tucked something under her feet, raising them up. A second later, she felt a blanket covering her. It wasn't quite a heavenly blanket like Dana's, but it was darn close.

"Dad?"

"Everything's okay, Jase. Just an electrical issue."

"Mrs. Cardinale!" Looking frantic, he let go of the puny brown-and-white puppy he was holding and rushed over to her. The puppy came, too, scrabbling his way up onto the couch with single-minded determination.

General Grant. Okay. Made some sense now.

She worked her hand out from beneath the blanket, wanting to soothe both of them. "I'm fine, Jason."

He grabbed her hand and sank down on the floor beside the couch. His face was pale and his eyes were the size of saucers. "There are two firetrucks outside. Are we burning down?"

"Nothing's burning down," West said calmly. He removed General Grant's teeth from the arm of the couch and set him on the floor again. "I want you to sit here quietly with Alexa for a minute while I go out and check on things. Make sure she stays covered up." Then he pointed at the dog. "Stay."

Neither dog nor boy listened. "How come you're here?" Jason's questions practically tumbled over each other. "Are you sick? Did you get hurt? Is that why the firetrucks came?"

She cupped his cheek. "I'm fine, Jason. I just came to see your dad and, uh…um—"

"She was standing too close when something went wrong with one of the lights outside," West said. He moved the puppy again, away from his attempted ascent up the side of the couch. But this time he kept hold of him. "She's had a bit of a shock. But we'll take care of that."

"Is she gonna go to the hospital?"

"What?" Alexa sat bolt upright. "No!"

"I don't think that'll be necessary." West nudged her back down. "But I want a few tests all the same, which we can do at the clinic. Jason? You good? I'll only be a minute or two."

"I'm good." Expression set, Jason wedged his butt next to her on the couch. He pulled the blanket right up to her chin and patted it in place with all of the care and precision that he applied to everything he did. "We're going to take care of you, Mrs. Cardinale."

God help her. How was she supposed to withstand this?

"I know you will, Jason." She closed her eyes, because it seemed a little more likely that she could stem another wave of tears that way.

She realized the sirens had been silent for a while now. "So, you ready for your grandma's turkey tomorrow?"

"I don't think she's gonna cook it, 'cause she said she didn't take it outta the freezer in time."

Despite the cocoon he'd made of the blanket, she managed to work out one arm, and she pinched the bridge of her nose for a moment. "Maybe you all can come to my Thanksgiving then," she said huskily. "We're apparently having a potluck on the beach."

"How encompassing is that *you all*?"

West was back. Even quicker than he'd said.

She was glad the lights were still off. It made looking up at him a little easier. "Sorry?"

"There are three of us."

"Aren't you gonna work, Dad?"

"Not unless there's an emergency of some sort."

"Cool!"

"But—" he handed off the puppy to Jason and moved aside as two young men came in, rolling a stretcher "—I don't think Mrs. Cardinale's plans of a beach day are likely to work out. It's supposed to rain until Friday."

"Of course." Alexa was feeling more wary of the ambulance stretcher than the rain. "Because it always rains in Cape Cardinale just when you don't want it to."

"Mother Nature is a contrary soul."

"As long as she gets her act together before my brother's wedding." She pointed at the stretcher. "I don't need that nonsense."

"Let's err on the side of caution," West said smoothly.

"But—"

"No buts." Smoothly, but unyielding.

"All right, ma'am…" The first ambulance kid who was probably ten years old smiled at her. "We're just going to slide you over, nice and easy."

"Ma'am." She pushed at his hands. "Why does that cause me physical pain to hear? I can move myself, thank you." She proved it by swinging her legs off the couch and standing.

And very nearly fell on her face when the room spun and tilted.

West beat the young ambulance attendants and lifted her off her feet himself. "You are a stubborn one, aren't you?" He settled her gently on the stretcher.

"Damn straight," she muttered.

"Mrs. Cardinale swore, Dad."

"I heard her, Jase." He was tucking in the almost-heavenly blanket around her. Just as thoroughly as his son had done, though his fingers lingered a little longer than was strictly necessary.

"Maybe she needs a swear jar like you used to have," Jason said.

Her head was still swimming as they began rolling her out of the house and she decided maybe it was better all around if she didn't argue too much about the stretcher. "You didn't have a swear jar," she said to West.

"I did," he admitted.

"And he says he filled it, too," Jason said, trotting alongside her. He was holding General Grant like a football and the puppy's floppy ears bounced with every step. "More than once."

She looked from Jason to West. One on either side of her, though West was holding her hand.

It was the only part of her entire body that felt comfortably warm. "Must have been a little jam jar."

"Two-gallon pickle jar," he corrected. "How do you suppose I afforded buying my first car for cash?"

They reached the front porch and West told Jason to put on his shoes and get his coat and the puppy crate while he helped balance the stretcher as they carried it down the steps. Then it was back on the wheels as they rushed her speedily to the ambulance parked crosswise in front of Betty.

"I'll meet you at the clinic," West told her.

"What about Jason?"

"My mom's going to meet us there. It'll be faster." He started to back away to allow the attendants to slide the stretcher into the ambulance.

She grabbed his sleeve, feeling suddenly panicked. "It's just a precaution, right? All of this?"

He leaned down. Brushed her hair out of her eyes. "Just a precaution," he said. Then he kissed her softly.

"Whoa. Doctor D."

West straightened and eyed the gobsmacked attendants. "Not another word," he warned. Then he stepped away, allowing them to do their work.

Alexa felt the stretcher lift slightly then lock into place.

West held her gaze until the doors were closed.

Then she finally exhaled. Touched her lips with fingers that were entirely too shaky.

No. She definitely was not going to fall in love with anyone.

Just West D'Angelo.

Chapter Fifteen

Following the lack of electricity—save the excess that had still been shooting out of West's yard lights when the ambulance drove past—the clinic was almost painfully bright.

As he'd promised, he arrived at the clinic only a few minutes after her ambulance.

But she realized the arrivals hadn't stopped when she finally entered the waiting room following West's thoroughly, clinically impersonal, examination.

Half a dozen people were there.

Dana and Cutter. Meyer and Sophie. Even Jason and his grandmother, who had clearly not completed the task of picking Jason up from the clinic. General Grant's crate was even there, though it seemed to be empty.

"Well?" Meyer was the first to ask, though he directed his question at West rather than Alexa, which she found a hair annoying.

West had at least left his lab coat back in the examining room. He'd worn it—as well as gloves—while he'd done a lot more than just a few tests. He'd even drawn in another office down the hall from his clinic where she'd undergone a CT scan. Then it was back into the clinic where he hadn't even cracked a smile over her attempted joke about playing doctor.

It was like he possessed the same light switch her sister did. On. And off.

Ever since they'd gotten to the clinic, it had most definitely been off. Capital O.F.F.

It made her question her own sanity and she didn't appreciate it one little bit.

"Her EKG's fine. BP's back to normal. She has no burns. No evidence of trauma. Ears are fine. CT was good."

"Hey." She waved her hand. "I'm right here. Just because I said you could tell them how I was didn't mean you need to stand around like the town crier about it." West had insisted on rolling her from the examining room in a wheelchair and they were talking right over her head.

At least Jason's grandmother paid her some attention as she tutted around. "And now that he's seen you for himself, it's time Jason gets back to his own bed."

"Grandma! I'm not even sleepy,"

"Your grandmother's right, Jase. It's two in the morning. And you're not sleepy because you're *beyond* sleepy."

"Blame me," his grandmother said. "He was so worried, I just couldn't make myself take him."

"As everyone can see, there's no more reason to worry. Come here." Alexa gestured at Jason and he shuffled closer. She held out her arms. "Give me a hug."

He blinked. Then wrapped his arms around her neck, squeezing so tightly it was nearly painful. She pressed her cheek against his tousled brown hair and squeezed him back. She had a headache like she'd never had in her life, but his hug was still like a breath of life.

"Okay," West said eventually. "Let her breathe, Jase."

He finally let her go. His eyes were red-rimmed. "I'm just glad you're okay, Mrs. Cardinale."

"I'm glad, too. And I think you can call me Alexa when we're not at school," she added conspiratorially.

He beamed and went over to his dad. An eight-year-old version of the original.

"So, Happy Thanksgiving." She managed to tear her eyes away from the two D'Angelos long enough to look at Sophie. "But I think I'll give the beach potluck a pass today, if you don't mind."

"We've already decided against that," Sophie said breezily. "We're going to meet at West's place at five."

She could tell he was surprised. A lot. Though all he did was raise his eyebrows. "We are?" he asked mildly.

"We are," his mother said firmly. "My mother's table is just the perfect thing for a Thanksgiving meal. Though I really think I should try getting that turkey thawed—"

"No," West said quickly. "I was thinking more of the electrical."

"Oh, that's already fixed." His mother dismissed his concern. "I called my friend Stanley at the rental management company, and he went right over. The fire department was still there. They've cut off all the lampposts, but the house is just fine. The fire inspector says what hit Alexa were the sparks. Not lightning, though there *was* a strike that took down a tree a few blocks away. Maybe that had some effect on the power to the first light that exploded, but he doubts we'll ever know for sure."

"Let this be a lesson," Cutter said. "Don't stand around in the rain."

Alexa couldn't keep from looking at West again. He was studying the ground, pinching his lower lip and nodding slightly. Jason was still leaning against his side. He had shadows under his eyes and his lids were drooping.

"Good to know the only things fried were my raincoat and my cell phone." She patted the arms of the wheelchair with her palms. "And as sweet as it was for everyone to come here, can we all just call it a night now?"

"Seems like a good idea," Meyer was eyeing Sophie. "Technically, it's already Thanksgiving and thanks to my future father-in-law, *where* we spend the next four nights is up to us."

Sophie flushed brightly even as she took his hand and pulled him toward the door. "See you all later. Marjorie gave us the address. Cutter, don't forget you're bringing ice."

"I won't forget." But he was just saying it to the empty doorway. "Dana, you and Lex'll have the beach house to yourselves. I'm heading to the closest hotel with a king-sized bed and a showerhead that I don't have to bend down to reach." He went out the door, too, but stopped. "Don't worry about a new cell phone," he told Alexa. "I have extras. All the bells and whistles you could ever want. I'll bring one later."

"Of course he has extras," Dana said when the door closed after him. "Tech, he has coming out his ears. The ability to finish a simple outdoor deck? Not so much." She stood, too. And even as late as it was, she still managed to look magazine-perfect. She focused on West. "Any precautions our patient still needs?"

"I *can* speak for myself."

West ignored her. "Just watch for anything unusual. Avoid any strenuous activity for a day or so. Limit alcohol."

Dana nodded. "I'll bring my SUV closer to the entrance."

"Maybe Alexa should stay with us at our house, Dad."

She felt heat run under her skin. "That's not necessary, Jason."

"I don't know." His grandmother's brow knitted as she peered at Alexa. "Maybe it *would* be good. You do look peaky, dear. I'm sure your sister would do an admirable job of looking after you, but there's nothing like having a doctor under the roof."

"I don't need looking after. I just need my own bed. A few hours of sleep and I'll be right as rain." She regretted the choice of words as soon as she said them. For the rest of her days, she would equate rain with West. "Besides, I have to help move all the food collections from the school to the community center for the Thankful Friday event. The volunteers are supposed to meet at Howell today around ten."

"You definitely need looking after if you think you're going to be hefting around hundreds of pounds of canned food," West said.

"You've just said there's nothing wrong with me. And we *do* use carts, you know."

"That doesn't mean you need to go out and run a marathon, either."

"Who said anything about a marathon!"

"You know what I mean."

"We'll just get General Grant from the crib and let the two of you work it out." Jason's grandmother picked up the crate and pushed Jason through the swinging doorway that led to the examining rooms. "We'll go out the back way. Good night, honey."

Which left Alexa alone again with West.

"Crib?"

"It's a drawer with a cushion and a plexi wraparound. First thing we've actually found that he can't climb up or sneak through. Dog's a terror."

"He's a puppy."

"He's a five-pound demolition crew."

"Jason's obviously happy."

"Strangely, he has us all wrapped around his paw. Which is not to say I wouldn't prefer to know my shoes were still safe."

She wrapped her hands around the wheels and started maneuvering herself toward the door.

"Not so fast there." With what seemed like no effort at all, he stopped her forward progress and swung her chair around to face him again.

"Oh, right. You probably want my insurance card. A guarantee for payment of services rendered."

He locked her wheels in place and planted his hands on the armrests, leaning down until he filled her vision. His eyes were almost black and a muscle kept flexing in his jaw. "Do you know how relieved we all are? How grateful? Jason didn't get to say goodbye to his mother, and he adores you."

Whatever flippant response she might have dredged up died a quick death. "It's mutual," she said huskily. "He...he knows I am not trying to replace his mother. That would be—"

"His idea of perfection," West said. He leaned in and brushed his mouth over hers and all of the longing that she kept shoving under a bushel started shooting out sparks as surely as that lamppost had. And she had no protection against it. "The more he sees us together," he murmured, "the worse it's going to be for him when you leave."

Regret squeezed inside her just as tightly as Jason's arms had squeezed her neck. "All the more reason for me *not* to stay at your house."

"Right." He rested his forehead against hers. "If I thought you needed observation, I'd have hauled your sweet butt to the hospital whether you liked it or not."

She was a modern woman who should be offended, not secretly shivering. "Sweet butt? Really, West?"

"It is sweet." He kissed her again. "I've seen it now, re-member?" His lips slid along her jaw toward her ear. "Even the little daisy tattooed on your right cheek."

"God." She turned sideways, trying to slump away from him in the chair. "This is humiliating."

He wasn't deterred. He simply kissed the side of her neck, extracting more shivers out of her. "It's all of an inch. Now, if it was the size of a dinner plate, maybe it'd be humiliat-ing."

"You're not helping!"

"How old were you when you got it?"

"Eighteen, and I thought I was living wild, I can tell you." She turned again, nearly knocking noses with him. "It's not fair. You know what my butt—not to mention *everything* else—looks like."

"Goddamn right it's not fair."

She gaped. "Dr. D'Angelo, that was a pickle-jar worth of swear."

"Deservedly. I'll donate it to your playground fund. My imagination was slacking. Now I know what reality is like and I'm never gonna sleep dream-free again. And every dream is going to be about you and I'm going to wake up every damn time hard as—"

"Hey!" Dana pushed open the door. Her eyes skittered over Alexa and West, who'd jumped a foot away as if he'd been bitten by a snake. "Everything okay? I've been out there waiting."

Alexa released the brakes on the wheelchair. "I'm coming," she said.

West covered his snort with a cough. "Not yet."

Dana narrowed her eyes. "What's that?"

"Nothing," Alexa said hurriedly. "Let's just go. We're all stupid with exhaustion."

Dana took command of the chair. "Should we take this wheelchair with us back to the beach house, West?"

"No!" Alexa vetoed the idea before he could answer.

"We'd bring it back," Dana chided.

"I said *no*."

"She'll be fine without the chair," West said. He held open the door for them so Dana could push her through. "Just watch for anything—"

"Unusual," Alexa interjected. "Right. We got it, Doctor D. Come on, Dana. Let's *go*."

"Now who's in a hurry all of a sudden?" Dana shook her head as if Alexa was a mystifying child. She gave West a quick hug. "Thanks for everything. And for being a good sport about Thanksgiving dinner and all. You won't have to do a thing, though. We'll bring all the food. All you have to bring is your appetite."

His gleaming gaze roved over Alexa, leaving her feeling more singed than her poor raincoat. The corner of his lip tilted slightly. "Guarantee it. Drive carefully. Roads are still wet out there."

"I'm always careful," Dana quipped.

Then she was pushing Alexa out the side door where the Escalade was purring softly, the passenger door open and waiting.

"What the heck was all of that?" Dana asked under her breath as she needlessly helped Alexa out of the wheelchair and into the SUV.

"That—" Alexa let her head fall back against the soft leather "—is someone who does it right."

Dana's lips parted. "Ohmigod. You and West had sex?" Her voice rose practically to a squeak. "When? While we were all waiting to see if you were okay?"

Alexa shook her head. "No! We have not had sex, and certainly not...not tonight. He was painfully professional." And she was suddenly extremely thankful for that.

"Well, you could cut the vibes with a knife." Dana closed the door and quickly went around to get behind the wheel. "Felt like some sort of voyeur walking in on you."

"Good thing you didn't wait a few more minutes, then, or you would've been."

Dana's eyebrows shot up. She fanned herself. "Alexa Marie."

"Tell me about it," she said with feeling. "And I even have a *headache*. Imagine if I didn't!"

Dana snorted out a laugh.

And then Alexa did, too.

"I gotta have some of that, too."

West looked at Jason. He was sitting on the bathroom

counter. They'd both just "shaved." Though, in West's case, it was with an actual razor. "Aftershave?"

"Yeah." Jason held out his palm.

West unscrewed the cap again.

"When you marry Alexa, are you gonna have more kids?"

He practically upended the bottle. "Jase." He snatched a towel and sopped up the mess. "You need to stop talking like that." He glanced in the mirror and grimaced.

Janine was sitting on the edge of the tub behind them. Particularly translucent, but only because of the morning sun shining through the windows of the second-story bathroom. She lifted her hands as if to say, *Well?*

Go away, he thought.

"I can stop talking about it," Jason said, "but that doesn't mean I stop wondering."

"I wish you'd apply some of that logic to the matter of Ms. Cardinale."

"She said I could call her Alexa. So can you."

He flipped on the water and glanced in the mirror again. Janine was gone.

"Wash your hands," he told Jason. "And use soap. You're going to reek of too much aftershave."

Jason obediently pumped soap into his palms and worked up a lather with his usual thoroughness. "It'd be cool to have a brother. But I guess a sister would be okay, too."

"Very democratic of you. Alexa's your teacher. There's not going to be any marriage. Nor any babies." He went into the closet and felt like an idiot when he realized he was debating what to wear. All because he couldn't get the image of Alexa's daisy-decked derriere out of his head. He rubbed his eyes and yanked a random pair of jeans from the drawer.

"Yeah, but you're friends, too. Arntcha?"

They were something. Putting a name on it felt dangerous, though. "I guess we're friends." He pulled on the jeans. "And the answer's still the same."

He wished they could go back to when Jason seemed most interested in manipulating things around to just a simple puppy. Now he wanted baby brothers and sisters.

What state would he be in by summer when Alexa went back to California?

For that matter, what state was *he* going to be in?

He looked out to see Jason was still washing up. He was taking his full twenty seconds—and then some—to do so, just as he'd done ever since Janine had once told him.

"Finish up," he said. "We need to be at the school by ten if we're going to help with Thankful Friday before everyone starts showing up here for dinner." He didn't trust for a second that Alexa wouldn't overdo things. And because of it, he'd decided they'd just have to be there, too, to make sure she didn't.

He selected an equally random shirt, pulled it over his head, grabbed socks and his boots and walked through the bathroom to his bedroom where General Grant's crate—now partially lined with plexi West had purloined from the clinic—was gnawing his way through the corner of his cushion bed.

Jason finished rinsing his hands and hopped off the counter. His skinny chest was bare. The latest flannel pajama pants West's mother had gotten hung on to his hips by a prayer. "I'm glad Grandma's not making turkey," he said.

West was pulling on his socks. "So am I, bud. Don't get that dog out of his crate unless you're planning to hold him while you're in here." He pointed at his dresser where a corner had been chewed to a nub. "It took him only thirty minutes to do that. Remember?"

"How's he gonna learn not to chew on stuff if he's always in his crate?"

ALLISON LEIGH

221

"He chews because he's a puppy. He'll learn to behave and chew on the things he's allowed to chew when the dog trainer starts coming next week. We'll all learn. For now? He's in someone's arms, in the crate or outside." He gestured with his sock. "Dogs like dens, bud. It's his palace. He's happy doing exactly what he's doing.

Jason rubbed General Grant's ears through the metal wires. "I put the bird back in the freezer," he admitted. "Twice."

"Probably shouldn't have done that," West said. Though privately he was glad. His mother's turkey had always been terrible.

"Probably. She needs to use a thermometer. I see it on the cooking shoes. I bet Alexa uses a thermometer." General Grant turned his focus back on his gnawing and Jason climbed onto the bed. He walked around on the mattress, clearly gearing up to sneaking in a jump or three. "I think she likes Stanley."

"Alexa?" West stopped what he was doing and looked at Jason. "What are you talking about? And, by the way, you have a trampoline in the playroom that you've rarely used. Don't even think about jumping on my bed. What's this about Stanley?"

"Not Alexa. *Grandma*." Jason flopped down and crossed his legs—with a definite bounce along the way. "She likes him. I'm pretty sure they gotta thing going."

"'A thing,'" he echoed. More lovey-show terminology or just osmosis from the world at large? "What makes you say that?"

Jason shrugged. "I can just tell. Plus, she has his phone number on her *speed dial*." He made the term sound like it was a hotline to the President.

West's mother was the only person he knew who still had a landline phone in addition to a cell phone.

"I guess if they do, that's their business." He swatted Ja-

son's thigh. "Move it. Dressed and downstairs in five minutes or you're doing laundry this weekend."

Jason scooted off the bed and ran out of the room.

"Finally," he murmured. "The key is *laundry*."

I told you that a long time ago.

"It's too bad Owen didn't live, Janine. You could be haunt-
ing him."

"Did you say something, honey?"

His mom had stopped in his doorway. She'd already come
armed with supplies for Thanksgiving dinner before he and
Jason had even dragged themselves out of bed. "What's that
you're carrying?"

"Just some linens that I don't need anymore. I thought I'd
stock up your linen closet." She patted the stack in her arms.
"Everything is as good as new." She smiled and started
down the hallway again.

"Mom." He followed her. "Are you getting rid of all your
stuff so you can finally sell the house?"

"Your father loved our house."

"He's been gone a long time. It's okay. Sell it. Rent it.
Whatever. Move to that retirement community you talk
about. You can do what you want with your life."

"So can you, honey."

"What's that supposed to mean?"

"Just that sometimes the things we want to fit forever…
don't."

He had a cryptic ghost. He didn't need a cryptic mother.
"It was a long night, Mom. My translation's feeling rusty."

"I know about the job offer you turned down to come here."

He exhaled. "Ruthie," he muttered, thinking of all the
phone messages she'd passed on from Sean. "It's not exactly a job offer."

"It sounds lucrative. Whatever it is."

"Medicine isn't about money. Isn't that what Dad always said?"

"Yes, but neither does it mean you have to be a pauper."

"You and Dad weren't paupers."

"We didn't live on Seaview Drive, either," she said wryly.

"You could if you sold the building."

"Beach Medical's been part of Cape Cardinale since before you were born. I'm not going to sell it. It's an institution."

"Some would say an albatross."

"The rent from Cardinale Cares is going to take care of that. You were right to talk me into leasing to them." She opened a built-in cabinet that was entirely empty and tucked her armload inside. "This house is too large for you."

"*Now* you realize it?"

She propped her hands on her hips. "I was trying to do the best that I could."

"I know." He gave her a kiss on her forehead. "And I love you for it."

"Dad! It's almost ten."

He looked at Jason. He'd dressed in jeans and a shirt that hung almost to his knees.

"You need to stop buying him clothes that are so big," he told his mother. "It's going to be two years before he fits that shirt."

"That's what you think. I remember when *you* were his age. One minute, just a little boy. The next, half a man."

"Dad!" Jason was thumping down the stairs. Both feet at one time, making as much noise as any kid could make. "Last one out has to do the stinky yoga laundry!"

Chapter Sixteen

West pressed the buzzer again next to Otto's front door, and he could hear the faint gong of the bell ringing beyond the doorway. He stepped back a few feet, eyeing the security camera that was above the door. "I know you're back, Otto," he said loudly. "Your trash is full of takeout from the Highland Pub."

The door suddenly opened and Otto stood there. His hair was standing on end and the silk robe he wore displayed his bony knees. A complicated-looking camera hung from a strap around his neck. "Son, you need to learn to take a hint."

"Nice robe." West wasn't touching the topic of the camera. "Wouldn't have expected hot-pink tulips on you, but whatever."

"A man grabs what he must." Otto looked over his shoulder back into the house. "I have *company*."

"Bring her with you. I'm here to invite you to my place for Thanksgiving dinner."

"Bland turkey and blander mashed potatoes? No thanks."

"Considering the group at my place, I doubt anything will be bland." He frowned. "Your cast is off."

"Huh." Otto held up his arm. Rotated his wrist. "Look at that."

"At least tell me you didn't cut it off yourself."

"I didn't cut it off myself."

"Without lying."

"I cut it off myself."

"Otto?" a feminine voice called from behind him. "Sweetie, I can't find the caviar—oh." Gwendolyn Hightower stepped into the doorway next to Otto and she smiled. Brilliantly. She extended her long, graceful arm. "How do you do? I'm Gwendolyn."

He stared stupidly at her hand. What did she expect? For him to kiss it? Feeling like a bumbling fool, he lightly shook her fingertips. "West." His own name barely came out right. She was standing there entirely nude except for what were obviously men's boxers.

Otto's, he supposed and figured he was going to have to scrub out his eyes with bleach over this one. "I came to invite Otto over for dinner."

"Isn't that nice." Gwendolyn cuddled her famous body next to Otto. It was like watching a cat cozy up to a bean pole with light-socket hair. "You didn't tell me you had such nice neighbors, sweetie. Should I get dressed?"

"We're not going to impose on West," Otto said.

"It's not an imposition. I invited you, remember?" Even before he'd left to pick up ice, his house had been full of characters. Otto and—his eyes strayed to Gwendolyn despite his efforts otherwise—his friend would be icing on the unexpected cake.

Otto lifted the camera though. "Appreciate the gesture. But my time's limited here."

West got the message and stepped back from the doorway. "Pleasure meeting you, Ms. Hightower. See you later, Otto." He'd only stopped at Otto's on the spur of the moment when he'd spotted the trash bin at the curb.

Gwendolyn Hightower.

He had to give the guy credit.

He practically dove into the car, glancing back only when he had tinted glass that could hide the fact.

Otto was still standing in his doorway, grinning. Gwendolyn had disappeared inside again.

West lowered his window enough to give the old guy a thumbs-up, and then he drove on to his own place.

Alexa's yellow VW was at the curb where it had been since the night before and now it had companions. A luxury SUV, a few pickup trucks, and a massive Harley.

He parked behind the Harley blocking the garage and walked past the pillars riddled with black pockmarks. Residue from the night before.

It didn't bear thinking about how much worse it might have been.

He yanked open the front door and laughter and music spilled out.

Not only were Alexa's siblings there with his mother and Jason, but since he'd been gone, several more unfamiliar faces were now crowded around the island in his kitchen. He dumped the ice in the deep freezer where another bag exactly like it already sat.

"I said I'd remember the ice," Cutter said. He cradled a long-neck beer in one hand and a leggy redhead in the other.

"And we also said five o'clock," Dana noted. She was holding a martini glass and smiling, but it went only surface deep. Maybe because her cool gaze was trained on the guy wearing a motorcycle jacket who was scooping up a handful of tortilla chips and talking to Meyer and Sophie.

"Ice never goes to waste," he said. He stuck out his hand to the stranger in the motorcycle jacket. "I'm West."

"Ty." The other man shook his hand. His gaze slid briefly toward Dana. "Gate-crasher."

"More the merrier." He sidled around them until he reached Alexa where she was propped on a barstool next

to Maxwill's cage. On the other side of the birdcage was
General Grant's crate. Presently empty.

"Dog?"

"Outside with Jason and your mom."

That was okay then.

He slid the mug Alexa was holding from her fingers and
sniffed at the coffee before taking a sip.

It was hot as blazes. But just coffee with a heavy helping of cream.

She raised her eyebrows. She'd twizzled her hair up in
some clips and a few whorls hung down over her forehead.
"Don't trust me with coffee like you didn't trust me with
the food barrels this morning?"

"Jason and I were the only *volunteers—*" he air-quoted
the word "—who showed up to help load the truck from the
community center. Aside from the driver who was eighty
if he was a day. Can you blame me? Besides. It's coffee.
And you're drinking it out of my favorite mug. Seems fair."

"That's terrible logic."

He shrugged. "Sue me. Who's Ty?"

She leaned her head close. "Mercer." She offered her finger through the cage to Maxwill and he hopped right on.
"Dana's husband," she provided under her breath.

He gave the man another look. He looked more suited to
breaking up bar fights than fighting zoning commissions.

"She doesn't look like she's thrilled he's here."

"They're having issues," Alexa murmured. She was looking at the bird as he flew from one side of the cage to the
other. "Can't let you out, Maxie. Too many people." Maxwill dove down to the bottom of the cage and started throwing around seeds. They bounced off the plexi on the side of
General Grant's crate.

"Temper tantrums from a canary," West said.

She chuckled and gestured with her coffee cup. "The

guy in the suit over by Cutter is Fitzgerald Lane. Sophie's dad. Francesca is his wife. They got married a few months ago. And the girl with Cutter is anyone's guess. They arrived right before you did. Introductions haven't made it around yet."

"What about the guy outside?" He'd looked over Alexa's shoulder through the window where a complete stranger was crouching next to the koi pond while Jason ran back and forth across the wood bridge, General Grant nipping at his heels.

"That is Stanley," she said.

He did a double-take.

The balding guy couldn't have been more different than his dad.

Apparently tastes can change, Janine mused.

Alexa had her finger through the cage again. She glanced back at him. "Change about what?

He stared at her.

She raised her eyebrows again. "You said tastes change? About what?"

He shrugged. "Liking Thanksgiving," he improvised. He took another drink of coffee.

If he'd ever needed confirmation that Janine was his own mind talking back at him, Alexa'd just given him proof.

It was what everyone had always said.

Just felt hard to believe that his mind kept projecting a physical form of his dead, cheating wife.

Enough whining about cheating, Janine said. *You were never there. I got lonely. It happens. Let it go and move on already.*

He pushed the mug back into Alexa's hands. At least she wasn't looking at him like he'd just spoken *that* aloud. "Shouldn't we be getting dinner on or something?"

"Dishes that need warming are in the oven. Everything

that's cold is in the fridge." She was looking at him closely. "And we have a couple million appetizers, too." She waved generally at the island. "Nobody's in danger of starving yet. Is something wrong?"

Nothing that a lobotomy wouldn't cure. "I want to meet Stanley."

"Okay." She set aside the mug and hopped off her stool, showing no aftereffects from the night before. She was wearing a pumpkin-colored sweater dress that skimmed her figure, along with tall burgundy boots. Tiny seashells dangled from her earlobes and she'd done something with her makeup that made her eyes even more luminously teal than usual. "I'll go, too. Unless you're wanting a man-to-man moment with him."

In answer, he took her hand. Led her through the house and around to the enclosed sunporch that overlooked the statues. "Need a jacket?"

"I don't know where your mom put it. She collected everyone's coats when we began arriving. Only ones she missed were Ty and Cutter." She grabbed a ratty flannel shirt that his mom used when she worked in the garden from a hook. "I can use this, if that's okay?"

"Sure." He held it for her while she pushed her arms through and wondered if his dad would approve. The shirt had originally been his. He smiled faintly. Straightened the twisted collar and leaned down to kiss the back of her neck, exposed by the sparkly clips that were designed to look like real butterfly wings. "You smell good," he murmured and kissed her neck again. The boots added several inches of height, which placed her hips exactly where his hands naturally fell.

"Lilacs," she said breathily. She angled her chin and looked back at him. "Probably shouldn't be doing this. Jason might see."

Knowing she was right didn't make it easy to step away. Like one would expect, the sunroom was made of windows. He reached out and flipped off the light. It wasn't quite dark outside yet. But it meant seeing into the sunroom was at least less likely.

He closed the door leading into the house and flipped the lock.

Then he settled his hands back where they'd been. He drew her into him. "I'm imagining your daisy," he murmured against her temple.

She let out a long breath, her head tilting against his shoulder. She slid her fingers through his, drawing his hands forward over her abdomen. Tightening the distance between them. "I noticed." Her voice had dropped. Turned even more throaty. "It's enough to make the boots actually worthwhile." She suddenly spun in his arms and twined her arms behind his neck. "Just kiss me really well, okay? And then we'll pretend that nothing's—"

He kissed her. Ran his hands down her spine. Pressing her even closer. Feeling her fingers slid up his nape. Along his collar. Her breasts were soft. Her arms strong. She was sweet and darkly mysterious and when she finally dragged her mouth away, she was panting as hard as he.

"That, uh, that was really...well." She dropped her forehead to his chin. Started backing away. Hips first. Breasts next. Her hands slid over his chest. Fisted briefly then straight-armed herself back. She lifted her chin. Her seashell earrings glinted slightly in the darkened room. Her face was a pale blur. Her eyes dark pools. She reached up and rubbed her thumb over his lips. His chin. "Lipstick," she whispered. "Wouldn't want anyone to think we've been—"

"Doing what we're doing?"

"Exactly." She did a little shimmying sort of move.

Tugged at her dress and shook back her head. A few more curls came loose from her butterfly clips.

He reached for her again. He'd been dying of thirst and she was liquid from heaven. "Spread your legs."

She hauled in a hissing breath. "West. We can't. What if someone comes in?"

"We won't. And the door's locked. Can you hear the music out there? Nobody's going to hear a thing. He was already inching her dress up her thighs. Her hips. He hooked his finger through the band of her panties. Her skin was the warmest velvet.

She gasped. Shifted a little. Another shimmy. Her thighs parted and his fingers slid between. She was wet. Hot. And so, so soft when he delved deeper. She gasped again. Laughing a little. "We won't, huh?"

"You will." He ran his other hand up her ribs. Feeling his way through the soft knit dress. Palming her breast. "It'll keep me sane," he murmured.

"Now there's a line." She was arching into his hand. Throwing out her hands behind her. Looking for purchase.

He stepped into her. Pushing her back until her shoulders hit the built-in cupboards. She arched even more. Braced one hand over her head. Wrapped her other around his wrist, stalling. "Wait. Wait. Too fast. You—"

"You're not waiting. Not if I have anything to do with it." He stepped closer still. Felt deeper. Swirled his thumb. He was engulfed in the heat and the pulse and the essence that was only her. And he realized she had her fist to her mouth. Stifling her keening groan. And she was flexing here. Straining there. Reaching. Reaching.

And suddenly…breaking free.

West knew the physical body. He knew the technical. The whys and the hows. But Alexa's orgasm, the feel of her turning molten in his hands, was something else.

Something magical.

Divine.

"I can't go out there now," Alexa whispered.

They were sitting on the floor. Fully clothed. She felt positively wrecked.

"Yeah, you can."

"They'll *know*."

"They won't."

"You don't know my sister."

"What do you want to do then? Hide out here until morning? You think that won't be noticeable?"

"This is your fault," she accused. "If you weren't so—" She lifted her hand. Dropped it again. *Perfect*. Nobody was perfect. But that's the only word that kept circling in her mind.

West D'Angelo. Perfect.

"It's your fault," he returned. "You've got the daisy."

She laughed weakly. Then she leaned forward, bracing one hand on his thigh. She pushed to her feet and pulled off the flannel shirt that had never been needed after all. She returned it to the hook, trying to smooth out the new wrinkles. Something sharp from the pocket jabbed her. "Ouch." She sucked the tip of her finger for a second before drawing out the offending object. "Scarf pin."

"Let me see."

She fastened the pin and held it out.

"I meant your finger. But I haven't seen that pin in forever." He angled it so the colorful yellow and orange flowers filling the octagonal head caught the light. "Was probably my great-grandmother's. She collected cloisonné. Her name was Poppy. Her things always had poppies in the pattern." He handed her back the pin. "By the time my parents got married, it'd become a tradition for the D'Angelo brides to wear a particular brooch. Way fancier than that thing. To this day, my mom says she only wore it because of expectation. But she hated it. My dad, though, always claimed she wore it just so he'd have to make up for it in every anniversary gift from then on."

"If any of the jewelry I've seen your mom wear is from him, I'd say he did a good job of it." She turned the pin over to look at the back of it and the worn clasp fell open again. In contrast, the enamel portion looked in perfect repair.

"Sophie makes jewelry." She swung her earrings. "She made these. I bet she could fix the clasp."

"I guarantee if my mother cared at all about that pin, it wouldn't be in her gardening shirt."

She slipped the pin back into the pocket. "They've probably already gotten through dinner and are onto pecan pie by now."

"There's pecan pie?"

"I wasn't about to bring pumpkin. Hate the stuff."

"So do I."

"Guess we're meant to be," she quipped lightly. She waved her fingers in front of his nose. "Up and at 'em, Doctor D."

"It's because I've been *up* that we've been sitting in here for so damn long."

"Should've just left it at a kiss then."

"Might as well ask me to stop breathing." He pushed to his feet.

They looked out the windows. Spotlights illuminated the statues. The wooden bridge over the koi pond was lit as well. Nobody was out there.

"Shield your eyes," he said. "I'm turning on the light."

They both squinted when he flipped it on.

"Where's the closest bathroom in this hotel?"

"I'll show you. I smell like your lilac perfume."

"It's soap."

"Whatever it is. I need to change." He flicked open the lock and cautiously opened the door. The music got louder. Voices, too. "Sounds like everyone's still in the kitchen." He drew her into the hall. Went the opposite direction. "Powder room's there." He pointed. "I'll be back down in a few."

Alexa quickly ducked into the bathroom and carefully closed the door. As if *that* soft snick would be noticeable.

Fussy rosebud-patterned wallpaper covered every wall of the powder room. But it was still better than the walls at the beach house. She looked at herself in the gold-framed mirror over the pedestal sink.

Aside from her lack of lipstick, she didn't *look* as if she'd just had the most erotic experience of her life.

Erotic.

She closed her eyes and shook her head. "Doesn't even cover it," she whispered. She flipped on the faucet and mopped herself up as best she could. She couldn't do anything about her drenched panties, but nobody would know.

Except West.

She shuddered a little. Her breasts still ached and there was a hollow feeling inside her that she knew would only be perfectly filled by him.

"Wrecked," she murmured again.

She turned off the water. Tried to bring a little order back to her hair, but it wasn't exactly as if it had ever been particularly orderly in the first place. She adjusted a few of the sparkly butterfly-winged clips. Pinched some color into her cheeks, pasted a bright smile on her face, and went out to face the world.

Or—as the case was—her family and his.

Everyone was still in the kitchen.

Dana's eyes shooting daggers at Ty. Fitz and Francesca still talking with Cutter and his latest pickup.

"There you are." Jason latched onto her hand. He was crunching on a carrot. "Wanna see my room?"

Bemused, she studied the digital clock glowing on the front of the wine cooler.

Not even an hour had passed.

That's all it had taken for her world to change.

"Sure," she told Jason, and followed him back down the hall and to the same rear staircase that West had used. It was much more utilitarian-looking than the *Gone With the Wind* version in the foyer. "I just need to—" she reached down and unzipped her boots "—get these things off."

She left them where the lay and went up the stairs barefoot after Jason. The walls held a lot of framed artwork along the way, and she could just tell that it had come with the furnished house. At least *Pietro's Last* hanging at the beach house made a person feel something.

As soon as she entered Jason's room, though, all that changed. His doodles—his *art*—was everywhere. Not only zombies and dinosaurs, either. Lifelike dogs crowded against abstract spiderwebs. They were tacked up in a haphazard way that formed a sort of wallpaper. A few were in colored pencil, but most were just black and every shade from there to white. The spaces that weren't covered with drawings were occupied by shelves cluttered with uneven stacks of books. A juvenile-sized desk was host to another stack of books. A door stopper of a textbook lay open and she glanced at the cover of it. Trigonometry. "Jase?"

"Yeah." He bounced against the edge of his bed, rendering the untidy comforter even more so.

"You understand the problems in this textbook?"

"Some of 'em."

"Your dad know?"

"I dunno. I found the book in his closet. He has a bunch more, too. Lotta literature. Got bored with that."

"A lot of literature *is* pretty boring." She smiled at the collection of plain old rocks that sat on a shelf next to a brain-teaser puzzle. "How long did it take you to figure this one out?" She held up the twisted contraption of metal and beads.

"That came from Santa. Dad solved it in two minutes."

"He's good with his hands," she murmured. She studied the mismatched collection of framed photographs tucked among the books. Recognizing Marjorie and West's father as a young couple. The man's similarity to West was strong. Aching a little, she picked up a small snapshot of a newborn held in the arms of his mother. "I like this one of you and your mom," she told Jason. "You have her eyes."

"My dad says that, too. I was a baby," he said needlessly. "It's my favorite."

She replaced the snapshot and sat in the chair at his desk. Everywhere she looked, something of Jason's own creation was pinned. It was almost dizzying. "What do you like better, Jase? Math problems or drawing?"

"Drawing. Way better. Sometimes I hide equations in my drawings, though. Like a puzzle that nobody knows is there." He looked around, as if trying to see his room from someone else's eyes. "Kind of messy in here."

"I think it's exactly right for you."

"It *is* messy."

She jerked. Looking over to see West in the doorway.

He'd changed into another cashmere sweater. Black this time. His jeans were darker than the other pair. His hair was slightly damp. And when he walked into the room, the scent of his aftershave wrapped around her senses.

"And it is exactly right for him," he finished. His eyes met Alexa's and he smiled slightly, sending warmth streaming through her. "But we should get downstairs, right?"

"Right." Jason scooted off the bed. "Francesca is making

spaghetti. We never had spaghetti before at Thanksgiving."
Clearly, the prospect appealed, because he raced out of the
room ahead of them.

West tucked a strand of hair behind Alexa's ear. His fingers lingered. "You good?"

Aside from feeling like a vice was slowly tightening
around her heart? She couldn't seem to get out simple words,
so she just nodded and started to leave the room.

But West caught her hand, halting her. His gaze roved
over her face. "I'm glad you're here."

In her mind, all she heard was the echo of *I believe*.

"So am I."

He cupped her nape. Brushed his lips over hers in a nearly
chaste kiss. "I wish you wouldn't have to leave."

She felt even shakier. "It's best. Right?"

"Logic says so." He held her hand until they reached the
staircase and, when they reached the kitchen, Marjorie and
Dana were pulling pans out of the ovens. Sophie was peel-
ing back plastic wrap from a salad bowl.

Needing something normal to counter West's effect,
Alexa rinsed out her coffee mug and filled it again from
the wildly fancy coffee maker.

"Jase."

She glanced at West standing near Maxwill's cage.

"Is General Grant outside?"

Jason stood on a chair, peering into the big pot on the
stove that Francesca was attending. "We brought him in
when we came inside."

"You put him in his crate?"

"Of course he did," Marjorie chided. "He's right—" She
broke off. "Oh, dear."

The crate was empty.

Plexi in place as usual. But the door was standing open.
West crouched next to it, studying. "That little bugger's

figured out how to open the latch." He sounded almost impressed.

He pushed to his feet. "Jason, get the dog treats. General Grant's on the loose again."

Jason darted into the pantry.

"Should we be worried? He's such a little guy."

"He's a terror. And no. No reason to worry. Jason's figured out all his hidey holes." He leaned closer, his voice dropping. "But if you want, I know another room with a sturdy lock, while they're all busy—"

She muffled a laugh. "Dr. D'Angelo. You're scandalous."

His smile widened. "You should meet my neighbor sometime. He's the one with a lock on that."

"The sooner we find General Grant, the sooner we can get on with—"

West raised his eyebrows, waiting. "With…?"

She slid off the stool and looked up at him through her lashes. She took his hand. "Let's find out."

He laughed. "Turning out to be the best Thanksgiving I've ever had."

Chapter Seventeen

"Twenty-five days to Christmas!" Regina Bowler entered the teacher's lounge the following Monday morning with a Santa hat on her head. "Who's excited?"

She earned a chorus of less-than-excited responses.

"Bunch of Grinches," she chided and tossed the hat on one of the lounge tables. She joined Alexa where she was debating the wisdom of a second peanut-butter cookie after the long weekend that had been filled with excesses of every sort. "I heard from Ernestine. She went home yesterday."

Alexa felt a stab of dismay. She glanced at the wall clock. "Is she going to come walking in any minute?" She wasn't entirely joking.

But Regina chuckled. "She's not quite ready for that yet." She leaned against the counter. "I did have to tell her that you've been taking her class."

"Bet that was fun." She determinedly replaced the plastic wrap over the homemade cookies. She'd already had a piece of leftover wedding cake for breakfast that morning. She did have *some* self-control.

"It was something," Regina agreed. "You have the fundraising committee this afternoon?"

Alexa nodded.

"Come and see me after. We'll talk." The principal slid

a cookie from beneath the plastic wrap and hurried out of the lounge.

We'll talk.

Two words that didn't inspire comfort. Not when Ernestine was most certainly involved.

Alexa grimaced and took another cookie. So what? She'd run extra laps up and down Cardinale Beach after work.

With the cookie and a full coffee mug, she headed to her classroom.

How many more days before Ernestine rightfully reclaimed it?

She'd planned to come in earlier to prep for the day, but West had phoned just before her alarm went off and she'd spent all that extra time—and then some—floating around in a bubble all because he'd wanted to tell her, "Good morning."

When she reached the classroom, she sat down at Ernestine's desk and looked at the span of desks. They'd have to move them back where they belonged. And the art supplies needed to be sorted back into their proper bins and stacked away in the cupboard again.

It was a depressing prospect.

She pulled open Ernestine's desk drawer and studied the disorder. She was putting it to rights when her cell phone rang. The one that Cutter had given her was larger than her previous fried model, but it operated a lot more easily.

She smiled as she put it on speaker while she kept separating pens and pencils. She had no idea when she'd made such a mess of Ernestine's desk. "We just talked an hour ago, Doctor D."

"Blame Jason. I don't know that it was a good idea to take him to your brother's wedding."

The wedding had been amazing. Beautiful. Chaotic. And perfectly emblematic of Meyer and Sophie as a couple.

"Why? He had a ball. Particularly when we all ended up

at the beach afterward. He was having a blast with Meredith's son." The bonfire that Cutter built had burned until the wee hours. Ironically, though they'd all had the freedom to spend it away from the beach house, with the exception of the newlyweds, none of them had gone anywhere.

All in all, it had been a pretty perfect weekend.

Plus. Cake.

"He was studying tide charts on the way to school because he's decided when you and I get married, it should be on the beach."

She nearly knocked her coffee mug sideways.

"Still there?"

She snatched tissues from the box on Ernestine's desk and mopped up the coffee that had sloshed over the side of the mug. "I'm here. What…what did you tell him?"

"I told him the same thing I always tell him. That we're not getting married."

"Wait. You *always* tell him? How often is this a topic between the two of you?"

"Often enough. But he seems to be digging in deeper. Decided I'd better warn you."

"Great," she said faintly. The first bell rang, making her jump, and she took the phone off speaker to hold it to her ear. "What do I say if he brings it up with me?"

"You set him straight, obviously."

Obviously. Of course.

The ordinary noise of kids in the hallway was a welcome distraction. "I have to go," she said abruptly. "Bell rang."

"I'll see you this afternoon."

"For what?"

"Your fundraising committee?"

She felt foolish. There was no reason for her to feel so sideswiped by the mention of marriage. "Right. See you then."

"And send me the info for that psychologist friend of yours when you can. The one who can do Jason's assessment."

"I will." She ended the call, closed the phone in the desk drawer, and got up to greet the kids as they began pouring through the door. With Ernestine out of the hospital, each day was going to be a gift.

But that didn't stop the heat from rushing into her face when Jason jogged through the classroom door and gave her a wide smile. She didn't know if he was still preoccupied with the notion of her and his dad, but she certainly was.

It was a problem that hadn't abated even by that afternoon when she headed to the committee meeting. So much so, that she was actually relieved when West sent her a message that he had a patient emergency and couldn't make it.

The two women in charge of the Winter Faire attended as they'd promised and agreed far more easily than any one of them had expected to their participation in the event. They even offered to waive the fee before Alexa could bring it up.

"That's another thousand to the pot," Donna said as the meeting disbanded a short while later. She was the self-appointed tally-keeper. "Since Doctor D said he'd donate the fee to us if we ended up not having to pay it."

Alexa felt like so much had happened since that first meeting. "What are we up to now?"

"Sixty-nine thousand." Donna tucked her notepad in her oversized purse. "The Highland Hotel agreed to donate a two-night lover's package for the silent auction. Plus, the pub's kicking in free chowder for six months. That gives us twenty-two items to auction off so far."

Alexa began putting the folding chairs away on the cart. "Sounds like you should be chairing this committee," she told Donna. "I haven't managed to get anyone to donate anything at all."

Donna shrugged. "I work there. They don't want to listen to me complaining if they didn't."

"Well, you've gone above and beyond," Alexa said. Donna didn't even have children enrolled at the school.

"I may still try and hit up Tanya's. I wasn't sure I should after all that with Tater, but now that he's out of the woods..."

"What happened to Tater?"

"He had a heart attack." Donna gave her a look. "Doctor D didn't tell you? He had it right in his office last week. Tanya said if it would have happened anywhere else, her dad would've died. The doctor went with him to the hospital, even. You know how Tater is. Doesn't trust anyone who isn't from Cape Cardinale."

"But he's doing better now?"

"Ask Doctor D. You're the one dating him."

Alexa felt her face flush. "I'm not dating him!"

"That's not what Shorty White says."

"Who?"

"His son's a paramedic with the fire department?"

Alexa pressed her lips together. Now she understood. "Regardless of what Shorty White's son thinks, I'm not dating Dr. D'Angelo." Not dating. Not planning to marry. Just pointlessly falling head over heels for him.

She shoved the last folding chair a little harder than necessary onto the rack.

"Would be worth talking to them, don't you think?"

She realized she'd missed half of what Donna had been saying. "Sorry?"

"JCS. Your brother runs it. Maybe they could donate one of their scenic flights or charter tickets."

"I'll ask."

"It's not like you'll have a Pietro photograph to give out."

The disgust in Donna's voice came out of nowhere. It was a reminder of the early days after the funeral when Alexa had felt almost accosted by the sentiment. "*Pietro's Last* was given out," she said now. "It was the last thing my father did in this life."

As if Donna realized she'd poked a toe over the line, she quickly left the library, muttering about all the things she had yet to do that day.

Alexa finished restoring the room and headed to the principal's office. Regina was on the phone, but she waved at the chairs in front of her desk.

Alexa sat in one of the chairs and pulled out her cell phone, needing a distraction of her own. But she'd already sent Sandy's information to West during the morning recess and not even Alexa's mom had been leaving text messages. Which left a pendulum swinging in her mind. West. Pietro. West.

Finally, Regina ended her call. "Sorry about that. Gerta tells me the donations for the fundraiser have leveled off the last few days. How're the Winter Faire plans coming?"

Alexa smiled weakly. Clutching the phone, she tucked her hands between her knees. "They're placing us right near the entrance, so we'll have plenty of traffic. Donna has a ton of items already lined up for the silent auction. With enough of the right advertising, I think we'll raise more. I just don't know that we'll hit the goal."

"I have faith." Regina folded her hands atop her desk and Alexa felt an alarm gong join the pendulum.

"Just tell me. Bad news. Whatever."

"Becky Newberry's husband has been transferred to Texas. She turned in her resignation this morning."

Alexa had been so convinced this would be about Ernestine, all she could do was sit there.

Regina, however, didn't seem to notice as she blithely continued. "Obviously, you're my first choice to take her position. Not just to fill out the rest of this academic year, either."

"I have a position waiting in California."

"I know you do. And I can't offer that kind of salary, but I can offer a much more affordable place to live." Regina sat forward. "Our community is growing. We need teachers like you, Alexa. The Ernestines aren't here forever." She smiled wryly. "Nor are the Reginas. You have growth potential here and—"

Alexa stood so abruptly that Regina looked concerned.

"I… I can't stay."

"Can't? Or don't want to?" The principal stood and rounded her desk. "I understand either way, but at least take some time to think about it. We'll have Becky only a few more weeks. At the very least, I hope you'll agree to take the offer through the remainder of the school year. I'll have the district send you all of the salary and benefit details."

"What about Ernestine?"

"Teachers are rarer than hen's teeth around here. An aide is easier to find."

"Even for a teacher who doesn't want one."

"She stopped having that choice when her class size hit twenty-eight. Which was already a fact before Jason D'Angelo was enrolled," Regina added.

Taking over Becky's first-grade class ought to be a no-brainer. "Do I have a choice?"

Regina's eyebrows shot up. "Between remaining an aide and taking a classroom for your own?"

It sounded so ridiculous that Alexa's cheeks felt hot.

"Does this have to do with Jason?"

Alexa lifted her palms. "Maybe." She sighed. "I don't know. I'll feel better when his situation is resolved, though."

"That's probably not going to happen in the next week," Regina said. "Or month, for that matter. I can wait a few weeks for your decision, but beyond that—"

"I understand." Alexa knew the principal couldn't wait forever. "I'll think about it."

"That's all I can ask. Oh. Except." She picked up a thick manila envelope from a side table. "These were all the get-well cards your class made for Ernestine. I thought I could get them delivered when she was in the hospital. They'll be for naught if she doesn't get them before she returns to school."

"We couldn't have just mailed them?"

"Gerta was going to, but she called in sick last week. And then we had the holiday break and—"

"And here we are." She took the package. An address had been handwritten on the front.

Regina beamed. "I knew I could count on you."

"That makes one of us." She tucked the envelope under her arm and went back to the classroom long enough to retrieve her belongings and her jacket. Then she plugged Ernestine's address in the GPS and she and Betty set off.

It didn't take long. Ernestine's small, boxy house was only a few blocks from the school. If an inanimate object could reflect its owner, the house did, right down to its paint that blended right into the dull gray sky.

She parked at the curb and walked up the narrow path to the front door. She rang the doorbell and studied the two urns with nothing but dirt in them positioned on either side of the door.

As bad as the beach house was, it still had more character than Ernestine's abode.

The door finally opened, and Ernestine stood there wrapped in a thick faded-blue robe. Alexa was shocked by the frailty in the woman's appearance.

But Ernestine's tongue was acerbic as ever. "What are *you* doing here?"

Alexa extended the thick envelope. "Get well cards from your *students*. It's not their fault we couldn't get them to you when you were in the hospital, so try not to burn them to a crisp with your fire-breathing." The second Ernestine relieved her of the envelope, she turned on her heel.

"I hear you've been subbing for me." Ernestine punctuated it with a spate of coughing.

She didn't stop walking. "Someone needed to."

"Thank you." The words were accompanied by more coughing.

Certain she'd misheard, Alexa looked over her shoulder. Ernestine had sat down on the porch step. She had gone pale and looked suddenly exhausted while she hunched over the envelope clutched to her chest.

Alexa swallowed a whole lot of misgivings and walked back to her once again. "You don't sound like you should be out of the hospital." She tugged the package out of Ernestine's grasp.

"What're you doing?"

She set the envelope on the porch and slid a hand beneath Ernestine's arm. "Helping you back inside."

"I don't want help."

"Yet here we are." Ernestine was thinner than Alexa expected. And undeniably shaky. "Come on," she said more gently. "On three. Ready?" She counted off and lifted while Ernestine pushed.

She made it to her feet but still leaned heavily against Alexa's side. Successfully stepping onto the porch felt like a monumental achievement and by the time Alexa got Ernestine back into the dim living room and settled on a floral-patterned couch straight out of the eighties, it was a toss-up who was breathing harder.

Ernestine was the only one who compounded it with her coughing, though.

Alexa didn't ask. She just went over to the kitchen that opened directly onto the living room and filled a glass with water. She took it back to Ernestine, who wearily waved it aside.

She set the glass on a round cork coaster atop the wooden coffee table and moved it within reach. Then she perched on the edge of the adjacent side chair. "When did you get home from the hospital?"

"Two days ago."

The kitchen had been practically sterile in its cleanliness. "Who brought you home?"

"A cab."

"No family or friends? What about food? Have you eaten since then?"

Ernestine's continued silence was less stony than exhausted.

"Can I fix you something? Soup? Tea?"

"I'm not hungry."

"Don't you think after two days that you ought to be? Did they send you with medication?"

Ernestine's gaze flickered almost guiltily and Alexa spotted a small white sack with the pharmacy's prescription labels sitting on the kitchen counter.

She retrieved it and pulled out the two amber-colored pill bottles inside. She didn't know what they were for, but the fact that Ernestine was to have been taking each of them three times a day seemed cause for concern.

"You haven't taken any?" she asked Ernestine. Just for confirmation.

The teacher's answer was to scoot sideways on the couch and tuck her robe tighter against her scrawny chest as she closed her eyes.

Alexa pulled out her phone and called West. He answered immediately and she explained. "I can give her the medications now, but what happens when she should have the next dose? There's nobody here to help her."

"What's her address?"

Alexa told him.

"Sit tight. I'll be there in a few. I'll drop Jason off at my mom's on the way."

She pocketed her phone. "Dr. D'Angelo is coming."

"No!" Ernestine jackknifed forward, coughing into a tissue she pulled from her pocket. "Not him."

"For Pete's sake, Ernestine!" Alexa pushed off the chair and paced in front of the couch. "Would you rather I just call 9-1-1?"

Her answer was another round of hacking.

She left the living room. The kitchen was on one side. Didn't take a genius to find the bedroom on the other side. She snatched the two bed pillows from the four-poster and took them out to the living room and situated them behind Ernestine. Then she went back into the bedroom and glanced around until she found a folded blanket on a shelf in the closet and she took that out to Ernestine as well. She lifted Ernie's stocking-clad feet onto the couch and tucked the blanket around her.

"You don't have to stay. I'm fine."

"Yeah. Sorry. I do have to stay because I don't think you're fine." She wandered around the living area then picked up the envelope with the get-well cards. "Shall I read these to you? The kids worked for two days on them."

"Waste of time. They have more important studies."

"Spelling and composition," Alexa countered. She tore open the envelope and slid the pile of handcrafted cards onto the coffee table. She picked one at random. "'Dear Mrs. Tone. I hope you come back soon. I have a new dog. We named him Ernie. But after my grandpa Ernie.'"

Ernestine actually cracked a smile. "Duwan."

"Yes." She slid the construction-paper card under Ernestine's fingers and plucked another from the pile.

She'd read through five messages when the doorbell rang.

She went to the door and let West in. "Since I called,

she's had a little water but no pills yet. I'll go wait in the bedroom. Give you some privacy."

He nodded and shrugged out of his jacket, tossing it onto the back of a chair as he went over to Ernestine. Alexa walked down the hall again and into the bedroom. Had there been anywhere else to go in the small house, she would have. Instead, she paced around the small space, feeling awkward and invasive. The only personal items were the trio of framed photographs that sat on the dresser where Ernestine's pendant watch lay in a heap. She straightened out the long chain as she peered at the photographs. A young Ernestine wearing a graduation cap on her head of brown curls. An elderly couple sitting on what looked like a park bench. And a young couple standing arm in arm. Ernestine beaming adoringly at the tall man at her side. She had a small ring on her left ring finger.

Alexa snatched up the photograph, looking closer at the man. Dark-haired. Blue eyed. With a dimple in his chin.

She slowly set it back in place and looked at the pendant watch again. And the faded red pattern of enameled flowers surrounding the watch face.

Cloisonné.

The puzzle box suddenly slid right open.

Ernestine's antipathy for Jason and West wasn't about either one of them.

It was about West's father.

She scooped up the chain and watch and went back out to the living room. "Where's West?"

Ernestine pointed at the front door. "Outside." She coughed.

"You didn't kick him out, did you?"

"Wanted to." Ernestine snugged her robe closer around her wrinkled neck. "He said he was calling someone." Alexa sat on the coffee table, earning a baleful look. "Now what?"

Alexa opened her palm, letting the pendant watch hang from her finger. "He gave this to you, didn't he? West's father."

Color filled her previously wan face. "That's none of your business." Ernestine reached out with surprising speed to grab the watch.

Alexa was faster, though. She dangled it out of the other woman's grasp. "It is West's when you're taking out your anger or…whatever…on his *son*. What happened?"

"We were engaged. Then we weren't. Give it to me." She sounded winded.

Conscience nipping, Alexa handed her the pendant. "He broke it off?"

Ernestine's thin lips pinched together. "He wouldn't have if he hadn't met *her*. It was disgusting. She was ten years younger than we were. A silly receptionist in his office."

"Who? Marjorie?"

"Who else?" She lowered her head, coughing again.

Alexa went back into the bedroom and returned with the box of tissues that had been sitting on Ernestine's nightstand.

Ernestine grabbed several and bunched them in her fist, which she waved at Alexa. "Now please leave."

Alexa would've liked nothing better. "You've spent what? Forty years nursing a grudge? Doing it for so long you can't even tell when you're taking it out on an innocent kid?"

"The only reason I left Edison was after West's—*my* West's—*son* began kindergarten there." She pointed her finger at Alexa. "And you should talk about nursing a grudge. I remember your father. Peter."

Alexa narrowed her eyes. "What about him?"

"You'd rather pretend he didn't exist. Not that you don't have cause. He was the worst rounder of them all. Even his own parents wanted nothing to do with him. Didn't have a faithful bone in his body."

"Try telling me something I don't know."

Ernestine coughed into her fist of tissue. She pointed a bony finger. "You're just like me."

Alexa bolted off the coffee table. Ernestine was a bitter, old woman. If she wasn't in the state she was in, Alexa would have been more than happy to tell her so. "I am *nothing* like you."

"I can read between Regina Bowler's constant praise of you. No personal life. All you have is your career. We're the same, all right." Ernestine's hands shook as she pulled the gold chain over her head. She clutched the pendant against her chest and leaned back against the bed pillows. "So, take a look at your future."

Alexa felt just as breathless as Ernestine looked.

When the door opened and West entered, she just stared at him.

He gave her a questioning frown, but his focus was on Ernestine. "Cardinale Cares is sending over a healthcare aide beginning in the morning," he said. "They'll come three times a day to help you with meals and medicines and whatever else you need until you're stronger. A visiting nurse will come as well."

"I don't need all that nonsense."

West glanced at Alexa again. "Where've I heard that before?" he asked under his breath.

Then he sat on the coffee table in front of Ernestine. "Maybe you don't want all that nonsense," he said in what Alexa considered his cajoling Doctor D way. "But for a few days, what'll it hurt if it helps ensure you don't land back in the hospital, Ernestine?"

When he spoke her name, it was like watching sand shift under a retreating wave. Ernestine's resistance faded.

"Whatever you say," she said, closing her eyes again. "West."

Chapter Eighteen

"Am I like her?"

Alexa's words burst out of her as soon as they left Ernestine's house.

"What do you mean?"

She waved her hand back at the house, looking agitated. "Like Ernestine? Is *that* who I'm turning into?"

"Whoa." He caught her arms. "Where'd this come from?"

But Alexa didn't want to stand still. She pulled away. Paced toward her car, the long sides of her hairy purple-and-green sweater flapping around her legs. Then she paced back. "I *do* only have my career, you know."

"No, I don't know."

Listen, West. Not her words. What's she saying? It was no longer Janine he heard. Just his own voice chiding him.

He pushed his hands in his back pockets just to keep from reaching for Alexa again.

"And I hold grudges," she said on her next round between him and their cars at the curb. "Forgiveness isn't in my nature."

He started to open his mouth. Thought better of it yet again and walked toward the curb instead. It was nearly dark. He wasn't concerned about Jason. His son and his mother had an evening of zombie reruns on the television menu.

Apparently, Stanley was joining them.

But Alexa's sweater wouldn't be warm enough against the growing cold.

"I'm judgmental." Alexa strode past him again. "And selfish. I don't like to share."

He reached his car. Leaned against the side. He glanced up and down the street. It wasn't unlike the one he'd lived on growing up. An eclectic collection of homes. Some large. Some small. Most well-kept.

Alexa stood in the middle of Ernestine's yard, staring at the house, hands on her hips. Beneath the sweater, her leggings were purple. Her high-top tennis shoes hot-pink. She was a swirl of color.

"What exactly do you dislike sharing?"

She rounded on him. "What?"

He repeated the question. "Seriously, Alexa. I'm genuinely curious. Because since I've met you, the generosity you show to others is even more noticeable than your entirely unique sense of style."

"If that's some dig about the way I dress—"

"Did I sound like I was making a dig?"

Her lips parted. Firmed as they pressed together.

"You of all people should know I like the way you look. Clothed." He waited a beat. "Unclothed."

Her cheeks turned pink. "You're a doctor. You're not supposed to talk about that."

"I wasn't looking at my medical degree the other night at my place. I was looking at you. And only you. Don't pretend otherwise."

"That was four days ago. And you…we still haven't—"

"Actually slept together?" He smiled ruefully. "Not for lack of interest, sweetheart. More like lack of opportunity. Between your family and mine, privacy is hard won. But back to this 'dislike of sharing' notion."

She narrowed her eyes. "Are you making fun of me?"

He spread his arms. "Where did *that* come from?"

Her jaw worked back and forth. "I don't like sharing peanut butter," she muttered.

He raised his eyebrows. "Sorry. What was that?"

"Peanut butter! Okay? I want the entire jar for myself."

"This existential crisis is about peanut butter?"

She glared.

He couldn't help smiling. "Okay. That was teasing. A little." He pushed away from the car and caught her hands. "Alexa. You are *not* Ernestine Tone. As far as I can tell, the only thing you have in common is a classroom. And maybe the ability to cut a man to his knees with a single look from those robin's-egg eyes of yours."

"I'm not trying to cut anyone to their knees."

"Not currently," he agreed. He slid his hands to her elbows. Her shoulders. "But if you think someone's not doing their best where their child is concerned?" He leaned down and kissed her lightly. "You're lethal." He straightened and nodded his head toward the house. "A career of teaching is admirable. But I'll bet you she's never stretched herself out on behalf of a student the way you have for Jason."

"He's special."

"As are a half dozen others, apparently. When I spoke with your friend Sandy, she told me you've footed the bill for more than one student in the past when it was the only way to accomplish it."

"She's not supposed to talk about that. And she cuts her rate nearly to nothing, too. You're going to let Jason see her then?"

"First week of the new year. It's her earliest opening. I already arranged a JCS charter to fly her in and out for the day. So, tell me again. Aside from peanut butter, what are you so selfish about?"

"Regina offered me a teaching position," she blurted, looking consternated.

"Your own class?" He jerked his chin at the house behind them. "Not hers?"

"The first-grade teacher is leaving in a few weeks."

"You don't look delighted. Don't like teaching six-year-olds?"

"I know what it's like putting my husband's career ahead of everything else. What if it doesn't work out for her? She's going to have a baby, too."

"It's their life, Alexa. Has she told you she doesn't want to go?

She shook her head. "For all I know, it's her dream come true," she admitted. "Dom and I were supposed to have kids. And we put it off and off again because it was never the right time for him."

"Would having a child or two have made his cheating easier for you?"

She scrubbed her hands down her face. "No. I know. There's nothing logical about the way I feel."

"Then let's go eat."

She dropped her hands. Raised her eyebrows.

"Come on." He opened the passenger door of his car. "I didn't have time for lunch or dinner. The Highland Pub's practically around the corner."

"I'll just follow you." She aimed for her vehicle.

"Don't want to be seen riding in the same car?"

"Rumors get started on less. And you're the one who just told me this morning that you're always telling Jason we're not involved."

"No, I'm always telling Jason we're not getting married." He closed the passenger door. "A car ride is more innocuous than a Thanksgiving dinner."

"True. At least at the pub, there's no sunroom."

"Just an entire hotel attached with rooms."

Her eyes widened. She gave him a startled look.

"Just saying."

"Well don't!"

"Why? Puts ideas into your head?"

"I don't need any help on that score." She climbed into her car.

He rubbed his hand around the back of his neck. On the bright side, he wasn't suffering alone. On the other side, now he knew it.

When they arrived at the pub, the place was already packed. "We can wait forty minutes," West told her, "or we can sit at the bar."

Alexa peered around him. "Donna's bartending," she said under her breath.

He waited a beat. "Room service?"

"Tempting. But ill advised."

He sighed. "Good thing I had them put my name on the wait list then."

She smiled. Then laughed. "I guess it is."

The wait was nearly an hour, but the chowder was hot and more than worth it.

Even when Alexa told him about his father's engagement prior to marrying his mother.

"It explains a lot." He poked his fork into the wedge of strawberry cheesecake they were sharing for dessert.

"Doesn't absolve Ernestine, though." She sipped her coffee. "What do you think the likelihood is of her returning to class this week?"

"A few more days could make all the difference," he said. "She's a regular patient of Stu Hayes', though. She admitted as much before I contacted Cardinale Cares."

"Any progress on them finishing the construction at your building?"

"My mother's building," he corrected. "And not that I can see. The hard-hat in charge left me a message, though, that they were still on schedule."

Just ask her, for Pete's sake.

"Are you going to take the job?"

Her lashes swept down again. "My home's in California."

He'd expected nothing less. But the answer still made something inside him sink. "I'm thinking about moving."

"*What?*" She practically rose out of her chair.

"It's only a six-month lease on the house. We need something that fits us better. Smaller."

She subsided, her shoulders sinking back down below her ears. "No statues or koi ponds?"

"Something like that."

"Makes sense. Though I do like that *Winged Victory* one. I've always wanted to see The Louvre."

"Never been to France?"

"Never been anywhere," she said. "Except California. And here."

"I'll take you."

She smiled wryly, shaking her head. "Yeah. Right. I make my own way, Doctor D. Or I don't make it at all."

"It'd be a life experience for Jason."

"Dragging me along isn't the way to convince him we're not—" she waggled her fingers "—whatever." She suddenly set her coffee down. "It's late. I have things to do before tomorrow." She tossed her napkin on the table. "Don't get up. Finish your dessert."

He ignored her and tossed cash on the table.

"I told you—"

"A bunch of nonsense." He held her sweater for her. "My dad would roll over in his grave. I may not have wanted to take over the clinic, but that doesn't mean I ignored everything he tried to teach me." His knuckles brushed the warm curve of her neck. It was hard not to let his hands linger.

"What would have happened to the clinic?" She swept the ends of her waves out from the collar of her sweater as she turned to look up at him. "If you hadn't come back?"

"We would have found another doctor to run it, like we've been doing for years."

"What changed?"

"Janine died."

"I'm sorry. I didn't mean to bring up sad thoughts."

"Irony is, she came with me." He didn't know why he said it.

"We don't forget people we love just because they're gone from our lives."

"I mean literally. Her ghost came with me."

Her eyebrows rose. "Oh. Kay."

"There are lots of explanations. Grief hallucinations being the most prominent."

"I haven't heard of that before."

"I could bore you with statistics, but—"

"No need. I understand. You loved her very much. Despite...everything."

"I didn't give her what she needed. And she found it somewhere else. Her ghost was my guilt. Knowing it didn't make it feel any less real."

"And now?"

"I've realized the present is a lot more interesting than the past."

She moistened her lips. Her lashes shielded her expression. "And the future?"

"Right now, the only future I'm working on is tomorrow."

Her lips stretched. She looked relieved. "Works for me."

He pulled open the door for her. It was raining. Not hard, but enough to make the parking lot gleam in the night.

"More rain." She sighed as she pulled out her car keys. "It makes my hair a mess."

"Then it should rain all the time. It's a great mess."

She just smiled and shook her head as she started across the parking lot.

He slowed his pace to hers. His imagination was running riot. Alexa in his gaudy mauve shower, hair sleeked back from her face, teal eyes gleaming.

She was silent until they reached her car. "Thanks for coming to see Ernestine when I called."

"What're friends for?"

She angled her head, looking up at him. A scatter of raindrops dazzled on her hair. "Is that we are? Friends with benefits?"

"Benefits yet to be fully explored."

Her lovely throat worked. She fumbled with the key in her car door. "As long as we're still agreed. None of that serious stuff."

He leaned down and kissed her cheek. "I can be pretty serious about benefits."

She made a soft sound that went straight to his gut and softened toward him. But then headlights swept over them as a vehicle entered the parking lot and she straight-armed him and wrenched open her car door, sidling around him. "Good night, West."

"G'night, Alexa." He stepped back and waited while her car engine cranked a few times. He thought about all of the private rooms in the hotel behind him. What if her engine didn't start?

But it did.

And he exhaled slowly, watching until she'd driven out of the parking lot.

"We're agreed," he said under his breath. "Two of the stupidest words you've ever said, West."

Then he walked to his own car and went home.

* * *

"Coffee." West handed Alexa an insulated cup. "More coffee." He handed her another insulated cup and then sat down beside her behind the folding table she'd covered with the "Excel at Howell" school banner.

The Winter Faire had finally arrived. The culminating event of her fundraising efforts for the school playground. And after she'd let the students use the banner as an art project, it was transformed into a perfect backdrop for their Winter Faire booth.

"Any more people stop by while I was in the pub?"

"It's been almost constant." They'd had perfect weather all day. Clear. Cold. For what felt the millionth time that day, she had to force herself not to lean into his warmth as he sat beside her. She still couldn't believe he'd been there the entire day. Not a single phone call to summon him away to work. Not even Jason had needed him, since he was having his first overnight stay ever with Aidyn Savage. The last time West had called to check on him, they'd still been playing a marathon session of ZombieCart.

"The silent auction closes in ten minutes," she said. Needlessly since West had been checking the time routinely. "The bidding has been amazing, right? Even Gerry's golf bag has several bids. It's up to a hundred dollars."

"No accounting for taste," he said dryly. "What about our headliner?"

She tapped the framed photograph that was displayed on an easel next to her. After Donna's comment about her father's photography, she'd done the unthinkable and called Lotus. Two days later, a package had arrived with one of her father's early works. *Light Dance*. Signed by the artist himself. It, along with the hotel package and a JCS charter flight were the only items they'd put online for bidding and she pulled the site up on her phone. "It's still at ten thousand. The hotel is three hundred. Charter's up to five."

"What's that bring us up to altogether?"

"I don't know." She uncapped the coffee and sipped gingerly. "After Ernestine stopped by this morning and left us that check for five thousand dollars, I've barely been able to add two plus two."

Following the episode at the teacher's home, the woman had been full of surprises.

Not only had she attempted to rectify her treatment of Jason once she'd resumed her class two days earlier by sending in her own recommendation for the gifted program, she seemed more intent on providing him the kind of work that would challenge him until that time actually arrived.

Meanwhile, that left Alexa still with the decision to make about taking over Becky's class. Her last day at the school had been the day before.

West grabbed a pencil from the array waiting for Winter Faire participants to use as they noted their bids on the various items that Donna had helped curate for the sale. "If we ended right this minute and Ernestine's check doesn't bounce, that gets you up to eighty-seven thousand and some change." He turned his scribbled numbers around for Alexa to see. "Not bad."

"Not bad!" She felt almost giddy. "It's *way* more than I thought we'd get." She grabbed his arm and shook it like a rag doll. "That's only thirteen thousand shy of Regina's crazy-high goal. I am *not* a failure after all!"

He laughed and tossed aside the pencil. "Sweetheart, you are the antithesis of failure."

She suddenly stood. "Can you watch things for a few minutes? I need the ladies' room."

He spread his hands, the picture of male insult. "What do you think?"

She rolled her eyes and walked away. She didn't need the ladies' room. She just needed a breather. Because every time West called her sweetheart, she felt such an intense longing that it was true, she wished he'd never say it at all.

She walked along the rows of booths, not really paying much attention to the wares on offer. Dana had come by earlier, bearing bags of purchases. "Christmas presents," she'd excused when she'd stopped at the school's table. She'd cast her eye along the silent auction stuff then pulled out her checkbook. "The last thing we need is more stuff at the beach house," she said, dropping the check into the slot of the donation box sitting on the table.

Meyer and Cutter had dropped by, too. Meyer with Sophie and Cutter solo for once. Even though Alexa had told them they didn't need to make donations, they had. Not to the degree of Dana's. But then, Dana could buy and sell them all twice over.

The crowd packed into the closed-off street was staggering and the further away she got from her own booth, the worse it seemed. After bumping into a second person, she turned and started back. The mayor would be announcing the winners of the silent auction on the stage where different groups had been offering entertainment all day.

Then, even though the street fair was scheduled to last until well into the evening, the school fundraiser could call it a day. Thirteen thousand was a small price to pay for some needed space from West D'Angelo.

A woman in a black coat and bright red beret stopped short in front of her and Alexa plowed into her. "Sorry."

The woman laughed, reaching down to rescue her bag of sparkling Christmas tree decorations from being trampled. "No worries." She straightened again and held up one of the little angels that dangled from a gold strand. "Perfectly unharmed." She dropped the angel into the bag on top of the others. "Did you ever expect to see so many people here?"

Alexa shook her head. There was something familiar about the woman, but she couldn't quite place her. A parent she'd seen in the drop-off at school, no doubt. "Cape Cardinale's doing itself proud, that's for sure." She nodded toward the bag. "Are you buying or selling?"

"Depends on the customer." Beneath the beret, her dark eyes danced. "I'm back over there." She waved vaguely. "Stuck in a forgotten corner." Her voice was light. Clearly joking.

Alexa wondered where they'd have room for a Christmas tree at the beach house, but she was suddenly determined that they would have one. "How much are they?"

"For you?" The woman handed over the angel. "My gift." She winked. "Promise you'll have a merry Christmas, Alexa?"

"Um. Sure. You as well." She waved the small angel. "Thank you. I'm sorry. I should know your name but—"

"Just call me JJ. And I should thank you. It's taken me forever to find them homes." Then she turned and walked away, disappearing into the crowd swelling around the stage.

Alexa hurried faster back to the table where a short line of people had queued in front of the bid sheets, obviously intent on getting their bids in at the last minute.

She slid behind the table again, next to West.

"Guess you found something to buy."

She set the angel on the table between them. The nearly translucent wings were opalescent in the overhead lights that had just come on while she'd been walking around. "I'd have bought it, but the woman selling them gave it to me. I nearly ran her over. She's got to be a parent from school."

"Pretty."

"If you see a brunette with a red beret, that's her. I

wouldn't mind having a few more angels. Oh." Alexa heard the announcement coming over the PA about the silent auction and grabbed West's arm. "That's us." The announcement ended just as the alarm clock on the table went off with a jangle.

"That's it, folks. Time's up." West leaned over the table and swept up the clipboards with the auction sheets.

"Could've given a buddy a second more."

"That's what you get for trying to work the system, Doc." West handed the sheets to Alexa. "It's your party. Go get 'em."

Alexa paged through the sheets. The last-minute entries that had come in during her brief absence made her goggle-eyed. She circled the winners as she worked her way back to the stage and joined the mayor.

"Thank you, Alexa." He dropped his hand over her shoulder and pulled her closer to the mic. "Everyone, say hello to our very own Alexa Cardinale!"

She managed not to gape as cheers went through the crowd. She was about as far from being the town's "very own" as she could get.

"Do we have the winners of the silent auction?"

"We do." She handed him the sheets and would have stepped back if not for his hold on her.

He made a production of clearing his throat. His version of building suspense. Which wasn't ineffective, if the faces turned toward them were any indication.

"We'll work our way up," the mayor said, and began reading off the final names that Alexa had circled. "First off, the winner of a golf bag, clubs *and* a round of golf at Cardinale Country Club is none other than Councilperson Andrea Webb! Andrea, step on up here, hon. Let's have a hand for her, everyone."

Inviting the winners up onto the stage hadn't been part

of the plan and by the time the mayor made it through all of the smaller prizes, Alexa decided there wasn't room for her, too. She stepped off the backside of the stage where West stood, carrying the locked wooden donation box and her father's autographed photo. The angel was dangling from his little finger.

"Your silent auction has taken on a life of its own," West said in her ear while the cheers—and jeers—continued.

"He's running for reelection next year." There wasn't even a need to lower their voices. They had to practically shout just to hear each other.

"Onto our big-ticket winners," the mayor boomed. "The first of which is the—" He glanced at the sheet that Donna was holding up from where she stood almost directly in front of him. "The Highland Hotel Lover's Package won by Ruthie Charles!"

"Wonder who's going to share *that*," someone yelled as Ruthie went up onto the stage and waved her hand.

"You're just jealous, Burt," the mayor said, and gave Ruthie a broad wink. He cleared his throat again. "Almost to the end, folks. JCS Aviation, also one of sponsors today, donated a fine, fine charter flight. And the winner is Hayden Bash!" Hayden jumped on the stage, waving his hands together above his head like a champion prizefighter. "Last but not least…" The mayor took Donna's final sheet of paper. "The grand prize, autographed and award-winning *Light Dance* by Pietro Cardinale, goes to Otto Nash thanks to his winning bid of—holy cow. Fifteen *thousand* dollars!"

He scanned the crowd, but nobody was moving toward the stage. "Good thing ol' Otto doesn't have to be present to win."

Donna hopped onto the stage and snatched the microphone. "Which gives us time to talk about the real winner tonight. The kids of Howell Elementary School! Because with your help, the playground fund has officially topped one hundred and ten thousand dollars!"

"Where's our Alexa?" the mayor asked.

"Go."

Feeling dazed, Alexa let herself be nudged back up onto the stage. She stared at the mic that the mayor pushed in front of her then out to the crowd. So many faces that she knew now.

Marjorie and Stanley near the entrance, where they'd been volunteering all day.

In the other direction Meyer, Cutter and Dana, toasting her with mugs from the Highland Pub.

West, standing in the tangle of power cords and sound equipment next to the stage where Regina Bowler and Gerta had joined him. They were all beaming.

She cleared her throat. "First, the person who deserves all this cheering is really Donna Blankenship." She grabbed Donna's arm, though she didn't really think the woman would slink away from more of the spotlight. "Without her, the silent auction wouldn't even exist."

"Go Donna," someone yelled.

"And thank you to the mayor and the whole Winter Faire planning committee who graciously allowed us to be part of your celebration today. And mostly..." She looked out at the blur of faces. "Thanks to all of you for opening your wallets and caring about the kids in our community. You make Cape Cardinale a very..." Her throat tightened. "Very special place to call home."

As if it had been perfectly planned, a premature firework streamed across the evening sky and blossomed into a snowball of stars.

Taking advantage of the distraction, Alexa made it off the stage again. She took all of the items from West and handed them off to Regina and Gerta. "Mr. Meacham has the padlock key. West can deliver the photo to Otto later. They're neighbors." She slipped the angel ornament off his little finger. "And this you can put in my new classroom," she told Regina. It would go on the Christmas tree at the beach house. Once they had one.

"New classroom? Does that mean you're going to take Becky's position?"

"Yes. We'll have to talk about the details later, though." She took West's hand and pulled him away from the stage. "We don't have much time. I want to see the fireworks before the concert."

"Where are we going?"

She pointed at the Highland Hotel. "See how good you really are at benefits."

He dragged her to a halt. "Now? The hotel's probably full up with people in for the Winter Faire."

"It isn't. I have it on good authority from Donna." She tugged. "Are you interested or not?"

"Not."

Horror swept through her with the speed of a firework. "You've changed your mind."

"Never about you. Only about what we've agreed on." He reeled her closer.

She eyed him warily. "Meaning?"

"Did you mean what you said on stage? About calling Cape Cardinale home? Because if you didn't, you need to know that if you're going back next summer to California, Jase and I are going to follow."

Her eyes prickled. "What?"

"We will follow you," he repeated. Slowly. So, there was no chance of her misunderstanding. "Wherever you are is where I intend to be."

"But your clinic—"

"Ruthie's been the heart and soul of that place since my

father died. We should have made her the director years ago. Whether I stay or go, that's changing as of now. She'll be the first one to tell you the physicians are the last in line of importance anyway. A far distance behind our nursing staff and probably even the janitor. And I can get out of suits and back into scrubs, where I belong." He smiled slightly and drew her an inch closer. "But if you *did* mean it about Cape Cardinale being your home—"

The lump in her chest was growing. "I did."

"Then that makes it even simpler."

"Nothing about this is simple and I can't take another broken—"

"Heart?" His eyes stared into hers.

"Yes," she whispered.

"Then let's agree not to break them." His voice went husky. "Not yours. Not mine." He threaded his fingers through hers and closed the distance between them. "If we're happy, we say so. If we're mad, or sad, we say so. We don't walk away. We stay. We work it out. And we never make a promise we don't intend to keep." He kissed her knuckles. "And, for the record, I'm not looking for a replacement for Janine. The only one I'm looking for, Alexa, is *you*."

"What about Jason?"

"Oh, he'll plan on us being married with three-point-two kids in no time. But maybe if we get him and General Grant another puppy, he'll be satisfied for a few months until his old man has a chance to catch up."

She suddenly laughed. Went to wipe the tears from her cheeks only to have him do it first. Brushing his thumbs gently over them.

She realized the pressure in her chest was just her heart. Filling up again after having felt empty for so, so long. "You haven't even been to the beach house. It's *not* anything to brag about. And I still have half a year to go where my father's will is concerned. I won't let my sister and brothers down."

"I wouldn't expect you to. And half a year's a blink of an eye," he said, "in comparison to an entire future. Let Jason figure out the math of it all."

She glanced at the hotel. "I just figured on us, you know. Finishing what we started in your sunroom."

"We'll finish," he promised. "Over and over and over again. And some day, maybe sooner. Maybe later. You'll wear the ugly D'Angelo brooch."

She inhaled shakily. "I'm sure it's not that bad."

"I've seen the pictures. It's hideous. You'll deserve diamonds every anniversary thereafter."

She traced her finger along his lower lip. It was perfect, that lip. Mesmerizing, in fact, particularly in the light of another firework overhead. "You've only seen it in pictures?"

His voice dropped. "Yeah." He caught her hand in his. Pressed his lips to her palm. "I love you, Mrs. Cardinale."

"I love you, Doctor D." How easy it as to say when it was true. "We're running out of time before the fireworks."

"We'll make plenty of our own. But at my place. I'll make sure you're back in your own bed before morning. Meanwhile, the tile might be gaudy, but I've got a helluva shower. There's no way the hotel would compete."

"Well then. I guess that seals it."

He kissed her.

"Come on, people." A grouchy voice accosted them. "Move it, would you please? We're trying to get equipment through here."

West laughed and practically lifted her off her feet as they ran through the crowd until they broke into the relative freedom of the parking lot just when an explosion of color boomed to life above them.

Alexa, who had loved fireworks all of her life, barely

even glanced up. The fireworks in store for her and West would outshine anything.

They made the drive to his house in record time. Raced through the kitchen and up the stairs, clothes dropping where they may.

Neither one of them noticed General Grant sitting happily on top of the kitchen table, free yet again from his latest of crates, while Maxwill Sing sat on his perch in his uncovered cage beside the table, his head cocked at the fireworks shining outside the window.

They definitely didn't notice the shoe the puppy was gnawing.

Or the fact that, at long last, the canary sang.

* * * * *

Look for Dana and Cutter's stories,
next in New York Times' *bestselling author Allison*
Leigh's new miniseries, Cape Cardinale
Coming soon to Harlequin Special Edition.

And catch up with Meyer's story,

The Pilot's Secret,

Available wherever Harlequin books and ebooks are sold.